NEW YORK REVIEW BOOKS
CLASSICS

T0243305

A LOVE AFFAIR

DINO BUZZATI (1906–1972) came from a distinguished
family that had long been resident in the northern Italian
region of the Veneto. His mother was descended from a noble
Venetian family; his father was a professor of international law.
Buzzati studied law at the University of Milan and, at the age
of twenty-two, went to work for *Corriere della Sera*, where he
remained for the rest of his life. He served in World War II as
a journalist connected to the Italian navy and on his return
published the book for which he is most famous, *The Stronghold*
(first translated in English as *The Tartar Steppe*). A gifted artist
as well as writer, Buzzati was the author of five novels and
numerous short stories, as well as a popular children's book,
The Bears' Famous Invasion of Sicily.

JOSEPH GREEN was the pseudonym of Gordon Sager
(1915–1991), who contributed Talk of the Town pieces and short
stories to *The New Yorker* from the 1930s through the early
1950s. Among his novels is *Run, Sheep, Run*, a roman à clef
about his friendship with Jane and Paul Bowles and their circle.
As Joseph Green he translated works by Giovannino Guareschi,
Luigi Santucci, and others.

OTHER BOOKS BY DINO BUZZATI PUBLISHED BY
NEW YORK REVIEW BOOKS

Poem Strip
Translated by Marina Harss

The Stronghold
Translated by Lawrence Venuti

A LOVE AFFAIR

DINO BUZZATI

Translated from the Italian by
JOSEPH GREEN

NEW YORK REVIEW BOOKS

New York

THIS IS A NEW YORK REVIEW BOOK
PUBLISHED BY THE NEW YORK REVIEW OF BOOKS
207 East 32nd Street, New York, NY 10016
www.nyrb.com

Originally published in Italian as *Un amore* in 1963.
First published as a New York Review Books Classic in 2023.

Library of Congress Cataloging-in-Publication Data
Names: Buzzati, Dino, 1906–1972, author. | Green, Joseph (Translator), translator.
Title: A love affair / by Dino Buzzati; translated by Joseph Green.
Other titles: Amore. English
Description: New York: New York Review Books, [2023] | Series: New York
  Review Books classics | Identifiers: LCCN 2022020989 (print) |
  LCCN 2022020990 (ebook) | ISBN 9781681377124 (paperback) |
  ISBN 9781681377131 (ebook)
Subjects: LCGFT: Novels.
Classification: LCC PQ4807.U83 A813 2023 (print) | LCC PQ4807.U83 (ebook) |
  DDC 853/.914—dc23/eng/20220718
LC record available at https://lccn.loc.gov/2022020989
LC ebook record available at https://lccn.loc.gov/2022020990

ISBN 978-1-68137-712-4
Available as an electronic book; ISBN 978-1-68137-713-1

Printed in the United States of America on acid-free paper.
10 9 8 7 6 5 4 3 2 1

I

ON A FEBRUARY morning, in the year 1960, in the city of Milan, Antonio Dorigo, architect, forty-nine years old, telephoned Signora Ermelina.

"This is Tonino," he said. "Good morning, signo—"

"Well! I haven't heard from you in a long time. How are you?"

"Pretty good, thanks. I've been awfully busy, that's why I.... Listen, could I come around this afternoon?"

"This afternoon? Let me see. What time?"

"Oh, I don't know. Around three, three-thirty."

"Three-thirty would be all right."

"By the way, signora—"

"Yes?"

"The last time, if you recall?...well, that material, to be quite frank with you, wasn't just what I wanted, I'd like—"

"I know. Unfortunately sometimes *I* myself—"

"Something a little more modern, if you know what I mean."

"I do. As a matter of fact, it's a good thing you phoned this morning, there's quite a remarkable opportunity...well, you won't be dissatisfied, I can guarantee."

"A dark cloth, preferably."

"Dark, dark, dark. I know, like ink."

"See you later then. And thanks."

He put down the receiver. He was alone in the studio; Gaetano Maronni, his associate who used the room next door, had gone out that morning.

It was an ordinary morning of an ordinary day. Work was going well. From the big window on the eighth floor he could see the building opposite, a modern building like all the buildings around, like the building where Dorigo was. Agreeable enough, all the same, in Via Moscova, a vast complex of co-operatives broken by tree-planted avenues where you could park your car.

It was one of so many gray Milanese days, not raining, but with that unreadable sort of sky; you couldn't be sure if it were clouds or only a haze on the other side of which the sun might be shining. Or was it nothing but smog issuing from the chimneys, from the vents of the oil furnaces, from the smokestacks of the Coloradi refineries, from the roaring trucks, from the drains, from the piles of rubbish spilled over the industrial areas of the suburbs, from the windpipes of the millions and the millions—were there so many of them?—gathered into cement, asphalt and passion around him.

He lit his third cigarette. It was a quarter to eleven ("*This is Tonino. Good morning, signo—*" "*Well! I haven't heard from you in a. . . .*") by the electric clock on the wall opposite, supplied by the co-operative; every once in a while a thin wisp of music came from the next room where Signorina Maria Torri kept her radio going. A little Japanese transistor, whether it was on her desk, or in her bag, or in her lap, it never stopped, even during conferences, and Dorigo hadn't the courage to forbid it. Actually he wouldn't have minded having one himself. He'd even bought one on the black market, a little pocket set, for ten thousand lire—in the downtown shops they sold for twenty-four, twenty-five thousand—but after only a couple of days Giorgina had wormed it out of him. Not that Giorgina excited him very much, but they'd known each other a long time; he'd run into her under the arcades of the Corso while from the pocket of his overcoat came one of those little Viennese waltzes, the kind he couldn't stand but out of sheer laziness he hadn't turned it off, and she had said, "Oh, let me see, how cute, will you give it to me?" After all, what was the little radio to him?

He lit his fourth cigarette. There was some work he might have finished up but he didn't have the slightest desire to: Anyway there was no rush, if he had it ready to show by Saturday that would be soon enough and it was only Tuesday now. When he got the urge to make love it was very hard for him to work, not that Dorigo was an especially sensual type or overburdened by virility, but every now and then, suddenly, without any obvious reason, his imagination began to work and then his entire train of thought went off in that direction.

Once the date was made, his whole body began to wait; it was painful but at the same time marvellous, hard to explain, almost the feeling of being the victim offered in a sacrifice, the whole body naked, with an abandoned outpouring of burning energy that flowed through every part of his limbs and his guts and his flesh. A charge of tremendous power, not at all animal or blind—on the contrary, poetic, full of dark obscenities.

At such times Dorigo went so far as to forget his own face—which he'd always hated, which he'd always considered loathesome—and deceived himself into believing he might even be attractive.

At the same time, waiting for a woman *("This is Tonino. Good morning, signo—" "Well! I haven't heard. . . .")* took away all his self-confidence, of which in his work he had so much. In the presence of a woman, he was no longer the nearly famous artist, internationally known, the clever scene-designer, envied and easily liked. He himself was always surprised that people liked him so easily, but with women it was all different: he turned into a nobody, and a rather objectionable one. He'd seen it happen a thousand times; women were intimidated by him and the more he tried to seem easy and witty the worse it got; the woman kept looking at him as though she were bewildered by him, maybe even frightened. To recover his own personality and appear natural again, he needed familiarity and trust; but that took a lot of time. So first meetings were always halting and labored. He envied Maronni who with a few words put women at their ease. Sometimes he even hated Maronni, for his own favorite jokes never worked with women. He knew it well. Instead of laughing the women grew uneasy, then bewildered, then they decided he was making fun of them or trying to snub them. He was consoled a little by the thought that in the long run his true quality almost always saved him and allowed him to appear a fairly agreeable figure if not actually a likable one. Women indeed intuitively sensed, and sometimes disliked, that intellectual superiority of his, closed off and proud, which prevented his giving himself openly as he would have liked. Instead he hurled himself without reserve, like a child, into the enthusiasm of a game.

Who, he wondered, would Signora Ermelina get for him that afternoon? He tried to keep himself from feeling too optimistic; it was so hard to hit on the right type, but at Signora Ermelina's there were always, thank God, new girls who had youth if nothing else.

And after all, he thought, if Ermelina had got Britta to come, that wouldn't be too bad. He hadn't made love to Britta in several months. Britta wasn't sentimental but she was easy-going in bed. She was fair, with a hard, smooth, pliant body, and not a hair on it, even at the crotch. He didn't ordinarily like blondes, even false ones, but Britta was as well put together as a young seal. When she raised her arms, her armpits seemed like opened flowers, rosy, smooth, warm, damp, shadowless, swelling softly a little, for such was youth.

He looked at his desk. On top of it lay a confusion of books, folders, papers, symbols of work.

Dorigo worked in the middle of the city; at that hour above him, below him, around him, in the very same building, men like him were working; they were working in the building opposite, and in the very old house in Via Foppa that he could just glimpse through a gap in the buildings, and beyond that too they were working, in buildings he couldn't see, further and further, through the smog, for miles and miles. Papers, ledgers, forms, telephone calls, receipts, hands full of pens, tools, pencils, hard at work on a socket, a screw, a sum, a gear, a job of soldering, a statement of account, a film bath: an infinity of frantic ants intent on their own well-being; yet their thoughts— oh, he had to laugh—all around, for all those miles and miles, thoughts like his, both obscene and exquisite, prompted by the mysterious voice that calls for the preservation of the species, transfigured into strange, blazing vices, why had no one ever dared to say so? thoughts of *her*, always of *her*, of that particular mouth, of those lips made in a certain way, of an arrangement of taut muscles (do you remember?), soft and fluid, with a curvature unlike all the others, of a fold, of a fullness, of a depth, of a warmth, of a dampness, of a surrender, of a descent, of a burning abyss. Yet the newspapers spoke of Soviet intransigence, questions in the House on the subject of the Alto Adige, assurances from Nenni concerning the autonomy of the P.S.I., a fire at the Fiamma movie house, a crisis in the Regional Sicilian Council. What a crazy joke it all was.

He lit his fifth cigarette. He stood up, he felt the special excitement of a man both apprehensive and sensitive by nature (*"This is Tonino. Good morning, signo—" "Well! I haven't heard. . . ."*). But he was well, no part of his body bothered him: he felt altogether calm, strong and serene. It was, in fact, a morning like so many others. Outside, the sky was still gray and monotonous, but he felt well.

The next few hours didn't hang heavy over him, nor did the days to come fill him with any sort of fear. Nor the wide future. The telephone was silent. Dorigo felt calm, things were going well. He wore a gray suit, white shirt, solid red magenta tie, red socks, black shoes, as though—

As though everything would go on as it had gone on until then, until that February day, which was a Tuesday and bore the number 9. Everything safe and propitious for a bourgeois in the bloom of life, intelligent, corrupt, rich, successful.

2

SIGNORA Ermelina lived on the sixth floor of a large building in the neighborhood of Piazza Missori. The elevator was the kind where the door opens by itself and sometimes closes unexpectedly. Once Dorigo had been caught in it and for a second or so was afraid he might be cracked like a nut, but the pressure of the two valves wasn't actually very strong.

There was no name-plate on her door. The long marble corridor was deserted. You couldn't, however, mistake the door for the very reason that there was no name on it, all the other doors had a name.

He felt the usual vague impatience, not quite suspense, that these affairs engendered. Which girl would it be? It was the easiest thing in the world, as Dorigo knew, to destroy the point of meetings of this kind. What's the fun of having a woman when you know she's only doing it for money? What satisfaction is there for the man, aside from the purely physical one which, after all, is so quick and so uncertain? The old objection.

Yet there was a satisfaction. And a considerable one. An almost unbelievable one. And not for the physical activities either, however refined they might turn out to be. No, it was what preceded them that made the thing so tremendous.

Signora Ermelina opened the door at once. She was from the province of Emilia, hearty, good-natured, a handsome woman still, of familiar mold, with nothing equivocal about her. To listen to her talk, you'd have thought she played the madam solely in order to help those poor girls out.

He'd hardly got inside when she whispered to him, with the usual tone of complicity: "Wait till you see what a little baby she is, just wait till you see." (She lowered her voice still further.) "Remember, though, she's under age. A dancer, a dancer from the Scala."

She'd brought him, meanwhile, into her parlor.

What a wonderful thing, thought Dorigo, prostitution is! Cruel, ruthless, it destroys so many. And yet what a wonderful thing it is! It was hard to believe it could still exist in the regimented, dreary world of today. A dream comes true, with the wave of a magic wand, for twenty thousand lire.

For twenty thousand lire, often even for less, you can have, immediately and without any difficulty or danger, stupendous looking girls who would probably have cost you, if you met them outside the game, in ordinary life, a lot of time, trouble, and money, and then as likely as not you'd find when the moment at last arrives they hadn't turned up. While here all you needed to do was make a phone call, take a short drive in your car, ride six floors in an elevator, and there was your nymphette taking off her brassiere and smiling at you.

Was it wrong? Dorigo wasn't without moral scruples, but however often and however long he thought about it, he couldn't find the weak point. If everybody did as I do, he asked himself, would it be better or worse? He really couldn't see the harm in it.

Still there was something evil about it. Perhaps prostitution attracted him just because of its cruel and shameful absurdity. Because of the kind of childhood he'd had, women had always seemed to him like foreign creatures; he'd never been able to give a woman the confidence he gave his friends. For him she had always been a creature of another world, superior and incalculable. That an eighteen-year-old girl, in order to earn fifteen thousand lire, would go to bed with a man she'd never seen or met before, with no preambles of any kind, and would let him enjoy every part of her body, even entering into the game herself with a warmth that was more or less real, this seemed to Dorigo a matter of incredulity and disgust—as though there was something mistaken about the whole idea.

Yet out of this bitter, even painful thought, this inability to accept the situation as it was, there was born desire. A respectable woman who went to bed with him unselfishly, out of love, would have given him infinitely less pleasure.

Sadism? The perverse enjoyment of watching something young, clean, beautiful submit slavishly to the most degraded practices? Relishing the pangs of humiliation, of which the girl certainly isn't aware, on the contrary she plays and jokes and laughs but all the while at the bottom of her soul something writhes and rebels and feels sick, nevertheless she laughs, plays her little tricks, throws back her head, with her eyes closed and her sweet little mouth panting, as though she were in paradise?

Possibly the main motivation for his attitude was the indelible stain left by his upbringing which had been Catholic and sternly opposed to all sensual acts. Thus, between him and young women, there had always been a barrier. Women for him were something illicit and the act of sex almost a legend. From this arose his belief that for a woman going to bed with a man was an event of the utmost importance which, even if it lasted only for a few minutes, involved, so to speak, her entire life. His knowledge that thousands of women were willing to go to bed with unknown men for a trifling sum and his own experience of such women for more than twenty years had not served to eradicate this belief. Every time a prostitute undressed and stood naked in front of him, it seemed to Dorigo unbelievable, stupendous, something that could happen only in a fabulous story.

That was why, whenever he went to keep an appointment at the house of some madam (and the same thing used to happen to him when public brothels were still open), he would not have been surprised if they'd said to him, "Are you crazy? What's got into you? Do you think a girl can be had just by paying for her? Do you imagine this is still the time of Heliogabalus?"

Yet each time, instead, the miracle happened. A magnificent girl—not always, unfortunately, a magnificent girl but at Signora Ermelina's his chances were quite good—a stupendous creature, the kind that makes every man's head turn as she walks down the street, got undressed right in front of him ten minutes after meeting him and let him hug her and hold her and enjoy every part of her body. All for a miserable twenty thousand lire.

At such times he would wonder what she was feeling. Disgust? Resignation? A sense of degradation? To judge by their behavior, nothing of the sort. The girls behaved as though what they were doing was the easiest and most natural thing in the world. Sometimes, it was true, they didn't take the trouble to hide their desire to get it over with as soon as possible, but never did they betray the slightest sign of sacrifice or distaste.

There were so many girls like that, of such varied origin, education, and social position, that it was surely legitimate to suppose that prostitution was an activity normal to all women, except under certain conditions wherein, because of some rigid and unnatural discipline, this instinctive inclination had been opposed and thwarted. But it was always there, nonetheless, ready to wake again if fate offered it the opportunity.

The girl, the dancer from the Scala, was already waiting for him in the parlor.

3

In the parlor, as they called it, there was a sofa in a corner, a round table, another sofa, a cupboard, and a wall closet. So-called modern furniture, Swedish style, rather simple, a certain feeling of cleanliness. More surprising was the presence on the walls of two large reproductions of the elder Breughel: those famous paintings of peasants. How they had found their way there was a mystery, or who had happened to choose them.

The girl was sitting on the long sofa. At first glance he got an agreeable impression but nothing out of the ordinary.

A pale little face, quickened by a straight, prominent nose, a small mouth, round astonished eyes. There was a fresh quality about her, a quality of the people, but nothing coarse.

He looked at her, trying to estimate the pleasure he'd soon be getting from her. The oval of her face was very beautiful and pure but had nothing classical about it.

What struck him most was her long black hair that tumbled loosely over her shoulders. Her lips, when she spoke, moved in graceful lines. A child.

Her lips were thin but clearly outlined, not openly sensual, rather mischievous. Her lower lip protruded, the more so as her chin, relatively, was small, narrow, and receding. She wore no lipstick.

Her mouth was hard and somewhat tense, very small in proportion to the rest of her face, but very important. Her whole face was taut with the extreme tension of youth. It was a determined, lively, naïve, sly, clean, exciting face. It reminded him of a Madonna by Antonello da Messina. The line of face and mouth were identical. The Madonna, certainly, had greater sweetness. But the same clear, authentic stamp.

Dorigo was always embarrassed by preliminaries. Her private judgment dismayed him. He knew he wasn't handsome. On the contrary. His face had always made him unhappy—even as a boy, passing in front of a shop window, if he happened to catch sight of himself in the glass, he felt humiliated. A hateful face, the face of an idiot, what woman would ever be attracted to it?

"What's your name?" he said.

"Laide."

"Laide. That's a strange name."

"Short for Adelaide, that's all."

Seated on the sofa, intimidated as usual by the presence of some-body new, Dorigo lit a cigarette while he looked at the girl who was there to be bought. In a few minutes that fresh, pretty creature, of whose existence he had until then been unaware, in back of whom stood a family, an infancy, a childhood, a whole world populated by an infinity of people, made up of a complicated fabric of memories, habits, perceptions, hopes, physical peculiarities, happy days and sad hours, all completely unknown to him, in a few minutes nevertheless he would have her naked in his arms, stretched out in bed, and he would be naked too. And it would all be just as though they were man and wife, or old friends or lovers, or at least as though there had been some reasonable prelude of acquaintanceship, invitations, prom-ises, flattery, and maybe deception. Instead they'd never seen each other before, he knew nothing of her, nor she of him; all the same within a few minutes she would have received within her his flesh.

Ever since Dorigo had grown up, that possibility had seemed to him unbelievable and, in a certain way, terrible.

In the past, however, in the brothels that Antonio had so agreeably frequented, hadn't the same thing happened? No, Dorigo had never succeeded in explaining it very clearly to himself, but there was cer-tainly a difference.

Perhaps the difference lay in the legal sanction that had made of those women a category apart, like the army or some religious order. Do we think of policemen or priests as men like ourselves? Better than ourselves, perhaps, but belonging to a different world. Do we thing of nuns as women? No. Saintly creatures, but of a different race. And that was true also of the women in the whore houses. They might be very young and marvellously beautiful, that wasn't so very rare, but we always had the feeling that between them and us there stood an impassible barrier: so rigid are our habits, our prejudices, and the authority of the law.

Or the difference may have arisen from the fact that the girls in the houses appeared nearly naked, in ridiculous, flamboyant, ostentatious clothes, usually in the worst possible taste, that left their legs and breasts uncovered. All mystery was resolved at the start. A uniform is what they wore, nothing else, a uniform that certainly wasn't an evening dress although it tried to look like one. This fact also played a part in making them a group unto themselves, separate from the rest of humanity.

Then too, the girls in the houses themselves made no attempt to seem like other girls. They played their role without the slightest concession to sentiment. Often they were nice girls, sometimes even affectionate, but a tightly sealed wall separated them from their clients. Between the two—with a few exceptions, when the bureaucratic spell was occasionally broken, and then trouble ensued—there was only the rapport of the body. Every other relationship was barred. If some man happened to ask, out of curiosity, about their private lives, he received only the vaguest and most conventional replies.

As for the girls, it was a good rule that said they were not to be curious themselves. Who was the client? What work did he do? Did he have a family? Was he rich? None of these questions, which are so strategic in any normally amorous relationship, played any part in the game. Both sides followed the rules and tried not to break them. This mutual indifference made the whole thing easier, it kept people from getting involved.

But with these girls here, on the other hand, although they sold themselves one and all in the same way, the circumstances and conditions were so different, it became quite another situation. They were in no way unlike the girls in ordinary life, for the simple reason that they belonged to ordinary life. Outwardly they were no different from the women that respectable men saw all the time, at home or out. The same look, the same habits, even the same language. And their fathers, their brothers, their fiancés were no different from their clients. There was no separating wall, they didn't belong to some other race; the very evening before they may have been guests in the house of some good family where the client himself often went.

That was why prostitution in these circumstances took on a disturbing quality; it was irrational and it was also infinitely more attractive. And that was why Antonio, each time, experienced the feeling that he was crossing an unauthorized frontier; the rules by which he had always lived, the rules that made of woman a forbidden fruit, to be won only after extremely hard and often useless effort, were here, miraculously, to satisfy his lust, broken. These call-girls, certainly, when compared with professionals, experts inured to the most fantastic depravities, were only clumsy beginners. To make up for that, however, they had mystery.

4

At that point Signora Ermelina said:

"Would it bother you if we try on a dress?"

"Of course not!" Dorigo knew that Ermelina claimed, as camouflage, to run a *boutique*. In the bedroom, as a matter of fact, along one entire wall there was a cupboard probably full of clothes.

In addition to which, that little pastime lightened somewhat the ceremonial hypocrisy of the approach. There was a convention of decency that decreed that going to bed had to be preceded each time by a quarter of an hour of chatter on this and that in a tone of forced gaiety. Whereupon, when all the topics within easy reach had been used up, there always followed an embarrassed silence. Till Signora Ermelina cried, "Come on! Be good children. Don't you want to go in there?" Sometimes the girl would take him by the hand, pull him up—an imitation of desire that was not without effect.

Signora Ermelina carried in a coffee-colored heavy wool dress. "This will keep you warm," she said.

Without the slightest shadow of embarrassment, Laide took off the gray sweater she was wearing and the pleated Scotch plaid skirt.

She was wearing a black slip. Antonio looked at her legs. They were slender, strong, firm, the calves were developed but still youthful, without that hard lump of muscle that almost all dancers have.

He was struck also by the compact roundness of her arms, such a rare thing. He saw in them the natural vitality of the people, as well as a childish innocence. When she raised her arms to pull the dress over her head, he saw that her armpits weren't shaved, which was unusual, in a ballerina.

"It looks as though it was made for you," said Signora Ermelina. Without a word Laide went to a mirror hanging on the wall. Raising her arms she straightened her long hair which had got caught in the dress.

Her arms still high, her back to him, she turned her head, looking at Antonio with a little mischievous smile. Did she realize how beautiful, in that pose, she was? Had she become aware of it on her own, with a flash of female intuition, looking at herself in the glass? Or had someone taught her the pose?

Turned, yet facing him, with her air of authenticity and her impudent self-assurance, it was as though she were saying: Do you see me? I'm different from the others, don't you think? do you like me? But not wantonly, nor lasciviously. Little girls look like that, at their mothers, or their fathers, or their brothers, when they're being dressed for their first communion.

At that moment he felt in the deepest part of him a shock, a kind of mysterious knell, as when in a vast and empty countryside one hears a far-off voice calling. He had absolutely no idea what had happened to him nor could he possibly have suspected the importance of it. In one of those flashes by means of which faded memories of days gone by are sharply revealed to us, he suddenly remembered having seen the girl before.

In Corso Garibaldi, at Milan, there is a group of very old houses, backed one against the other in a tangle of walls, balconies, roofs, and chimney pots. It is a place where the spirit of the old city, not the city of the rich but of the poor, has survived with singular intensity. Bit by bit old Milan was destroyed. The only things saved were her stately mansions, but they, after all, were like the stately mansion of other cities; they expressed, in their various styles, the pride and vanity of the same kind of human being. Only out of the houses of the poor does the true spirit of a city rise, but the brutish fail to realize this, and using the money they have, and hoping to make more, they level off all the dusty dirty districts that have been standing for a thousand years or more.

In Corso Garibaldi, however, this stubborn island still stood intact though it had been hacked at all its edges by the axe. Between Number 72 and Number 74 a passage topped by an arch opened onto a short, narrow alley. A stone marker said: Vicolo del Fossetto.

So narrow is the entrance to this tiny street that most passers-by take no notice of it. But after twenty-five or thirty feet, the alley widens into a kind of small square surrounded by dilapidated buildings. It is a forgotten corner of Milan, a labyrinth of narrow lanes, passages, underpassages, courtyards, stairways, winding stairs, where life still teems and burrows. They call it, no one knows why, the Storta.

Who lives there? What happens in it at night? Is it a ghetto of the poor? A den of the underworld and of vice? The narrow strips that cut through such tangles of houses seldom have names. At night the light comes only from strange little yellowish lamps that glimmer dimly in entrance ways. Sounds of radios, shouts, echoes of quarrels, a dog barking. Then silence.

Some months earlier, it must have been September or October, one evening after the lights had already been turned on, Antonio was walking along Corso Garibaldi, going from his studio to his house, which was in Piazza Castello. After the Largo della Foppa, towards the center of town, the street becomes intensely Milanese. The houses on both sides are old, some very old indeed. Shops follow one after the other. Dark passages plunge into strange and gloomy courtyards. Sidewalks swarm with people, but it isn't that inexplicable, dreary, almost hopeless ferment which towards evening covers certain parts of Naples, for instance; rather it's life itself, animation, vitality and gaiety, not poverty and hopelessness, but hurry and a preoccupation with not arriving on time. The faces of the people—this, to be sure, is only an impression—seem less drawn and anxious and silent than in so many other districts of the city, even those that are more central and more modern and richer.

Suddenly Antonio became aware of a girl walking in front of him. She wore a dress the color of ash-lilac, with white trimmings, made of a material called *pied-de-poule*, a bolero of the same material, very tight at the waist, and a full short skirt, as the fashion then was. From her right arm, which fell straight down, hung a large leather bag; she walked resolutely, haughtily, almost arrogantly, without moving her hips, and with splendid self-possession, beating her high thin heels peremptorily on the sidewalk. Her young legs had a quick inner movement from the ankles up through the swelling of the calves and along the exciting series of muscles that were lost in her skirt.

Like all women, this girl, as she passed the windows of the shops, turned to look at herself in them, though the light from inside must have made it difficult for her to get an adequate reflection. She did this quickly, apparently without definite intention, as though a habit had become an instinct. Thus Antonio was able to catch glimpses of her.

The line of the cheek had been drawn without correction, the nose jutted straight out with an inquisitive look to it, the long, very black hair was drawn back and gathered into a tight chignon. He couldn't see her mouth but he could imagine it, given the sharpened line of her chin. It would be small, firm, and selfish.

She was clearly a girl of the people, full of their physical vitality, but she wasn't showy, she was a girl of whom you would become aware slowly, and only then would you discover her absolute natural elegance. She must have been about eighteen.

Apart from taking fleeting glimpses of herself in the shop windows, she walked with her head straight, as though looking directly ahead without even seeing the people coming toward her. Antonio slowed down, in order to be able to go on following her. Not since he was a student had he followed women in the street and tried to stop them, and even then he'd done it rarely, four or five times in all probably: not out of distaste but out of his unconquerable timidity, for he was convinced that he couldn't possibly be attractive to any woman. What's more, his few experiences of that kind as a boy had been unfortunate. With his friends Antonio was witty and *degagé* , but the minute he tried to pick up a woman, his inferiority complex turned him into an apparent idiot; he couldn't find a word to say, he stuttered, his voice, in his embarrassment, sounded false, hard, and repellent. He was aware of all this perfectly well, aware of it even as the unfortunate words fell from his lips, but there seemed to be nothing he could do about it.

Nor did he now seriously consider the possibility of a pick-up. Obviously the girl belonged to a world wholly apart from his. This fact strengthened his interest in her but at the same time made the difficulty of approaching her appear to him unsurmountable. What could he say? What could he offer? How could he enlist her sympathy? He felt enormously attracted to her, there was no question of that, and he wondered what work she did, shopgirl, or model, or mannequin, or whore. There was the difference in age as well of course, a difference he'd been steadily becoming more painfully aware of.

No, there was nothing to be done. In a little while he'd watch her disappear into a house or a shop, or onto a tram; and he'd never see her again.

The girl, in fact, slipped into the alley between Number 72 and Number 74. Just before she did so, however, she turned around, unexpectedly, to look behind her. Although there was very little light just at that point, Antonio was able to catch a glimpse of her face. Pale, thin, childish; round, astonished eyes. She seemed to him very beautiful, she looked a little like a Spanish girl.

For an instant their glances met. For a fraction of a second one touched the other. How he'd have liked to talk to her! To smile at her at least. But he lacked the courage. Her expression, as she looked at him, was one of absolute indifference. Then, her undaunted steps continued into the dark passage.

Should he follow her? Antonio paused at the entrance to the alley, watching her silhouette move swiftly away from him against the light, for at the bottom of the alley was a courtyard or small square that was fairly well lit.

Only after the unknown girl had disappeared into the darkness, did Antonio himself dare to enter. He continued to the end of the little street and to the diminutive square from which, among the old houses, radiated other small streets and passages. A delivery boy went by carrying a tray full of cakes. An old woman, leaning out to close the shutters of a window on an upper floor, watched Antonio curiously. Three children playing marbles under the light of a street lamp turned to watch him. From the jungle of houses around him, with their parallel balconies, came voices and noises and sounds. A hammer banged on a piece of metal. There was an appetizing smell of soup with garlic.

It was like a little country that had embedded itself into the rows of houses—an unexpected bit of Milan he'd never heard spoken of. Aside from the electric lights, and a Vespa parked outside a door, everything must have been just as it was a hundred or two hundred years ago.

Antonio would have liked to explore the little alleys. How far, he wondered, did this secret citadel extend? Were there more of these little squares? Could you get out on the other side, into Via Statuto or Via Palermo? He might even run into the girl again.

But as usual he was a coward. He felt like a stranger. After all, these were other people's houses. Even the narrow little piazza might be private property. If someone were to ask him what he was doing there, what on earth could he answer?

He left, resigned. He lit a cigarette. It was anybody's guess where the little Spaniard had gone to earth. Maybe she lived there. Maybe she'd gone to meet a girl friend. Or to a date. Anyway, he'd never see her again.

Yet in one of those intimations of the soul, apparently so meaningless, that at the moment may go unheeded but that endure somewhere within, to wake again after months or years, when the spring of fate is released, Antonio felt a premonition: it was as if the encounter had some meaning for him, as if the momentary crossing of their glances had forged between them a link that could never be broken, though they two remained unaware of it. More than once in the past Antonio had felt the incredible power of love, which, with infinite patience and wisdom, across breathtaking chains of apparently chance events, from one end of the world to the other, reties at last two very slender threads that had got seemingly lost in the bustle of life.

But time passes, with it comes work, travel, people. Antonio thought no more about her, about that disturbing little creature, forgotten, buried in memory's deepest vaults.

5

WHEN, HOWEVER, in Signora Ermelina's obliging parlor, the girl who was under age, with her naked arms raised like the arms of an amphora, turned to smile at him, suddenly there leapt to the surface of his mind the memory of that evening last September or October in Corso Garibaldi.

He couldn't swear she was the same girl. The girl of Corso Garibaldi seemed, at least in his memory, a bit prettier. However, there was a strange similarity of type, although this one, naturally, lacked the mystery of the other.

The very violent attraction the other girl exerted over him may, of course, have come from the fact that she at that time and in that place was unattainable, while this one was at his total and complete command. Or did the two different situations make them seem like different girls? Were they, in fact, the same girl?

Laide, meanwhile, satisfied by the fitting, had slipped out of the dress and stood there once again in her slip.

"I trust you're not going to get dressed again!" cried Ermelina with a laugh, for the girl had picked her skirt up from the sofa. "Children! Everything's ready in the other room!"

It was one of the ritual phrases. Preceded by Laide, Antonio started into the bedroom.

On the threshold, however, after the girl had already gone in, Ermelina signaled to him, calling him back. She whispered:

"Look, she's an odd little girl, do you know what I mean? She likes...." She made a gesture. "I'm telling you so you'll know what to do."

"Ah yes, of course," he replied, without, however, having understood.

The bed was made, there was a cretonne cover over it, evidently Ermelina had decided they'd make love in the open. The room, however, was anything but warm. Antonio pulled the cover away, undressed, and climbed into bed. She had gone into the bathroom and was washing.

This was perhaps the best time, these five minutes of waiting in bed while the girl got her body ready. The imagination, certain of immediate and undisputed satisfaction, could evolve the most exciting and licentious images—images that would, of course, go unrealized at least eighty per cent of the time.

When she reappeared, she was still in her slip. "Hi," she said, as she came into the room. Then, with surprise in her voice: "You got under the covers?"

"My dear, it's not very warm here."

"No, I suppose it really isn't."

With the unconcern she might have felt if she'd been alone in a closed room, without the least suggestion of embarrassment, she took off her slip, while he watched her and foretasted her, and then her stockings. Under her slip she wore violet colored panties and a *guêpière* of a slightly lighter shade of violet with vertical black stripes. All rather sophisticated. Ermelina required that the girls in her stable take good care of their underthings. That was the important item with a select clientele like hers, no one cared about their dresses or coats.

Head bent, lips clenched, Laide unclasped her *guêpière* at the back. Then she opened it out like a sea shell. She was naked.

It was the classic body of the ballerina, with slender narrow hips, long slim thighs, and the tiny breasts of a child. She looked like a drawing by Degas.

She leapt into bed. "You're right, it's cold!" she cried, as laughing she slipped into his arms.

He kissed her mouth. She returned the kiss, her tongue between her lips, not obscenely though, not excessively, with indeed a kind of restraint that was almost chaste.

Then Antonio raised his head to look at her, at that cheerful child-ish face beneath his, framed by the long flowing black hair. She seemed entirely at ease.

"Is it true you're a dancer?"

"Yes."

"Where do you work?" he asked, pretending that Ermelina hadn't already told him.

"A theatre where you go too."

What did that mean? Did she know who he was? Did she know he was a scene designer? Or was she only alluding in a general way to his social standing, as though everybody of a certain class went to the Scala?

"What do you mean, where I go?"

"A theatre where you go too."

"You're a ballerina at the Scala, aren't you?"

She nodded. The confession seemed to please her.

"Congratulations," he said. "I'll have to come to applaud you."

"Thank you."

"But—please forgive me for asking—how does it happen you haven't shaved under the arms?"

"Shh! I've got to go to the beauty parlor."

"But what do you do at the Scala when you dance?"

"Oh, that! There's a kind of shield you put under your arms, then nobody can see the hair." She made a wry face, curling her upper lip, as coquettish little girls do when they want to be forgiven.

"Tell me something," he said. "By the way, what's your name? Laide? Do me a favor, satisfy my curiosity, do you by any chance live in Corso Garibaldi?"

"Me?" She looked surprised. "Not even near there! Why?"

"No special reason. I saw you once, though, in Corso Garibaldi."

"Me in Corso Garibaldi?" Her voice lost its tone of banter. "When?"

"I don't remember exactly. Three, four months ago. It was in the evening. Around September or October."

"I haven't been in Corso Garibaldi in two years!"

"You went into an alley that leads into an inner quarter, a place they call the Storta."

"Me in the Storta?" She pronounced it Stovta, with a most engaging Milanese "r." "Fine places you send me to! I've never been in the Storta in my life, thank heaven!"

"Why? What's wrong with it?"

"What's wrong with it? In the Storta there's nothing but crooks and whores and pimps and pansies. My God!"

"What do you know about all that stuff?"

"Everybody knows about it. Why, what do you mean?"

"Nothing. I didn't even know the Storta existed."

"All right, but just bear in mind I don't set my foot in places like that." She seemed angry.

"What do you want me to say? I thought I'd seen you, that's all."

"It must have been somebody who looks like me. What was she wearing?"

"As though I'd remember!" Actually Antonio remembered very well.

"What did you see me do there? Walk the streets?"

"Why are you getting so upset? What did I say so awful?"

"Never mind, just remember with me certain topics of conversation don't go. Okay? Finished. Now. . . ."

She drew him to her and glued her mouth to his.

6

WHO WAS the girl? Where was she going? What did she want? Why was she leading the life she led? She seemed so young, so alive, so genuine. If she'd been born into a family like his, would she have come to Ermelina's? What had gone wrong in her childhood that drove her to this? Was it a passion for liberty, or rebellion, a love of clothes, or was it some wild desire to be humiliated, to squander herself, sell her body, abandon herself to anonymous desires, and to be destroyed?

As he dressed, in the particular state of mind, which is both serene and sad, that follows sensual indulgence, Antonio thrust aside the muslin curtain that covered the window, and looked out. He hadn't thought he was so high up. Across the way there was a house of the same height, maybe even higher. To the right of it opened a kind of passage over which one's eye could roam across an unlimited expanse of terraces and roofs—of roofs above all, black and crowded with chimney pots. He stood at the window and looked out, breathing in the city and its inhabitants:

Down below him lay Milan out of which Laide came. Balconied houses with the stench of cats, flower pots blossoming in May and underwear hanging from lines and the voice of a young girl singing freely, and the ghastly quarrel between *him* and *her*, with words it would be shameful to repeat. The sun beats down on the garden of a noble house, warming a little its yellowish walls with their coat of arms; the rag man calls in the mornings as he approaches slowly and then he's there underneath and before you know it he's gone; the squealing of the tram around the bend; every once in a while the accountant's eyes converge with a kind of hiss on the back of the neck of his fifteen-year-old girl employee; the communal wells in the court-yards glitter with rain, black and glassy. A phonograph on some seventh floor has been left to itself and says taa-taa taa-taa because she's been thrown across the sofa and panting he grabs hold of her. Eleven-thirty in the morning after the grain market's over Signor Marsigliani from Borgotaro will come and say a blonde girl please. The delivery truck unloads packages of bobbins, this time the boss is in a black mood, God only knows where to put all that hot stuff. All right if you'd like to, dear, what do you do? you're a waitress? here's my number if you like, but keep one thing in mind: cleanliness above all, perfumes don't matter but soap and toothpaste do, those creatures that hang around in the Carminati underpass they need the dark! The door creaked, no mother I was at Nora's listening to records and she talked and talked that's why I'm late, three thousand a night plus the sale of the flowers plus the extras if you know what I mean. You won't play the fine lady here in my house, the whole thing is to hook onto one of those old codgers who when you shake them make a clinking sound they're so loaded with gold; Milka made off with one this fall who was a sight he was so repulsive but she made up for it with a mink coat have you seen it? That humming of the elevator as it goes up and down. He takes her chin between two fingers and tweaks it angrily six seven times and then he grabs her and then he shakes her again, she looks at him frightened. And no more of that, baby, he says to her, you diddled me out of twenty tens, one after the other, and if you try it once more I'll settle your hash, you'll get such a beating you won't even be able to make a hundred a night, have you got that straight? and then maybe he wallops you as he knows how to and you think your whole face has exploded, and bang, down you go, and then if he really beats you up so much the better, that's the way you learn. And sometimes he takes his belt to your behind, you ought to see the marks you can't work for a week, your legs too. Kasparri the engineer's chauffeur gets out of uniform every evening but who gives him the money for the night clubs? he's as ugly as a gorilla but they say Signora Kasparri, who looks like an angel like a madonna, they say she goes out of her mind every night with jealousy knowing he's guzzling champagne with the whores but what can she do? It's like a disease. In the S.N.A.D.L. office the telephone rings in the dark, at that hour the telephone rings six seven times, the whole immense building can hear it, a really hopeless sound until around three-thirty. It's about a week now since a discrepancy of thirteen million was discovered. In the pit at the service station the attendant looks up and sees the bellies and the crotches and the private parts of the cars—the Seicentos and the Millecentos—always the same way with their filthy sores, and he's anxious to get away and between wheels he keeps glancing at the clock a quarter to six, ten to six. Also upstairs in the T.E.T.R.A.M. office the telephone rings. No absolutely no. Unmovable, he laughs sardonically, a cigarette in his mouth: at least three no's and again no; I sent you especially, I hope you're not going to make me sorry I did now with all those expenses we've had on your account, and meanwhile he thinks about the black stockings on the legs of a certain number and he feels a tightening in the crotch but that's ridiculous he's got a wife and children. And the heels the heels the vulgar noise of heels on the stairs with the weight of the hips surrendering to the law of gravity. Hurry up Ines there's a gentleman waiting for you, what gentleman? you know you know him, he's the one who always comes this time of day, don't hold back, make him squirt his heart out, you know what I mean. From the sixth floor balustrade a woman leans out, her eyes out, her belly out, waiting for him but he doesn't come. At last on the mezzanine the light of dawn and maybe the sky is clear and blue but maybe there are clouds, anyway there's the damned business of the dawn from the moment the sun comes up, but the city doesn't know it never knows it, the houses dark and shuttered and sleeping and the few, the very few, still awake feel something almost divine for an instant, for a fraction of an instant only, because then sleep comes, worries, time schedules, dark listless light of dawn over the big city—but is it really big? ridiculous, there are hundreds bigger all over the world. On the mezzanine the light filters through the chinks, which shows how serious it is. The naked girl looks at the man who's bought her for the night. She sees him satisfied and sleeping with his mouth half open like the manhole covers over the sewers in the street or like the flickering light at the altar of Our Lady of Sorrows where she kneels in the frost of dawn; she too this morning with a black veil over her head, she, she too, why not? she prayed, tears in her eyes, she prayed for her lover, for her future, for her home; a priest hanging about the nave watches her slyly, yet without loss of his ecclesiastical dignity; the smell of incense, the feeling of houses all about, one attached to the other, upright, gray, filled with human lives, huge stage curtains one after the other barricaded piled around the little nineteenth century church with the black scaling walls; kneeling hurt her she felt cleansed in spite of the night she'd spent at the mercy of an unknown buyer, indeed because of it because of the personal sacrifice that prostitution involves. Her mother at home sick maybe with a horrible disease pains down there every night every night, and all around the black outlines of the walls with the reflection they cast over her with her shadowy veil. A pale violet light in the dashboard of the Supersport while he puts one hand on her leg, like that, casually, as though to sample the merchandise and idiotic chatter all the time: do you know the one about the little boy that talked dirty? well there was this little boy and he comes into the parlor and his mother's there with a lot of her lady friends and the little boy says (turning the corner he almost ran into a taxi but got away fast in third, it's really nice this feeling of mechanical power). What's the difference what's wrong with him as long as he doesn't have bad breath, she felt something happen to her left stocking above the knee, she wasn't expecting that, damn him they cost money; the colonel on the floor above in the rooming house with his little mongrel dog who looks at her when he meets her on the stairs, how he looks at her, if he knew, my god if he knew... there's no question high heels are becoming, they're tiring but what they do to the legs, the eyes of the men are like threads, she feels them sticking to her like cobwebs, pigs! At school Sister Celeste always said to her that's enough, looking at yourself in the window panes is a sin, that's what she said, it was winter through the window the avenue was completely covered with snow and quieter than ever before and the street lamps one after the other as far as the eye could see, but that night there were very few cars while on the old worn stairs there were dim little lights on every floor, except on the third it was burnt out, and out of it comes the light that tells so many terrible things. God, God, the dark walls, the puddle, the car mysteriously parked, the peculiar laboratory in the basement where odd people come and go, the hideous photographic studio on the first floor that never seems to do any business, the fantastic snarl of chimneys on the roof, court yards being swallowed up, somebody's always peeing in the corner, the clicking of the latch every now and then from the lodging house next door, the tablet on the house where the Milanese patriot lived, the brick that sticks out, the nightly argument in the tavern in the little court yard, the terrible closeness of pullulating lives and nothing is known nothing is ever known. In a kind of silent roar, night was already falling, lights here and there but the tops of the houses still black enigmatic shapes steaming with mist. He, Dorigo, was on the edge of an immense dark pit, out of it came Laide out of that unknown kingdom and a voice inside Dorigo, not really a voice, more a deep knell, called him called him. . . .

What nonsense! he said to himself. He let the muslin curtain fall, turned from the window and looked at his watch. At that moment, coming out of the bathroom, he saw Laide: she'd drawn back her hair, beautifully tight, in a hard little chignon. Doubtless a bad girl but she, without makeup on her mouth, only said to him, "What, aren't you dressed yet?"

7

HE SAW her again a few days later, again at Signora Ermelina's. He telephoned as usual but this time asked for Laide. When he met her for the second time, however, in that parlor of Signora Ermelina's, he felt somehow disappointed. She'd let her hair fall onto the back of her neck and looked slovenly, and her features seemed to him common, and even vulgar, with her petulant nose that ended in a little bump and her sly lips parted in a provocative, self-assured expression. He was also amazed by the casual way in which, in front of him, Ermelina, and a rather ugly girl who had stopped by, Laide discussed subjects usually considered indelicate. When she spoke of her fellow dancers, she said they were all whores.

"Yet there must be some who are still virgins," said Ermelina.

"Oh, of course," replied Laide, with a laugh, "but they're worse than the others. There's one, a friend of mine, of good family too, who's such a pig," she made a dreadful little gesture, "her sides got as wide as that, so of course she had to stop dancing, you can imagine the goings on. However, she's still a virgin."

"But what difference does it make if she got heavy?" asked Dorigo.

"There's nothing worse," replied Laide firmly, with the air of one who knows.

When they got into bed and began to make love it wasn't like the first time either. Caresses and kisses seemed like bureaucratic formalities. He tried to find out something about her, but Laide wasn't inclined to confidences. He discovered only that she lived with a married sister, who was twelve years older than she, and that her mother had died a few months ago, her father fifteen years ago. Her sister was always ailing, her brother-in-law owned a small business. The fact that she was a dancer at the Scala gave her considerable liberty of action and the right to come home late at night.

It was on the subject of the Scala, however, that Laide was most secretive. In an effort to impress her, and to establish also a kind of professional bond between them, Antonio told her he was just then designing sets and costumes for a ballet by Lachenard, *L'Etoile du Soir*. Would she be in it too? Of course, she said, though she didn't like the ballet. "Were you at the rehearsal yesterday?" "Yesterday, no, I wasn't, yesterday I had a slight fever."

As for her last name, there was no way at all of finding it out.

"What's the difference?" she said. "We can see each other all the same, can't we?"

"Are you afraid of something?"

"No, it's the way I am, that's all. The less you tell the better off you are."

"You don't trust me."

"I don't give my name to people."

"Your phone number then."

"That, I can tell you, that, absolutely nobody in the entire world knows. There'd be hell to pay if people started calling at the house and asking for me, my sister would make a real stink."

"How does Ermelina telephone you?"

"I call her. Every now and then I give her a ring."

"To find out what's new?"

"Or else she calls me after midnight at the Due."

"That dance hall?"

"Yes."

"Do you go there every night?"

"Every night no, I don't go there every night. When I go, I do a number."

"What kind of number?"

"We call it a slow dance."

"What do you wear?"

"I'm dressed, don't worry, I wear tights."

Dorigo had been to the Due a couple of times with friends. It was called the Due in an allusion to the prison of San Vittore which was popularly known in Milan as "El do" because its doorway bore the number 2. It was in the center of town, underneath a bar, one of those so-called existentialist dance halls fantastically decorated with macabre or abstract paintings in rather a student sort of taste. Young boys and girls, very young indeed some of them, made frenzied displays of themselves in acrobatic boogie-woogies or rock'n'roll. On the whole it was a pleasant enough place—more sporting than sinning. The touch of the shady, of the underworld, that so fascinated the well-to-do middle class, was supplied by the narrow little stairway that led down to it, the rude inscriptions on the walls each with a double meaning of some sort, and the vulgarity however naïve of the murals, which were French surrealist. There were no hostesses, but the young girls who danced the numbers would hardly have been novices in a convent. They had no hesitation, doing their pirouettes and somersaults, about letting their partners handle them in every part of their bodies. Antonio remembered having watched what they called "a slow dance." It was a kind of modernized *apache*, where time and again the girl was flung down to the floor, dragged around by the hair, and brutally manhandled. It was apparently that sort of thing that Laide danced.

"How about the Scala in that case?"

"If there's a performance, the Scala's over at midnight, twelve-thirty at the latest."

"Does your sister know you dance at the Due?"

"God no! There'd be hell to pay."

"What time do you get home? Three? Four?"

"Listen, I get home at one, at the latest, one-thirty. Or else my sister—I hate to think about it."

There was a great deal in her stories that Antonio found unbelievable. That Ermelina, for instance, didn't know her phone number. Or that her sister didn't know the kind of life she was leading, and that she was unaware of the nightly exhibitions at the Due. Or that the Scala even allowed one of its ballerinas to dance in a place like that. But she spoke with such assurance and in a tone of such absolute sincerity he found it impossible not to believe her; he'd have had to think her a complete monster otherwise.

Anyway, what difference did it make to him? He'd have her another couple of times at most, then once his curiosity was satisfied he'd be bored with her. Laide wasn't one of those clever workers who know how to reanimate desire even after a long acquaintance. So if he asked her about herself and her life, it was only out of the fascination that her unknown world, the world of those girls, had for him. How, he kept wondering, did they live? What did they hope for? How did they manage to stand the life? Who were their real lovers? They belonged to the world of upright ordinary families and at the same time to the underworld, they knew the sons of the richest families, they went to their luxurious summer villas, they clambered aboard their Ferraris and their yachts, and they deluded themselves into believing they belonged there, but in fact, of course, they were only being tolerated as instruments of amusement and pleasure and so were inevitably despised. They may have gone as invited guests to the *garçonnières* of millionaires but if they made any trouble or if they refused to submit tamely to the most obscene and humiliating caprices, or if they asked for ten thousand lire extra, then maybe they'd get knocked around in a drunken way and insulted as if they were the lowest whores off the sidewalk. They displayed their knowledge of expensive dressmakers and great international hotels, they talked about their evenings at the most fashionable night clubs, in shops they were haughty and impossible to please, on the street they walked with the scornful air of the loftiest princess, but at the same time they'd run panting to some small hotel near the station to satisfy, in return for a five thousand lire note, the lust of a fifty-year-old broker, a fat obscene creature who treated them like servants.

Ermelina was waiting in the hall when he left. The parlor door was closed, he could hear a confabulation going on, interrupted by bursts of laughter. There was a man's voice. Another client, probably. Maybe Laide had been picked out for him. Antonio gave twenty thousand lire to Ermelina.

"Tell Laide goodbye for me, will you?"

"She's coming now."

Ermelina half-opened the bathroom door.

"Are you ready? Signor Tonino wants to say goodbye to you."

Laide came out of the bathroom in her slip. She smiled at him. "Bye, honey."

That "honey" annoyed him. It sounded too professional. As he left, he felt as though he'd been freed of her. Yet seeing her again had left him with an odd uneasiness. Maybe it was because of his memory of the girl in the Corso Garibaldi. It was as though something about Laide had touched him deep inside. As though she were different from the others. As though between him and her a lot of other things were still to happen. As though he would come away from their relationship changed. As though Laide was the whole perfect incarnation of the forbidden world of adventure. As though there was some kind of inevitability about it. As when a person, without any special symptoms, feels he's about to be ill yet knows neither the why nor the wherefore. As when you hear from below the squeak of the outside gate and though the building is enormous, though hundreds of families live in it and there's a continuous coming and going, nevertheless you know at once when the gate opens that someone is coming for you.

And so he felt a certain sense of fear at the prospect of a third meeting as well as a strong desire for it. Things could become complicated. He could get stuck, more firmly bound to her than he already was. But it didn't happen. Her fascination dissolved, of itself, in the commonplace act of paying money to make love. Laide after all was only one of many. Pleasing to be sure, real, physically vital. But empty. There had never, after all, been anything between them.

The next day he left with Soranza, and a friend of his, to go skiing. He stayed a week at Sestriere. Dede was there, a girl of good family, whom he'd met the year before at Cortina. They went skiing together every day. Laide might never have existed for him.

8

AT FOUR there was to be a rehearsal of Lachenard's ballet, *Evening Star*. They told him about it at the last minute, and Antonio had already arranged with Ermelina to meet Laide at four. "What's your preference?" Ermelina had asked him on the phone. "Shall I get Laide to come?" In her voice there had been a slight shadow of guile as though she had decided she knew something. "What's your preference?"

"Oh, I don't know."

"Shall I get Laide to come?"

"All right, Laide. Or else Lietta."

"Lietta?"

"She told me her name was Lietta."

"Ah, Lietta! A little on the heavy side, is that the one?"

"Yes," he said.

"Would you prefer Lietta?"

"Either one, I don't care, you decide."

It wasn't true. Lietta was a great husky girl with red hair he'd met a couple of months before and now he felt like having her again. She had the shoulders of a javelin-thrower, flat but powerful breasts, legs that could grip. As for Laide, he knew her well enough already, she promised no new sensation. Nice, yes, she attracted him. But...

"All right," Signora Ermelina had said on the phone. "One or the other."

But at the last minute they told him about the rehearsal and he phoned to break the date.

"Never mind," said Signora Ermelina, "the worst that can happen is I'll have to get her to the phone and tell her not to come."

"Which one?"

"I got Laide for you."

"I'm terribly sorry but it really isn't my fault."

Better this way. For, the fact was, he realized, that he had been going to Ermelina's more out of habit than out of need, for the satisfaction of experiencing, the vague pleasure of enjoying, some beautiful, virtually unknown girl who for twenty or thirty minutes would be his, a girl all the men on the street would turn their heads to look at. As he was about to go onstage, he realized that Laide should be there too, since this ballet was using the entire corps of the school.

He continued onstage. He felt a slight embarrassment. He was unaccustomed to the world of dancers, and ballerinas for him were women first and dancers second. This was the first time he'd seen them so close.

There were six or seven chairs on the apron. Sitting there he saw the choreographer Vassilievski, the woman who directed the ballet school, the composer who had come especially from Paris, the conductor of the orchestra, the ballet master, and a couple of others. Further back there was an upright piano to take the place of the orchestra.

The curtain was drawn but the place was sunk in darkness. A few bare bulbs cast a white light over the stage. Higher up, and back, opened the mysterious cavern of the theatre, that fantastic tangle of rolled-up back drops, ropes, boards, strange machines, and catwalks; it made a dizzying perspective that suggested another world, complicated, fascinating, and absurd. The sets he'd designed weren't ready yet, so as a backdrop they were using a classic trompe-l'œil perspective of a cloister, maybe the one they used in *Forza del Destino*.

Introductions were made, he was offered a chair, they all treated him with the courteous deference that was due a guest unfamiliar with family affairs. He could just as easily not have come that afternoon. Work hadn't even been started on the costumes as yet. When the piano player began the opening bars, the ballet master came over to say that Clara Fanti, the prima ballerina, wanted to ask him about the costumes he'd designed for her. The ballet master smiled as if to say: you know as well as I do these women can't live without making a little trouble.

It was then he realized the sets and costumes no longer really mattered to him. They weren't the reason he had come. Once a job was finished, his habit was to forget it, maybe out of laziness, but in practice it seemed to him a sensible rule. No, he had come because of Laide, and until that very minute he hadn't realized it. Now he experienced an agony of impatience.

A group of ballerinas came onstage, ten or twelve, they were the shadows of the evening. No one was in costume of course, they all wore black tights. Without make-up, their hair mostly drawn back with a ribbon or a kerchief around their heads, most of them rather skinny, the impression they gave was of an ostentatious lack of interest, of slovenliness even, with white powder marks on their knees, elbows, and backsides, of uncleanliness. But this very carelessness of theirs made them seem bolder and more exciting, the tights they wore showed off their young bodies so much more clearly, they were infinitely more desirable, Antonio thought, as they were than in the elaborate splendor of their costumes.

Seeing them so close, watching them work so hard, without their make-up or their peacocks' tails, simple and unadorned, nuder than if they were naked, Dorigo suddenly understood their secret, he understood why for countless centuries dancers had been the incarnation of femininity, of the female body, of love. The dance itself was a symbol, a gorgeous symbol of the sexual act. The regimentation, the discipline, the iron-hard often cruel imposition of difficult and even painful steps, the forcing into tense yet open positions of those young virginal bodies to reveal their secrets, the freeing of legs, torso, and arms to the utter-most: it was all for the satisfaction of the male. And to the accomplishment of this task the dancers devoted themselves with passion, with pain and with sweat. In this lay its beauty. It was display, it was an offering of themselves, it was an invitation to make love, and yet they didn't even know it. Those half-closed mouths, those pale tender armpits opened wide, those legs spread longingly, that thrusting forward of the breast as for a sacrifice—it was as though they were throwing themselves into the passionate arms of some invisible, insatiable god. All the great choreographers had, cleverly enough, stylized this sexual phenomenon into apparently decorous attitudes that anyone could accept. But deep within the core remained. For one with eyes to see, a sequence of classic ballet steps was infinitely more revealing than the most lubricious belly dance of a stripteaser in a night club. Yet these were matters no one dared to talk or write about—because of the insane though universal conspiracy of pretense that surrounds the world of love.

The dance—this was Dorigo's discovery—was nothing but a lyric outburst of sex: else it was only decoration or absurdity. The crude lascivious solicitations of the prostitutes were comic when compared with the allusive, cunning blandishments of the ballerinas, for the ballerinas went to the very heart of the matter. The greater the dancer, and the more daring, harmonious, skillful, airy her performance, so much the more intense, in the man who watched her, was his desire to embrace her, to hold her, to touch her, to caress her, her thighs most especially, and at last to have her entirely.

Now another group of ten or twelve came on. They were the shadows of twilight.

Laide hadn't been in the first group. Then he thought, with a start, that she was the third girl in the second group, a brunette of medium height. They danced so fast it was hard to make out. Then the brunette drew near and as she turned she paused, along with the rest of the company, one leg raised behind her and balanced on the toe of the other foot. He was able to see her clearly then. He realized that this girl's nose was altogether different.

The prima ballerina came on, there was a *pas de deux*, then the first group again. The thing began to drag. Although they'd been thoroughly rehearsed by now, and had all the steps well in mind, Vassilievski, wearing a kind of overall, kept interrupting them, oftener perhaps than someone else would have, maybe because he liked to show off, and he would redo one step or another, without music, accompanying himself with curious little cries: la, la, ta-ta, la. Vassilievski was getting on, he must have been around fifty, yet he still had the dash, the precision, and the elegance, if not the muscular power, of his youth, when he was considered one of the two or three great premiers danseurs in the world.

Eight fireflies came on, young and thin, all of them. They too had that slovenly, sloppy air about them, like workmen who take pains about their work only when they're in the mood: the people at the rehearsal weren't there, naturally, to judge the dancers' beauty; and as for Dorigo, so new to this world, it seemed to him none of the dancers was even aware of it.

Laide wasn't among the fireflies either.

Ten bats came whirling on. These were men, and Vassilievski did a lot of work with them, correcting, modifying, rectifying, occasionally inventing new movements. What with all this rehearsing and re-rehearsing, the bats alone took over half an hour.

Then, as Antonio was watching Vassilievski, a group of goblins burst in from the right. At the moment he wasn't even aware of them.

They were eight ballerinas. After a number of quick steps on the points, they began a series of cabrioles, now on their hands, now on their feet, making complete turns.

Antonio saw her. She'd pulled her hair into a chignon on the back of her neck, she wore no lipstick, her face had the wild-eyed look women wear when they wake up in the morning. He might not even have recognized her. It was not by her body he identified her, which was so much like the bodies of the rest of the company, of much the same height and weight—it was by the way she danced, as she walked, with a listless, haughty, somewhat malicious air. Of the eight, she was the only one who hardly even bothered to do the cabrioles, she danced lazily, without even throwing her arms and legs up all the way, just hinting at the movements. As if to say: These things are nonsense, so far as I'm concerned, they aren't worth the trouble, I could do them without half trying.

He kept his eyes on her but she never looked at him. It was Laide and yet it wasn't really Laide. With her costume, which wasn't a real costume, she'd changed even the expression of her face. And because her shoes had no heels, she seemed shorter.

She was wearing a black jersey with long sleeves and heavy black stockings that went nearly all the way up but he couldn't understand how they stayed up. Between the lower edge of the jersey and the top of the stocking a half-moon of skin lay exposed. She wasn't the only one dressed like that, evidently it was an accepted outfit. That patch of naked thigh had a special meaning, it was a kind of allusion, a reference to forbidden things.

She was not in tights, she was wearing a jersey with long sleeves that clung to her back, to her little childish breasts, and to her behind. A pair of black stockings covered her legs entirely save that the hem failed to meet the lower edge of the jersey, which, tight over the flesh, pulled away. Thus a strip of skin glowed whitely against the black. It was almost a provocation, a caress, a wink, an invitation.

The cabrioles finished, she'd have to pass quite near him, no more than a few feet away, and turning her head now to one side, now to the other, she'd be bound to see him, her glance cross his. But there wasn't a flash of recognition, not the least change of expression, not a sign. It was as though she'd never seen him before, as if he didn't in fact exist.

No. It wasn't his sets or his costumes or his work he cared about. The hell with them. She was the one he kept thinking of, kept hoping she'd stand out and be better than the others. But she wasn't, no better and no worse; probably she could have been if she'd wanted to but she made a point of not wanting to. Listlessly, she'd done the absolute minimum that was necessary if she were not to disrupt the harmony of the company.

Twice more she passed him, without doubt she saw him, but it looked as though she saw nothing at all.

Then Vassilievski stamped his foot down hard and made a gesture with his right hand; the piano stopped, the choreographer was giving them a rest. The dancers, boys and girls both, started to move off.

"Stay here, all of you! You've only got five minutes, you don't have time to go to your dressing rooms," cried the woman in charge of the school.

Then the director of scene production appeared. Himself a celebrated designer, he went up to Dorigo to compliment him on his sketches. He spoke enthusiastically, perhaps a little too much so, but it didn't seem hypocritical, rather as though he wanted to put Antonio, who was new to this world and clearly out of his element, more at ease.

"Thank you very much," Antonio replied. "It's very kind of you. This is the first time, you know, I've done anything quite so ambitious. I'm counting on your help. I know you can produce masterpieces out of a few squiggles on a sheet of paper."

As he spoke, he saw Laide joking with one of the dancers, a handsome husky boy taller than she by a head. She was standing quite near him. At a certain point, with a laugh, she punched him in the chest—and she was suddenly herself: impudent and mischievous, coquettish, common, self-assured.

It was like a pin, it was like a sharp point. The punch was so gay and comradely; it implied a long background of intimacy, or at least a free and easy relationship, an even footing, many things in common, memories, work, ambition, jokes, evenings in Milan, company gossip, dirty stories, secrets, nights of love perhaps, such a relationship as would have been impossible between Antonio and Laide, because of the difference in their ages if nothing else. He was old enough to be her father.

Signora Novi came over with Clara Fanti to discuss the costumes she wanted changed.

"You don't like them?" Dorigo asked the prima ballerina.

"No, no, I like them very much, but it's impossible to dance with that plume on my head."

He looked at her. Seen so close, wearing tights, the famous dancer was hardly that diminutive flashing sprite she seemed to be on stage or in the pages of the magazines. Yet—because of the rehearsal costume—she too looked far sexier. Her face was sharp and well-designed, her expression that of a stubborn child, her muscular arms might have been those of a woman of thirty, but her legs were still perfect and she made them seem even more exciting by wearing over her black tights a pair of long red stockings from her hips to her ankles. Because of this, her legs, her thighs, and particularly her calves, seemed stronger, harder, more authoritative, yet without losing their slimness, as though they expressed the whole personality of the dancer who otherwise appeared to have the lightness and fragility of a child. Antonio, strangely, felt no trace of desire for her.

"It's not a plume," he said. "It's got to be very very light. It's a kind of filigree."

"Made of what?"

"I don't know, I confess I don't know about those things, but without that plume, as you call it, I'd have to change the whole costume."

"No, no, I like the costume."

"Then you've got to have the plume."

"But how can I dance with that thing-um-abob on my head? Are you going to teach me how to dance?"

Signora Novi, in her pleasant, self-possessed manner, intervened. She proposed to make the plume a little smaller; she said the material would be extremely light, Clara wouldn't even know she was wearing it.

Meanwhile a group of boys and girls had gathered around, to look at the designs. Laide, however, wasn't among them.

The discussion lasted a few seconds longer, then the two women left him.

He found himself alone in the middle of the stage which was crowding again, the rehearsal was about to begin. He felt out of his element. He stood uncertainly, looking about.

He realized that no more than a step away, turning her shoulder to him, was Laide. Hands on hips, she was joking with a couple of the boys. The one she had been talking to first was not one of them.

It was a quick little scene, a dusting of time, but it stayed with him the rest of his life.

Another ballerina, a blonde, approached and said to Laide, "Mazza, could you come here for a minute, please?"

Laide waved goodbye to the two dancers with her left hand and turned to follow. And thus found herself face to face with Dorigo.

For a fraction of a second, inevitably, she looked at him. He was about to greet her. As she from the beginning had avoided making the least sign of recognition, Antonio guessed that she preferred, at the Scala, not to know him: out of a kind of squeamishness perhaps, not liking to mix the devil and holy water. But now they stood so close, face to face in fact, and so apart from all the others (certainly no one was watching them) that not to have said hello would have been absurd.

Antonio held back, waiting for her to greet him first. She, however, turned away to follow the other ballerina, quickly but without the least suggestion that she was trying to avoid him. That was the strangest thing: she showed no suggestion of pretense or of playing a part. Her indifference was absolute, rather it was a total absence of all reaction, for indifference is also a way of facing reality. It was as though, while looking him squarely in the face, she hadn't even seen him—he might have been a wall, a piece of furniture, someone so ordinary he was hardly visible. This was so unlike her, it seemed incomprehensible to Dorigo. There should have been something, a gleam of fright in her eyes, a gasp of surprise or annoyance, a mouth half-opened in apprehension. But there was nothing. It was impossible to explain. It made him feel very uneasy.

Yet it was also understandable, he thought, that she would want to keep her two lives apart, her life as a prostitute and her life as a ballerina at the Scala, and it was understandable too, he went on, that after the fun was over, she'd want to keep the client out of both her private and professional life; meeting him thus at the Scala, he'd become someone altogether unknown to her.

Nevertheless, Dorigo felt both snubbed and offended, as a man and as an artist.

What happened, or rather what hadn't happened, seemed to him, as he thought about it, ever worse and ever more humiliating. He began to feel a kind of agitation, anger, even rage, the reasons for which he tried to puzzle out. Was it because he no longer seemed to exist for her, even as a memory? Because his work as a designer hadn't made the slightest impression on her? Because she insisted on seeing Dorigo as a client and nothing more, an undifferentiated larva, and refused to think of him as a fellow-worker. Or was it because there seemed to be absolutely no way for him to catch her interest, not to mention her sympathy, no way at all for him to enter her life?

But why did all this upset him so? The question made him angriest of all. Why did he go on eating his heart out over her? What difference did she make to him? As a bed companion, he was bored with her, he already knew by heart everything he could hope to get out of her. And apart from bed, she was a little fool of no interest at all. Was it the romantic fascination of the ballerina, then? Could it be that? Was he so absurdly provincial? Anyway, who on earth was this ballerina? A member of the chorus, with no trace of an artistic personality. Anyway, anyway, was he sure it was really Laide he'd seen at the rehearsal?

9

THREE days later he telephoned Signora Ermelina. "Could you get Laide tomorrow afternoon for me?"

The fact that she'd pretended not to see him still annoyed him, he intended to have some sort of explanation from her.

"Poor Laide," said Signora Ermelina. "The other day—remember, Signor Tonino, when you couldn't come?—she arrived on the dot."

"At four?"

"On the dot."

He couldn't understand it. At four the rehearsal was starting at the Scala, and he'd seen Laide there on the stage. Or had she somehow managed to get to the theatre just in time for the entrance of the goblins? That might explain her listlessness as she danced.

Dorigo preferred, naturally, not to go into the matter with Signora Ermelina, it was nothing that concerned her. They made a date for the next afternoon at two-thirty.

The next morning, however, Laide telephoned him in the studio; it was the first time she'd done that, he found her voice with the funny little "r" strangely agreeable to hear.

"Will you do me a favor?" she said. "At two-twenty I'm supposed to leave for Rome."

"For Rome? Why?"

"I'm going to stay with my aunt and uncle for a week. They invite me every year. I don't want to miss it."

"What about the Scala?"

"I got a doctor's certificate."

"Then we won't be seeing each other?"

"Would you like to make it earlier?"

"How much earlier?"

"I don't know. One, one-fifteen. Then you could take me to the station."

"We'll have to do it with our hats and coats on, is that it?"

"If you can't, never mind."

"No, no, let's meet. One o'clock?"

"One at Signora Ermelina's. Bye."

Did Laide really want to see him? Or did she only want the fifteen thousand lire? Dorigo had a lot of work that day, but he arranged things so as to be free. He didn't mind skipping lunch.

At one he was at Signora Ermelina's. She told him to sit down in the living room. She went right back to the kitchen. She hadn't finished lunch yet. He heard the voice of another woman. He lit a cigarette.

One-five, one-ten. Signora Ermelina reappeared.

"They're all the same, those girls. Without a brain in their heads. Do you know where I had to go to dig her out last night? Her phone didn't answer."

"Where?"

"I had to go to that night club, the Due, where she dances a number."

"Does she do a number there every night?"

"When she's in Milan, she does."

"What do you mean? Does she go away fairly often?"

"Well, recently she's been in Modena all the time."

"Modena, why?"

"She says she goes there to work, to model for fashion photos."

"At Modena?"

"She says there's a big dressmaker there, I don't know."

"What about now? It's a quarter past one. And she told me she had to catch a train at two-twenty."

"She oughtn't to behave that way."

"She certainly won't come now." (He looked at his watch for about the twentieth time. How absurd it was. It wasn't as though he was waiting for someone he loved; after all she was only an ordinary call-girl, to be had by anybody who felt like spending twenty thousand lire, probably less. It was possible that in some other house Laide did her work for less, it was even probable. With those kids the more they earned the more they spent, they never had enough money, another five thousand lire are always a help, or four thousand, or even three. At this thought Dorigo felt some emotion deep inside him, annoyance, anguish, it was like being on fire, it made no sense to him. He looked at his watch again, it was one-seventeen.)

"No, no," said Signora Ermelina, "if she said she was coming, she'll come, don't worry," and she smiled wickedly "at my house they don't miss their appointments."

"Anyhow, there's no time now, if she has to leave at two-twenty. Time to get to the station...."

"She'll come, she'll come, there isn't any doubt of it," and she nodded her head three or four times, half-closing an eye. Did she mean that Laide certainly wouldn't let fifteen or even ten thousand lire go down the drain? Or that she'd never dare to treat Signora Ermelina that way? Why, she'd never set foot in that house again, the strumpet, there are thousands like her in Milan, prettier and younger and fresher, who wouldn't want anything better, and Ermelina's clientele was the best in Milan, the most respectable, the richest, the safest. The other madams either they took advantage of the girls or else they landed them in a mess, it's not very nice for a young student of a good family or a woman with a husband and maybe children to be found naked, let's say, in bed with a man she doesn't know and then taken away in a police wagon and kept twenty-four hours at least in a guard room with a lot of filthy old whores, and then the family is notified, the scandal, the scenes, and if by any chance a minor's involved then it ends up in the courtroom. While at Ermelina's no one has to worry, among her clients are some so highly placed nobody would dream of making trouble. And then—maybe she wanted to imply that too—the girls are afraid of her. She's an honest woman, a woman of good heart, how many she's helped in their difficult moments, poor unlucky wretches, she's like a mother to the dear girls, but it would be too bad if they tried anything that's all they'd need. Ah some thought they'd get away with it but they soon found they couldn't. It isn't hard to ruin a girl that's been around a bit; one thing about Ermelina she's always well-informed, she knows everything about all of them, sometimes a telephone call at home is enough, or else an anonymous letter, to set things right. She wouldn't be the first that Ermelina had ruined.

Suddenly Antonio realized he'd got up from the sofa, and was impatiently, nervously, pacing up and down, quite unable to control himself, while Signora Ermelina watched him complacently. In spite of his years, it seemed, the architect wasn't an old man yet!

"Wouldn't you like a coffee?" she said.

"No thanks," he let slip, "I haven't even eaten yet."

Ermelina burst into laughter.

"That's marvellous! A man like you! For Laide! A man like you to miss your lunch? You're really sweet, you know that? You're like a little boy!"

At that second the doorbell rang. It lacked one minute till one-thirty.

10

SHE CAME in breathless, pale, with the look of a hunted beast.

"What a face!" cried Signora Ermelina, as she gave her an affectionate tap on the cheek. "What happened to you?"

"I've been racing," answered Laide, without even saying hello to Antonio. "There was a rehearsal at the theatre, they wouldn't let me go."

"But if you're going to Rome for a week," said Antonio, "what does a rehearsal matter?"

"Well, that's the way they are in the theatre. What time is it?"

"One-thirty by now."

"Come on! Come on!" cried Signora Ermelina, laughing. "Don't waste any more time."

Dorigo, to make things easier for Laide, undressed in a flash. But Laide, strangely enough, appeared to be in no hurry at all.

"I'll be with you in a minute," she said and went into the bathroom. He kept on looking at his watch. For a long time he heard water splashing. She reappeared at one-thirty-seven.

"Tell me something," he said at once, as soon as he had her in his arms, "why did you pretend you didn't know me the other day at the rehearsal?"

"Forgive me," she answered immediately, "but I prefer it that way. You know what gossips and trouble-makers they all are. If I'd said hello to you, right away they'd have wanted to know where I met you and when and how and why."

"But a smile at least!"

"No, no, in things like that I'm very fussy."

"But now I know your name."

"How wonderful! My name's Laide."

"Your last name."

"You know my last name?"

"Yes."

She drew her mouth from his.

"What's my name then?"

"Mazza."

She began to pound her fists against the pillow. "Damn, damn! I told you there are certain things I don't like people to know. How did you find out?"

"It was easy. One of the girls called you Mazza, that's all."

"Well, I don't like it."

"Why? Don't you trust me?"

"What's that got to do with it. It's always better...."

What a pretty mouth she had, though, small, soft, alive.

He tried to hurry up, determined to show how thoughtful he was, a real gentleman: at eighteen minutes to two it was all finished. You could hardly call it making love. But there was a train to catch.

"What about your bags?"

"They're down in the porter's box."

"I'm ready. Are you?"

"Just a little lipstick."

They left the room together.

"My God, what a face you've got today, you don't even look like yourself," said Signora Ermelina.

"Am I really so ugly?" she asked.

"Of course not, only you look a little tired."

"I know. I'm not going to the theatre any more. I've decided to give it up. It's not what it used to be. The atmosphere's just terrible now."

They asked him to wait outside on the landing. The two women had their accounts to settle, apparently. He heard their voices. In a little while she reappeared.

She had two bags, rather nice ones. The larger, in black and white leather, was very heavy.

Carrying it, he started for the car, which wasn't far. It was five to two. The sun sparkled down on Milan.

"Why did you say it's a terrible atmosphere?" he asked, it seemed to him a strange remark for a girl like her to make.

"It is, it is!" she cried, in an irritated tone. "Please don't ask me about it! I'm up to my ears with it. Anyway, I've made up my mind."

They reached Antonio's car, a Seicento. They put the bags in.

"And when," she said, "are you going to get around to turning in this old rattletrap?"

"I'm not. For getting around the city it's still the best."

"I'm used to something a little better, you know."

"Such as what? A Jaguar, a Mercedes, a Rolls Royce?"

"All right, don't get mad, I was only joking."

They'd come out of 25 via Velasca, where Signora Ermelina lived. Dorigo had carried the bags to the Piazza Missori where he'd left his car and arranged them on the back seat. The parking lot attendant came over. He was a hearty man who looked like Pella the minister and Dorigo gave him a hundred lire tip. As Laide sat down, her skirt slipped up, exposing her knees and a bit more, a shadow of something to come. In Signora Ermelina's house the bedroom had been clean but bare, the bed wide, there were no crucifixes or Madonnas on the walls, only a horrible oleographic reproduction of a seascape.

She said: "Do me a favor. You've got to go down via Larga anyway, I want to stop by the shoemaker's to pick up a pair of shoes."

He started the car, the traffic was ruinous, they moved slowly. He looked at his watch, it was already two o'clock.

He looked at Laide. It was the first time she'd been in the car with him. She sat in profile, paying no attention to him at all.

He thought she might have turned to look at him, not because he was under the illusion that he was handsome but she ought to have been glad to know a man like him, out of vanity if nothing else, to feel herself under the protection of somebody as respectable as he was. After all she couldn't have been very accustomed to people that respectable, undoubtedly she'd never even met a man as respectable as he was, or rather yes she undoubtedly had met them and she'd gone to bed with them and they'd kissed her and done all the other things but not one of them had treated her as he was doing; they'd all treated her like a little twenty thousand lire tramp, politely but underneath they felt only the liveliest contempt for her—so he thought—while he made no distinction between respectable and not, he treated her like a lady, he wouldn't have treated a princess any better, he wouldn't have given a princess any more consideration. He felt he was owed in return at least a smile, a glance of acknowledgement.

But she didn't look at him, though he constantly turned to look at her. She looked straight ahead, at the street, with a tense almost anxious expression, she was no longer the arrogant and self-assured little girl.

She had almost no lipstick on, she wasn't pretty any more, she was like a frightened animal, as when she had turned up at Signora Ermelina's.

"That's it there. Can you stop here?"

"Hurry up, though, otherwise I'll be fined."

She was no longer the bold, proud girl, she was a hunted creature seeking escape. She got down from the car and went through a doorway. He lit a cigarette. It was already five past two.

Soon she reappeared holding a cellophane bag with a pair of shoes inside it.

"Are they new?"

"No, I had to have some new heels put on."

Hurrying toward the station, he continued to look at her, he couldn't help it. Not she. She looked ahead, her nose was no longer petulant and whimsical; it had become the most important thing in her face, it seemed to have scented danger.

She didn't speak, she was locked into herself, some preoccupation held her tight, she looked straight ahead, onto the street. It wasn't impatience, it wasn't fear of missing the train, it was something more. As though everything around her was unfriendly and she had to look after herself. As though whatever it was she was waiting for, in five minutes, or an hour, or tomorrow, constituted a threat. As though the voyage she was about to embark on wasn't to be fun at all but rather a disagreeable *corvée* to which she was being forced to submit.

She wasn't beautiful, she was pale, she was thinking secret troubling thoughts. He went on looking at her, she made no response.

The more she looked about her in that watchful way, the more certainly she became the remote, unattainable resident of a world forbidden to him. And the more he wanted her, though she had belonged to other men, unknown men, innumerable other men whom he hated as he now forced himself to picture them: tall, easy, moustached, at the wheel of some powerful car, men who treated her as something that was theirs, as one of so many girls who had belonged to them, not even worth the trouble of thinking about, but at the right moment in the evening, after the night club, a bit drunk, to take her to some room and not even to watch her as she undressed. Like antique satraps, they go into the bathroom to urinate or rinse their mouths with Odol, sure of finding her in bed, and naked, and if it so happened, then, if they felt like it, to squeeze her breasts a bit, and in the best of cases to spread her legs with their arms and bending over to sink their snouts in her groin. What a condescension for them, these selected types with their Ferraris and their yachts at Cannes, but the next day, on the links at Monza, they wouldn't even think about her. A little whore like so many others, not worth thinking about, neither more nor less than a drink taken at a country bar during a long trip in an open car with the sun shining down, just to quench the thirst and then away, the bar forever forgotten and the girl behind the bar too, a brunette, not bad, who at a certain point, as she was looking for the bottle of soda, leaned forward. And through the loose summer dress the girl was wearing, her round, hard, peasant breasts could be glimpsed, could in fact be seen perfectly well, and for an instant there rises the thought how fine it would be to stop here and in the hot night buzzing with mosquitoes, while outside from time to time trucks pass with their shattering racket, to throw her over the bed and undress her, revealing her muscular brown limbs, all so natural, with that good smell of sweat and laundry soap. She gives herself to the rich gentleman from the city, with the naïve vanity of the country girl who hopes thus perhaps to live a bit of the picture story she read a couple of hours earlier while Cavalier Frazzi and Signor Viscardoni were playing cards in the corner there at the back, and maybe, after having had me, he'll realize what kind of dish I am and take me with him in that wonderful car to Milan and he'll buy me a house and take me to the theatre and I'll show my build off to those mincing hags with their flabby breasts. I'll make them slobber with envy. But Claudia's waiting for him outside in the car, she's so sophisticated she bores him to death but he can't just leave her that way, for bourgeois conventions are very strong, they impose a code of behavior, and so he routs the desire for the waitress, he doesn't even say goodbye to her, he goes out into the sun, he gets back into the car, he continues on down the highway, while Claudia dozes asking every now and then lazily, "Where are we?"

Laide, the human being seated beside him in the small car, with all her childhood memories, her dreams, anxieties, school day worries, longings for toys and beautiful clothes, holidays begun bravely and hopefully and ended in the evening with disappointment in the dreary little room without a window, with her whole infinite world of memories, facts, hopes, worn shoes, home-made underwear, the illusion of being special, destined to the attention of fine gentlemen, able to make them fall in love, but instead this splendid creature is put up for sale like merchandise. The madam says: I have a little thing that's just what you like, dark, slender, sexy, do you know what I mean? and he says let's hope it won't be like the last time, the last time was a mess she didn't even know how to kiss. Then Laide is told to come in and he, without even asking her what her name is, sits her down on his knees and begins to finger her and then absentmindedly pulls the zipper down her back and she lets him do it and then he undresses her and unfastens the clasp of her brassiere and then plays with her breasts, the little virginal breasts, it's a well known game, and meanwhile with the other hand he gropes for her sex to see what her reaction's going to be, no no, that's enough! how ridiculous, how crazy, what did he care after all what this girl did, where she went and with whom? There were hundreds like her. He had not the slightest intention—a man like him at his age—of getting mixed up with a girl like that. It's all he needed. Let her go and do it with whomever she wanted and whenever she wanted, he had plenty of other far more important things on his mind although it's true he liked her, not only her face and body but also the way she spoke with her Milanese accent, the way she moved and walked. To have her next to him in the car was very pleasant, not that today she looked so wonderful, she was really beat pale and drawn, she even looked ugly. No, actually being near her was pleasant, and that she'd got into the car with him after all was proof of her confidence in him, he felt actually flattered by it, ridiculous maybe but that's the way it is: flattered as though someone above him had condescended to him. Anyway there she was sitting next to him in the car, for that fleeting moment if she wasn't his she at least wasn't anyone else's either; in a little while, in a few hours, this evening, yes, she'd be naked, embraced and held and possessed by the body of some other man, young, virile, well-muscled maybe, but not for the moment, not for the rest of this short ride. And he thought but said nothing. And she thought, he knew perfectly well that she was thinking about something that had nothing to do with him, she was thinking about something or other that might net her a little cash.

His respite ended. He stopped at the cab rank of the central station in Milan, she got down, rapt and tense, looking for a porter to carry her bags. Then she turned: "Give me your address."

"Why?"

"I'll send you a postcard."

Taxis pressed around him, thundering at him. He left, he glimpsed her a last time, from the back, as she entered the ticket office with her hard, self-assured, haughty dancer's walk. But did she really leave?

11

WHY DID it matter so much to him? Why did he go on thinking about her? What was he afraid of? that Laide would disappear out of his life? Ridiculous! A phone call was all it took to send her running for a taxi; and there she'd be, at his command, her linen impeccable, her body so well washed he could kiss her wherever he liked.

No. The argument was pointless. It wasn't enough. She'd come running, true, when Signora Ermelina phoned, and she'd go to bed with him, but all the whole thing came down to was half an hour an hour at the most, for her only a short interval of work, to be got through gracefully but also as quickly as possible (Dorigo knew well he didn't excite her, when he kissed her sex Laide kept her eyes shut, her lips half-parted, but there was never a real throb, a sigh, a moan; better that way though than the disgusting little comedies some prostitutes played, convinced that when making love all men with no exceptions are complete idiots). A half-hour, an hour at the most with him, a couple of times a week. And the rest of the time? All the other hours of the day and the night? Where did she go? Whom did she see? Her real life, ambitions, amusements, happiness, vanity, love, all lay elsewhere, not in the few moments she spent with Antonio. She was really *there*, and out *there* was all he wanted to know about her, out *there* was her world, mysterious, fascinating, maybe wicked and squalid as well, a world forbidden to him. How angry he'd get when, for instance, after making love, he'd suggest taking her home in the car and she'd say no, she had to stay on a bit longer at Signora Ermelina's to try on a dress and he knew perfectly well the dress was a meaningless excuse, what she was really waiting for was another customer. Or else, if they happened to meet in the evening, she'd leave before him; they were waiting for her at the theatre, she said, or she didn't want to get home late—if she did her sister would be up in arms—or else her girl friend was waiting for her downstairs in the car.

And then it wasn't even true that Laide, for those ten or fifteen thousand, was always at his beck and call. Today for instance they were supposed to meet at two-thirty and Ermelina on the phone told him she'd gone the evening before to the Due to look for her and in fact had had to get a friend to go with her because she couldn't go to the Due alone, and Laide said she'd come at two-thirty and Antonio went at two-thirty and in the living room there was only that mess Wanna, because Signora Ermelina was in the kitchen and Wanna told him Laide had telephoned a little while before to say she couldn't come because she had to go to Modena, and he sat there without quite realizing what was happening to him and Wanna watched him with a sort of pity in her eyes and then she said, "We've had a blow, haven't we?"

He didn't say anything, he lit a cigarette in the empty room and then Wanna moved nearer and began to touch him here and there and then Antonio to be free of that feeling of anguish, after having held out a little—he'd even decided to go—nodded yes if for no other reason than to show there wasn't a word of truth in it. So they went into the other room and Wanna got undressed and began to play those perverted little games that he always liked but not that day and the pleasure was like an animal's over in a few seconds.

While he in obvious dejection was getting dressed, Wanna from the bed watched him with a smile of commiseration:

"Quite a blow, huh?"

"What do you mean?"

"Laide, isn't it?"

He shrugged.

"Tell me," said Wanna, "is she that good?"

"What a question! I like her."

"Come on, tell the truth. Can she do it like me?"

"What's that got to do with it?"

"It's funny, usually when they go with Laide, after the first time they...."

"After the first time they what?"

"After the first time there isn't a second time, they don't come back, they've had enough, they want someone else."

"Yes?"

"You're the first. Usually with her once is enough, then they want someone else. She's cute, I don't say she isn't. With all that black hair. Don't you think she's cute?"

He looked at her and he hated her. That hag was talking about Laide as she would about one of her own kind, ready like her to sell her body to the first comer. Yet she was right! It seemed dreadful to him that a fresh young girl like Laide should be put in the ranks of professional whores and that they should consider her a colleague.

"Isn't she cute?" Wanna went on, teasing him.

"Drop it!" cried Antonio, exasperated at last.

Wanna burst out in laughter. "Look at him, he doesn't want naughty things said about the woman he loves! The little virgin! She's taken on a regiment, that Laide of yours. Listen, I'm telling you, I've known a lot of girls, but one that carries on as much as she does I've never known. However, if you like her!"

"Yes, I think she's very cute," he said.

"Very cute?" Wanna's voice grew sharp. "Do you know her specialty?"

"What do you mean, her specialty?"

"In making love, I mean. Haven't you found out yet?"

"Found out what?"

"You haven't? Then it's better if you don't know. I can see she hasn't gone all out with you."

"What specialty?"

"Better if you don't know. If you knew, you'd be through with her, I'm sure of it. Or maybe you'd like her even better. You men!"

"Well, what is it?"

"Nothing."

"Are you going to tell me or not? What's the specialty?"

"Better not. Not that it's any mystery and she's the first to tell you, with me she's always bragging about how she spent two years in those houses. She wants to show off, she likes to be at the head of the class, but the fact is she isn't. No, it's better if I don't tell you because if she really hasn't played those little games with you—"

"Little games?"

"Little games, exercises, filthy tricks, obscenities, whatever you want to call them, the fact she hasn't done it with you makes me wonder—"

"Why? Is it really such a terrible thing?"

"Terrible? It's marvellous—if it's well done."

"All right, are you going to tell me or not?"

"No I'm not, I told you, it's better not. But you've had a nice slap in the face, haven't you?" There was a note of hatred in her voice.

"I'm going," said Dorigo, folding two ten thousand lire notes and putting them under an empty glass vase that stood on a table. He went toward the door.

Wanna tried to mend matters. "Don't take on so!" she cried. "Don't you know I was joking, it was all a joke?"

"That specialty you were talking about too?"

"I don't even know that Laide of yours, I've seen her here a couple of times, hello goodbye that's all, what do I know about your Laide?"

"Then you made it all up?"

"Yes."

"You're a fine bitch."

She threw herself back onto the pillow, laughing. "Just to make you mad. I love to watch your face when you're mad."

He left, much annoyed. He realized it was best to let it drop. No telling what kind of nonsense Laide might have got herself mixed up in. As for him, he didn't give a damn. With all the girls far nicer than Laide there were around! He'd had a similar infatuation, he remembered now, once before, during the war, at Taranto, a very beautiful brunette from Trieste who worked in a house there. At that time licensed establishments at naval bases were provided with the best merchandise available. This one, Luana, was very fond of him. Well, he began to think a lot of her, he went to see her almost every day, and when his ship was transferred to Messina he even sent her post-cards, whether they ever arrived or not. He remembered how sad he felt when his vessel weighed anchor at Taranto, he couldn't even tell her he was going because of military secrecy. It was a summer morning, a vague blue haze shone over the roadstead, beyond the still sleeping city glistened whitely in the sun. From the deck, while the white band of houses faded further and further away, he looked intently, with a consuming, lyric sadness, toward the quarter where the brothel was. Tired, she was still asleep and assuredly she wasn't dreaming about him, one of the many hundreds who visited her, yet he liked her very much, with a quite disinterested affection; he'd have liked to do something for her, he even thought, if he saw her again, of giving her a ring or a bracelet and thus somehow or other become a part of her life. But after a few days he thought no more about her, the passions of war swept that ridiculous little infatuation away. He never saw her again.

After the broken appointment at Signora Ermelina's, Antonio decided to rid himself of his annoying preoccupation with Laide. The next day he went off skiing, he stayed away a week, he began to feel calm again, when he came back he resumed his work with a tranquil mind.

12

HE THOUGHT no more about her, almost two weeks passed, and he'd thought no more about her. In his studio, one noon, he was in rather a hurry to finish up some work because at two-thirty he was to pick up his friend Cappa to go to Saint-Moritz, and he was a bit worried about the weather which looked like rain, by now he really thought no more about her, and the telephone rang. Mechanically he lifted the receiver.

"Signor Dorigo?" That "r." It was the second time Laide had phoned him. Her voice went through him. He felt a sense of fantastic relief. Why? What did that feeling of relief mean? If he'd given up Laide, if he wasn't thinking about her any more, why the feeling of happiness?

"How do you happen to be phoning me?"

"No reason. Are you sorry I did? I just wanted to say hello."

"Sorry? Not at all, I'm very pleased you phoned. What have you been up to all this time?"

"What a bore! If only you knew. I've been working in Modena."

"Doing what?"

"Modeling for photographs."

For a fraction of a second he entertained the thought of letting her go, of liquidating her; all he had to do was say he was going away for a few days, and maybe later, after he came back, some such vague postponement. That was all he had to do. That was all he had to do and he'd be safe.

But why safe? What danger was he in? It was ridiculous. As if he couldn't make love to Laide now and then! She didn't have the plague. And don't forget, she was the one who was looking for him now. It was even possible she was telling the truth, maybe she had been away all that time. And the minute she got back, she phoned him. Maybe she didn't dislike him. Maybe her image of him had stuck in her memory as something clean and reassuring, maybe she felt a need for him, maybe she was tired of that phony life of hers, maybe she was sick of the vulgar people, the equivocal places, the faithless friends, maybe she felt lonely.

"Well," he said, "do we see each other?"

"Of course! How about today?"

"Today I can't. I'm going skiing. I'll be back Sunday."

"Oh.... All right then I'll phone you Monday."

"What time?"

"Noon."

"Right. See you then. And thanks for calling."

"Don't be silly. Bye," she said, and Dorigo thought he detected a shade of disappointment in her voice, as though she'd hoped he'd even give up skiing in order to see her again right away.

Better this way, he thought with a certain satisfaction, to make oneself wanted is always the best tactic. He still felt peaceful. More. Happy. Untroubled, self-assured. That it was the telephone call that had made him happy did not seem to worry him. Why worry? He was in control of the situation.

But Monday, when the clock on the wall said twelve o'clock, he realized he was beginning to feel impatient. And he realized also that all morning he'd been waiting for noon to come, in fact the waiting had begun the night before when he got back to Milan, the waiting had begun on Friday the very second that Laide said: Don't be silly. Bye. For three days he'd been waiting, and without knowing it.

Now he couldn't stop looking at the clock. Trac! said the spring once a minute, and the hand made its little jump ahead. Every trac! was a tiny segment of time gone, one probability the less that Laide would keep her promise. So many things might have happened to her since Friday, so many men might have wanted her and gone after her, younger, richer, handsomer than he, so many opportunities there were for a rather silly, rather desperate girl in three days' living.

At twelve-ten he got up, he couldn't stand it any more, he could no longer concentrate on his work, he was supposed to be answering a letter, he read it and re-read it without having the least idea what it said.

He thought: if she doesn't call in five minutes, it means she won't. Maybe she's not even in Milan now, maybe she went to Modena again, or to Rome, there's no telling.

He was called away by Maronni, it was the man Blisa, who owned the paper mill; they wanted to talk about the project for the athletic field. What if Laide phoned while he was there?

The door of his studio was the kind that closed by itself, with a spring worked by a piston. He opened it wide and put a chair against it to keep it open. The door of the other room he left ajar, luckily it had no spring.

He realized that Maronni was watching him.

"I'm waiting for a phone call," he said. "From outside."

Maronni smiled. "From outside?"

"Yes, they're supposed to call me from Como."

He'd lied fairly well. Usually lying was a terrible effort for him.

Here too there was a clock. Trac! every minute. Everywhere in the building there were those clocks that said trac! every minute. Visitors were always surprised. However, after a little while, one got accustomed to them, one no longer heard that trac! one was no longer shocked by it every minute. Maronni's studio, a very attractive room, also had a clock. It said twelve-sixteen, it said twelve-seventeen. The conference was about the façade facing the street. Blisa wanted something representational, he even spoke about columns. To change his mind to something more acceptable seemed a hopeless task.

Out of the corner of his eye Antonio saw the hand of the clock jump ahead. Twelve-nineteen. She'll never turn up again, she'll never call again, she'll disappear into the mist with other men other anonymous men young men self-confident men. Maybe a plain wall with a vertical curve would be better, but he didn't give a damn about anything, where is she now? Is there a telephone where she is? Is there a directory so she can find the number, she's hardly likely to remember the number, no she certainly wouldn't remember the number. To discuss the project took tremendous will power on his part but he succeeded, though with long pauses. He looked: twelve-twenty. Laide won't call now. Does she even exist? Does a girl exist with a name as comic as Laide? She never existed. She existed once but no longer. She exists but far away very far away twelve-twenty-one the clock said trac! now at last even he felt it. He would never see her again.

He made some excuse, left Maronni and Blisa, and shut himself up in his own office. He breathed a sigh of relief. How hard it is to control yourself in front of other people, maybe to laugh and crack jokes. Now at least he no longer ran the danger of not hearing the telephone if it rang. He lit a cigarette, after two drags he put it out, he felt it must be nearly midnight, there was such a darkness inside him, it was crazy, it was absurd, worse it was unworthy of a man like him to be so preoccupied with a call-girl. Some days she wasn't even beautiful, some days she was really ugly, well, maybe not really hideous but certainly nothing special—he held on to that thought consolingly, she wasn't beautiful, she was ordinary, she wasn't worth bothering about.

But that lively, spirited small face, that physical vitality of hers, her legs, he thought, those long slender thighs that as she walked revealed even under her clothes the vigor of her youth, her fantastic lack of modesty, more artless and chaste than the strict propriety of schoolgirls, if she felt warm she'd sit down and hitch her skirt up all the way without the slightest embarrassment, her childish gift of herself to her fellow creatures, like a little girl who has been led to believe that everything is fun and evil doesn't exist, the throng of anonymous shadows in her background, men and women who are part of her, dim lights in the corner of some modish dance hall, ambiguous phone calls, mad dashes along the highway in a racing car with some son of a rich family who at a hundred miles an hour puts his right arm around her and pulls her to him and gives her a long kiss deep in her little mouth; that way she had of walking, timidly and boldly at once, like a young warrior entering a dragon's cave; that mischievousness of hers, her profile that looked so like those you see in sketch books of nineteenth century artists where everything is mixed together, the upper class with the lower, sex with the family, even history is there; her round staring eyes, now frightened, now hard and pert, now happy and trustful like a country girl on her way to a fête; her selling of herself as though it was some little game girls were playing that year, that serene composure she had in bed never giving herself up wholly to the passions of the flesh, her abandon which was always restrained, the prostitution which was no more than some artless ritual of chastity by whose means she, though poor, gave her naked body to the rich to enjoy, that silly, mad, conventional lust for life which for her as for so many girls was a way of living, her "r," perhaps the subterranean reflection of high birth lost among damp labyrinths in decrepit palaces, amid a bustle of servants bearing torches.

The telephone rang. It's not her, he forced himself to think. It's not her.

"Hello," he heard. A slow, tired, suspicious voice, a wholehearted mistrust of the world that was inconceivable in a girl of twenty.

"Hi," he said.

13

Now they no longer met at Signora Ermelina's. Laide told him she'd had a quarrel with Signora Ermelina and took him to the house of a girl friend of hers. Then he also made use of the apartment that belonged to Corsini, a friend of his who was almost always away from Milan. It was a handsome apartment at the far end of Via Vincenzo Monti, near the Fair grounds, a pleasant apartment with a large living room and an inner stairway that led up to the bedroom. His friend was almost never there, so the apartment was almost always free in the afternoon. Laide liked it very much; anything that in any way connected her, as an active participant, with well-to-do, respectable middle-class life gave her an enormous pleasure. And though the furniture was contemporary, she guessed at once that the person who lived there was chic and at the same time substantial; it had no suggestion of the *pied-à-terre*, of the bachelor's hide-away.

Laide wandered about, looking into everything, as happy as a little girl trying to find a hidden present, she examined the kitchen cabinets and the refrigerator, she seemed to take pleasure, on the flimsiest pretexts, in making him wait indefinitely. Not that Antonio was so impatient to have her, but it was only in bed, when he held her naked in his arms for those all too brief moments, that he could allay completely the damned uneasiness that because of her coursed through his body. She was much happier and livelier in bed than usual, not that sex with Antonio gave her much pleasure, on the contrary it clearly meant nothing to her at all, but perhaps bed had become for her a kind of giant toy on which it was so entertaining to roll about, to play games, to slip under the covers and hide oneself (does a bed cover not represent, perhaps, for children, a mysterious and fascinating world, an immense cavern where no one can tell what he is likely to find and which no one dares explore to the very end for fear of being caught there, and while one creeps slowly into the dark cave one makes sure out of the corner of one's eye that the cover at one's shoulder doesn't shut the light out altogether but that there's always a gleam somewhere, a hole, a bright crack that guarantees one's escape in the event of some unforeseen danger?), in addition to which bed is the perfect place for minor quarrels, for showing how offended one is, for pouting, teasing, provoking, for all the many little spiteful duels that are so valuable in giving spice to love. About these quite indescribable caprices of hers, however, there was nothing professional or calculated, indeed it was their freshness and spontaneity that sometimes excited Antonio and sometimes irritated him and sometimes brought him to the verge of complete exasperation.

Laide, in bed, lost most of the scornful *aplomb* which out of bed seemed to her so important, as when walking down the street for instance. Naked she seemed more childish, her breasts being small and her pelvis narrow, and very likely she realized it herself and enjoyed it and finally felt herself master of the situation, the winner, and pretended to be unaware that in the struggle her chignon had come undone and her black hair was spilled all about her like ink from a broken bottle, and then smiling she'd allow herself to make conceited little confidences so transparent as to render her even more childish. "Do you know what there is about me?" she might say to him. "I'm still a child, yet at the same time I'm also terribly female."

"Once a boy told me," she said, "I was still very young then, I couldn't have been more than twelve, he said to me: 'Laide, you were born to drive men crazy.'"

"Do you know what I am?" she would say to him with the sudden excitement of a happy memory, one of the few perhaps that she had, as though solemnly uttering a magic formula destined to free her from all her troubles. "I'm a cloud. I'm lightning. I'm the rainbow. I'm a delightful little girl." And naked, kneeling on the bed, opened to him, she looked at him impudently. Then, characteristically, she thrust out her thin little lips, a childish provocation and a challenge. Meanwhile Antonio stared at her in adoration, overcome by so much instinctive wisdom, he with all his absurd literary equipment in that skull of his.

14

ALL AT once one becomes aware of something perhaps one has always known but until that moment has been unable to believe. Like a man who for a long time has noticed unmistakable symptoms of some ghastly disease but has stubbornly insisted on interpreting them in such a way as to be able to go on living his life as he did before, but the time comes at last when, in the violence of his pain, he must give in and then truth confronts him, clear and horrible, and everything in his life suddenly changes direction and cherished things fade away and become strange, empty, and even repulsive. Vainly he looks about him for something to which he might hopefully cling; he is altogether unarmed and alone, there is nothing in his world save the malady that devours him, and then his only means of escape, if indeed there is any escape at all, is either to cure himself or else to bear the disease and to keep it at bay and to hold on until the infection with the passing of time exhausts its fury. In any case, from the moment of revelation he feels himself being carried down into a darkness never conceived of save for others, and every second the speed of his descent accelerates.

On April 3rd, around five in the afternoon, Antonio was driving his car out of the Piazza della Scala. He wanted to take Via Verdi, but the traffic signal was red, jammed all around him were other cars, pedestrians walked in front of him, the sun was still high, the day was beautiful. In that flash of time he pictured Laide at the edge of the runway in Modena, where she had said she had to go to pose for fashion photographs, and the delight she felt in being admitted to that extraordinary world which the newspapers describe at such length and in such fabulous terms. And there she was at the edge of the runway in Modena joking with two young test pilots in white overalls, those fascinating beings, incarnate symbols of twentieth century virility. One is flirting with her and idiotically asks her why she's not in the movies (Someone like you would be a great success), but the other keeps silent; he's a stockier boy, dark, with a square hard face; he keeps silent, only once in a while he gives her a hardly perceptible smile, but it's a smile of complicity because soon, after the sun is down and the runway deserted, he'll take her to bed in his furnished room, as he did yesterday too, and she didn't make the slightest difficulty, as though it was the most natural thing in the world; in fact he couldn't believe a model like her could be so easy and free to boot.

The light turned green and Dorigo was startled by a horn just behind him (there's always some idiot ready to sound his horn), it would certainly be boys like that whom Laide would play with, and she'd go with them enthusiastically without asking a penny. It's not even impossible that she'd be the one to give the present if only to show she was a good girl, interested in sports that's all. To supply her with cash was the business of the older gentlemen who frequented the House of Ermelina, with them it was another matter entirely, with them it was a question of work, not that it was such a terrible sacrifice for her because luckily they were almost always proper people, decent looking and clean but certainly love didn't come into the picture for a second, nor the body's satisfaction.

My God, couldn't he think about anything else? His mind was fixed eternally on the same agonizing thought, and looking up at Brera he was overwhelmed by dismay because at that moment Dorigo realized how unhappy he was and with no hope of remedy. It was absurd and idiotic but it was also so real and so intense that nowhere could he any longer find peace.

Now he knew, try as he might to rebel against it, that the thought of her followed him every fraction of a second throughout the day, everything everyone every situation everything he remembered or read led him through the most agonizing and evil associations to her. A kind of interior thirst around the entrance of his stomach, up up toward the breast bone, a painful unchanging tenseness of his whole being, as when from one moment to another something terrifying occurs and one is immobilized by the shock, anguish, anxiety, humiliation, hopeless need, weakness, desire, his illness included them all and the suffering that resulted was total and complete. He knew that the whole affair was ridiculous, was foolish and disastrous, the classic snare for provincial boors, he knew that anyone had the right to call him an idiot and that therefore from no one could he expect consolation or help or pity. Consolation and help could come only from her, but she didn't give a damn for him. It wasn't through wickedness or the pleasure of watching him suffer, it was only that for her he was a client like any other, so how could she guess that Antonio was in love with her? It wouldn't even cross her mind, a man from a world so different from hers, a man almost fifty years old? The others? His mother, his friends? It would be a bore if they knew. And even at fifty a man can still be a child, as helpless, as bewildered, as terrified as a little boy lost in a dark wood. Restlessness, longing, fear, dismay, jealousy, impatience, despair. Love!

He'd been taken prisoner by a false mistaken love, his mind was no longer his own, Laide had got into it and now she occupied it entirely. In the most hidden recesses of his brain, in all the most secret subterranean caverns where he hoped to hide from her to find a moment's respite, there at the end he found always and only her: and she doesn't even look at him, she isn't even aware of him, she giggles on the arm of some boy, she dances wild dances, every part of her body handled by some greasy and sinister partner, she undresses under the eyes of a certified public accountant named Fumaroli whom she met a moment before. Damn the woman, barbarian occupier of his brain, who from his brain looks at other men, telephones other men, intrigues with other men, makes love with other men, comes goes departs, driven frantically by her many private affairs and her mysterious errands.

And everything apart from her, everything that didn't concern her, everything else in the world—work, art, family, friends, skiing in the mountains, other women, the thousands and thousands of

other beautiful women, more beautiful than she, and more sensual—
it all meant nothing to him, any longer, it was all dust and ashes, that
unbearable pain he felt only Laide could relieve, and it wasn't even
necessary that she give herself up to him or be particularly kind to
him. All he asked was that she be with him, beside him, and talk to
him, and be ready to admit however unwillingly that he too, if only
for a few minutes, was also alive in the world. It was only in those very
brief intervals that happened so seldom and lasted so short a time that
he found peace. Then the fire in his breast ceased burning, Antonio
became himself again, his life and work resumed their proper direction once again, once again the artistic world to which he had given
his life began to glitter with its old enchantments and an indescribable
sense of peace suffused his whole being. He knew, of course, that in
a little while she'd go and then almost at once the same old unhappiness would take hold of him, only this time it would be worse, but
it didn't matter, the sensation of liberation was so wholehearted and
so wonderful that for the time being he could think of nothing else.

It wasn't that Laide made him feel especially sensual. In fact, after
the first time, there had been a lowering of pressure. Only the first
time, without going in for a lot of tricks, had she entirely given herself
up to it. Now she was on the whole passive, it was almost as though
she'd guessed there was no need to be otherwise any longer, that he,
no matter, would always prefer her to the others. And one day when
he'd actually dared to say to her, "My God, you're lying there like a
log of wood, you don't want to do a damned thing, do you?" she'd
answered: "But it's the man who's supposed to work on the woman,
not the other way around."

He'd often heard tell about men, usually older than he, who'd
become slaves to some woman because she was the only one who
could still give them the pleasure they wanted. It was a kind of sexual
witchcraft.

At the start he'd wondered if that wasn't the very thing that was
happening to him. But he realized that his situation unfortunately
was altogether different, and far graver. If it had been merely a question of a sexual bond, there'd have been nothing to worry about. In

that case everything could have been worked out, with a girl like that, in a simple arrangement of giving and having.

No. To Antonio physical possession mattered relatively very little. If, for instance, some illness had prevented him from ever making love again, he would at the very bottom of his heart have been rather glad of it.

He daydreamed that Laide had fallen under a street car and lost a leg. How wonderful that would be! Deformed, cut off forever from the world of prostitution, and dancing, and sexual adventures, she would no longer be at the mercy of all those people. Only Antonio would continue to worship her. And that might be his only hope that Laide, if for no other reason than gratitude, would begin to love him.

No. He loved her for herself and for what she symbolized—femininity, inconstancy, youth, plebeian honesty, mischievousness, wantonness, daring, liberty, mystery. She was the symbol of a world that was common and nocturnal, gay and vicious, fearlessly wicked and sure of itself, a world that teemed with life insatiable, surrounded by the boredom and respectability of the middle class. She was the unknown, the adventurous, she was the flower of the old city that had sprung up in the courtyard of some unsavory old house, among the memories and the legends, the poverty, the sins, the shadows and the secrets of Milan. And though so many had trampled her down, she was still fresh, lovely, and sweet-smelling.

It would be enough for him, he thought, if Laide were to become just a bit his and live just a bit for him. This idea of being able to enter into her life and be someone important to her, even if not the most important, had become his obsession. He would be prouder of that than if some very beautiful and powerful queen, or someone like Marilyn Monroe, were to throw herself, overwhelmed by love, at his feet. A call-girl, one of countless bits of fluff at so much a time, a little prostitute that anybody could have!

It wasn't an infatuation merely of the body, it was a far profounder enchantment, as though some strange fate, a fate of which he had never even thought, had called out to him and now, with ever-increasing and irresistible force, was carrying him off to a dark unknown tomorrow. Looked at from any point of view, there seemed to be no way out. Awaiting him could only be humiliation and anger, jealousy and sorrow unending.

And he also knew that to persuade her to live with him, to establish her in some apartment, to construct a communal existence, would be madness. He'd become a figure of fun, and she after less than a week would begin to champ at the bit. With the habits she now had. And with almost thirty years between them.

Furthermore, to attempt to redeem her made no sense at all. For Laide prostitution wasn't punishment or slavery or a dishonorable yoke; for her it seemed rather to be some exciting and remunerative game that was no trouble at all to play. But what about the apparently unavoidable humiliation if, in order not to annoy the madams that she had to deal with, she was forced to submit to hateful and disgusting clients? When Dorigo had hinted at this, she'd answered at once, and with a proud sort of gesture, "Well, I can call myself lucky. I've always had nice boys." "Come on, sometimes you must have had to go with old men, maybe without teeth or something." "I tell you no. I must say I've always been lucky. And then, you know, I always try to have a look at them first. If I don't like what I see, you can bet I don't go with them." "But have you ever refused?" "Oh! There's never been any need to."

The sad thing was that though he really loved her, though he didn't only just want her, it was impossible for her to respond to his love. There was no question that she thought of him as an old man. And his artistic personality, which sometimes succeeded in fascinating women of his own world, was for her a matter of utter indifference. To win her esteem, owning a new Maserati would be far more strategic than having built the Parthenon.

At the same time that taking physical possession of her became a matter of secondary importance, the thought of her body became, in his jealousy, a kind of obsession. As the sick man can never resist the temptation to go on prodding the part of him that's unwell, thus making it worse, so Dorigo never stopped inventing scenes that could only increase his misery: he worked at them pitilessly, down to the most minute and obscene detail. He saw her going into the *garçon-nière* of some new and elderly client, to whom she had been sent by Signora Ermelina, and after the usual exchange of civilities she seated herself on the old man's knee and pulled up her skirt not so much to keep it from wrinkling but to let him feel her flesh and the heat of her legs and she smiled at him mischievously, and then while his hands worked their way into her dress and took hold of her breasts she put her mouth shamelessly to his, and then very excited he picked her up bodily, and the two of them lay naked on the bed, and then the convolutions and the contortions and the kisses, and her desire to unleash in him the greatest possible excitement and so find reason for pride in her own body with the hope of a little something extra at the end and she didn't even know his name or what he did, and probably she'd never see him again, but at that moment she did her best to excite him and she kissed him dutifully at the most sensitive places, amused by the shivers and the shudders of the old man as a little girl might tickle a toad just to see him jump. Everything that might mean degradation for a girl, the grossest filth, the most abject humiliation, unwound itself in Dorigo's mind, and then, maybe while he was at his work desk, he would sit motionless, far away, unbearably tense, and he would feel that this torture was eating away years and years of his life. Was there perhaps some dark pleasure to be got from those painful fantasies? Did those perverse day-dreams only serve to make Laide ever more exciting, strange, and unattainable and therefore ever more deserving of his desire and his love?

15

SHE PUT a record on. They were in the apartment that belonged to Corsini, Dorigo's friend; it was during the period of the Milan Fair. With the sun on the terrace, the shutters were lowered almost all the way down; still, if you listened, you could hear the roar of cars, of life, impatience, plans, bustling greed, motors, voices, footsteps, money, stupidity, music, sweat, animal desire. It mounted all the way to the eighth floor but neither of them heard it. She because she was aware of nothing—she was alive only to her own dark plans and whims— he because there was no longer anything in the world for him save this girl with the straight, petulant features, the long black hair, the heart—the heart?—what kind of heart? did she have a heart?

"What is it?" he asked.

"It's the best cha-cha-cha in the world. *Los cariñosos*," she answered, with the assurance of someone who says *Tristan* or *Rigoletto*, nourishment famous to all the world. And in a kind of childish over-excitement, she began to dance alone.

She's sure of herself. The undulating rhythm carries her up and down like a wave but at the same time she was the master, she controlled the impulse. Suddenly there's no longer anything false about her, or left out, or hidden, or vile, or mean. Her arms held up like two folded wings, her hips weaving to the rhythm of the music, her face set in an unmoving smile that is no longer hers but the smile of the music itself, artless thought of everything desirable, self-respect, provocation, proposal. In the movement that carries her forward and at once brings her back, she threw back her head in utter abandon as though just before her stood an altar, a god, life.

She stopped to look at the shelf of records. They were on their way upstairs to the bedroom. Lazily she paused and began to examine the records.

"What are you doing?" he said. "Let's have some music afterwards."

She didn't reply. The little white hands, the very soft hands have already drawn a large record out of the wrapper, she's lifted the top of the phonograph, she's turned it on, she knows how to work it. She knows how to work it so well a horrible suspicion enters his mind: has Laide been here before? has his friend known her in the past and brought her back to bed? Otherwise how could she possibly have handled the phonograph so easily, with its complicated automatic gadgets?

"How is it that you're so experienced?"

"A girl friend of mine has the same machine. Flora. I've played hers a hundred times."

At the right moment the pick-up automatically dropped onto the record with a sly movement like that of some reptile. The music poured out.

"What is it?" he said.

"It's the best cha-cha-cha in the world. *Los cariñosos.* Down at the Due they play it all the time. But it's not so easy to find it on a record."

"Do you dance the cha-cha-cha well?"

"I should hope so."

There's a note of angry pride in her voice, as though his doubt had offended her. Does she know how to cha-cha-cha? Ask Fangio if he knows how to drive a car.

Alone, in the middle of the large room, she began to dance.

No, thinks Antonio, it's impossible she could have been here with Corsini. Corsini has a regular girl friend, he doesn't go around with anyone else. And then Laide, when I brought her here for the first time, would have made up some story or other to avoid a mix-up. She leads her life but at the same time she's very insistent about not being considered one of *them.* If by chance she discovered that someone she'd made love with was a friend of mine, she'd invent some nonsense or other to keep me from finding out about it. Yes, her story of a friend who has the same kind of phonograph is plausible enough.

"What is it?"

"It's the best cha-cha-cha in the world. *Los cariñosos*." She began to dance. Her dress in the color of lilac, a cloth with a thick weave, tight across the breasts, held in at the waist by a belt, the knee-length skirt short and full. The cha-cha-cha doesn't come out of her legs but out of her back and her spinal column, it imposes on her body its own kind of loving undulation, of release, of giving and not giving, offering and not offering, like trotting along a road that always returns upon itself, like an insistent voluptuary, like a game between one wave and another, a rhythmic fulfillment of love, frenzied, measured, precise, tired, insatiable, like the imaginary evening fever of the African bush when the soul is lost in fantasies and memories, like the dim light in the alley from the depths of which a voice calls, like equivocal red lips that for an instant in the reflection of the searchlights open in silent promise, like sad youth that laughing heaves and twists happily in the darkness that will trample it down, an ambition, an ideal, a shattering vibration of the innermost organs, voices of the earth that we'll never know, rehearsals of the victory that will never happen, a soft cruel hammer beating one-two-three one-two-three with a short pause in the middle, beating one-two-three, beating one-two-three, and thrown down by the cataracts of April seventeenth, beating one-two-three, one-two-three, boulders and crashing water run riot, become a water snake, epilepsy, harp, perdition but she on her spike heels rises, flows, plays and smiles with the overwhelming conspicuity of a wise child that has found the true, the irresistible sap of life.

In the popular theme of the music, plain as a twig yet heavy with the weight of centuries, something said, very clearly, goodbye, with the power of love, to what was and will never return, and at the same time a confused premonition of things that will one day come, perhaps, because true music is all there in regret for the past and in hope for the future, which is likewise painful. And then there is the despair of the present, which is composed of both. And there is no other poetry than that.

"What is it?" he had asked her.

"The best cha-cha-cha in the world. *Los cariñosos*."

He sits down on the couch and he watches her, dismayed, lost. Like a hunter who lies in wait to kill a hare and sees a dragon. Like a young and trustful soldier who suddenly finds himself facing an entire army arrayed against him, with infantry, cannons, and armored cavalry. Like a man who realizes he's challenged someone a hundred times stronger than he.

She perhaps, as she danced, thought she was having fun, she had no idea what was happening. She danced out of some impulse of youth, out of a superabundance of energy, out of a desire to be admired. She knew, of course, that she was dancing the cha-cha-cha stupendously, with absolute command, so much so that she even pretended, coquettishly, every once in a while, to falter. She has no idea, however, as she dances, of what is happening in her soul.

For here, carried along by some mysterious force, the girl with the detestable habits, accustomed to renting her body at so much the hour, without being aware of it, draws herself up from the miasma below stairs toward the light.

Or does she perhaps in her confusion believe that as she dances she has become another being? Does she perhaps in the deepest part of her imagine that this is a delicious way to be revenged? In this losing of herself in the rhythm of the music does she perhaps find freedom? There, in front of her is a man much older than she who in a little while will have her because he's paid for her, and yesterday and today and tomorrow she'll sell herself to other men like him, who need the release she gives them, and she doesn't suffer overmuch on account of it, yet she knows that other girls like her live and have fun and travel—flirtations, receptions, parties, cars, minks—without having to take off their brassieres for money. She even knows that other girls like her get up at six in the morning and work for eight or nine hours for forty thousand lire a month, which is what she often earns going around in a couple of days, and so she feels envy and shame, a sense of uselessness and ever-increasing destruction. Yet now, dancing the cha-cha-cha, she tastes the marvellous sensation of being free, light, and chaste, of belonging to no one but herself, not even to herself but to something even more marvellous, to music, to dance, to poetry.

Her dress is the color of lilac, a cloth with a thick weave, tight across the breasts, held in at the waist by a belt, her skirt short and full. She smiles, in the ecstasy of the dance, her thin lips half-closed and puffed out like the petals of a flower, mischievously. How true she was, how real she was, how beautiful she was. He could never catch up with her. She was an outsider, she was a stranger, she belonged to a different race, she was unreachable, she was the incarnation of . . . of . . . of the . . . of the . . . damn everything that he hasn't had until now and has despised: madness, daring lost nights, so-called adventures that consist of murmurs in forbidden corners, corridors of great hotels, doors that can be opened without creaking, soft words spoken on the edge of the bed, those sexual transparencies, the whirling story that bewitches her, the burst of laughter, the arm that hugs the waist and she gives in, slowly, oh yes, yes, slowly while outside, in the garden, in utter silence, hangs the moon.

Not this time either, he thought bitterly. She danced the cha-cha-cha alone in the middle of the large room. In a little while she would go up the stairs with him, she would take off her bracelet, her necklace, then she'd ask his permission to go in the bathroom, then she'd come back half-dressed, she'd stretch out on the bed, entirely his. But what's the good of it? It's not the girl who in a little while will be lying beside him on the bed that he loves. Let her make love with him under those conditions ten thousand times and she'd be his then no more than she was now, which was not at all. It's this other being who has got into his head, the Laide of these very moments, the girl who having glimpsed bright fortune from the other side of the pit has put her foot with a shudder into the water in order to cross over, but the water isn't water, it's mud, it's wet sticky clay, it's the wide quicksand of a great city which slowly draws her in, into which each day she sinks a little further and meanwhile the golden light on the other bank recedes, recedes, becomes a mirage, unreachable. The pit is a boundless swamp, a thick dead sea of mud; yet she insists on going on, they've told her that the important thing is to go on, it's better to begin and lose courage than never to begin at all; moreover that sticky mud in which by now she's thigh-deep is soft and warm and imparts a strange sense of well-being, but every once in a while she turns and looks back, at the bank she left, and she sees it clearly for the distance that she's come is horribly short, she sees people there, men, women, girls like herself who haven't even considered taking the shortcut of the pit and who live and work in seeming calm and in the evening they close the doors of their houses, and their houses become clean and safe, there are no peculiar phone calls, the lock on the big door downstairs doesn't squeak at three in the morning, the powerful specially built cars don't stop just around the corner, so as not to be seen, with a red-faced forty-year-old man at the wheel. That's the way proper families live, an orderly, ordinary, boring life, so easy to despise though from time to time the suspicion must arise that it would be nice to live that way, even perhaps that living that way is one's truest deepest desire, a happy haven to reach, but a different world from hers, a world denied to her.

And so she struggles to climb out of the pit, she wants the people on the bank who smile at her but no longer respect her to realize that she too is a being worthy of life and, forgetting everything that's happened, she becomes a child again, as though she'd like to begin her whole life over. Such is Laide dancing the cha-cha-cha alone for a man who's a stranger to her, and in this unselfish act of beauty she's transformed, she becomes a rose, a cloud, a harmless bird, remote from every ugliness, fulfilling thus her one moment of purity.

16

LAIDE that day seemed happier and more carefree than usual. Did it mean that finally she was beginning to feel at ease with him? That somehow a formula for human intimacy was going to be worked out between them? A good-sized chunk of sun came slanting into the bedroom beating down on the green carpeting and by reflection palely illuminating the whole room.

They were already lying on the bed, she was still in her slip. For Dorigo, in the imminent certainty of love, these were the rare moments of respite and peace. No further doubt that she wouldn't phone again, that she'd disappear into nowhere, that without warning she would have left Milan forever, no more the torture of waiting as the time of the promised call drew near, with the minutes dripping horribly away one by one after the agreed-on time had passed, and then the conjectures, the suspicions, and the hopes slipping away all slipping away in a whirling crescendo that transformed him at last into a kind of brainless automaton. The unbelievable had once again come true. Laide was at his side, she spoke to him, she undressed, she let him caress her, kiss her, possess her, for an hour, an hour and a half she'd be with him, in the privacy of a comfortable house that was utterly and entirely theirs. How simple, how easy everything became. And his sick anguish seemed, even to him, absurd. Why on earth would Laide ever refuse him? He was well-bred, trim, polite, he offered her hospitality in a more than proper atmosphere where even a princess might well have come. It was crazy to imagine that a girl like Laide would let two bank notes of ten thousand slip out of her fingers quite so easily. The situation seemed to him then so obvious and so reassuring as to exclude even the possibility of further torment. Dorigo suddenly felt strong and self-assured; the sensation of having been cured restored to him a sense of total well-being, which was something he'd thought he would never feel again. No, he must have been out of his mind to have worried like that, there couldn't have been anything stupider. After all—so he told himself, convinced that he was being sincere—all he cared about was seeing Laide once in a while; otherwise she could do as she liked. Certainly he had no intention of taking over her entire support; where would he find the money?

("How much money do you need to live on?" he asked her once, while they were in the car on their way to Corsini's house. "Well," she answered, "I get fifty thousand at the Scala, if I had another fifty thousand I'd be all right." But all you had to do was think about it a minute to realize it must be a lie. Otherwise why would she go on leading the life she did?)

He felt so sure of himself that it seemed to him he could now afford to have a little fun. Why not confess to her what an hour earlier had been for him a burning question? He couldn't have done it an hour ago, he'd have thought it too dangerous, but what could he lose now? Now he felt sure of never losing her. He understood now. Now he could allow himself that little luxury.

Or was this confession a final attempt to rouse her, to make her realize that he wasn't like the others, that he didn't think of her as only a bed companion, but that, on the contrary, making love to her didn't matter greatly compared with what he really wanted from her?

"Listen," he said, resting his hand gently on her naked leg, "you could do me a great favor."

She looks at him suspiciously: "What?"

"Well, you could sort of lend me a hand."

"What do you mean?"

"Well, you could help me out. You can."

"Help you how?"

As he spoke now he realized that it was only a school boy's trick, that the stratagem was altogether too naïve. But he'd found nothing better. He who considered himself a man of talent, an inventor of wonderful fantasy, had found nothing better. But she was rather simple and the men she knew fairly unimaginative, so maybe the little trick would work; it might even seem funny to her.

"Oh, it's a bad business," he said.

"What is?"

"I've fallen hard, I've really got it bad for a girl I know."

"Do I know her?"

"Yes. And if you wouldn't mind, you could put in a good word for me."

"Has it got to be me you ask to do you a favor like that?"

"Well, I think of you as a friend."

"A friend yes, but I still don't think it's very nice to ask me to do something like that."

"Never mind, if you don't want to."

"No, tell me."

"Better drop it."

"No, please, tell me. Is she very beautiful?"

"I think so."

"You say I know her?"

Smiling, full of curiosity, she sat up. Her breasts were no longer beautifully tight and firm, they sagged a little, but small as they were they were always pleasing, the nipples high. She paid no attention to them.

"You say I know her?"

"Yes."

"Well?"

"Yes."

"What's her name?"

Then like a child he threw himself flat, hiding his face in the pillow. Had Laide understood? Had she got the joke? Did she get it the minute he had begun to talk? Or had she got it several days ago, when he took her to the station? Or was it such an old story for her that she knew all about it the very first day—by the way he looked at her when she was trying on the dress at Signora Ermelina's? Women were tremendously sensitive, even the least cunning of them, to what a man felt at certain times; there was a mysterious flash that ignited and burned the soul. Perhaps the man had no idea of it and didn't even suspect it while she at that very moment mounting her invincible throne had begun the delicious little game of driving him crazy.

"Who is it? What's her name?"

He raised himself, bent over her, and whispered in her ear: "Her name begins with 'l'."

At last she turned, laughing, but made no answer.

"Did you get it?" he asked.

Smiling she nodded yes.

"And will you put in a good word for me?"

"Is it necessary?"

Antonio was astonished that she had got into the game.

"Certainly it's necessary. Love is a terrible disease."

"No, no," said Laide. "On the contrary. It's so wonderful."

"When it's reciprocated. But in my case...."

"No, no, it's fine to be in love, it's a very fine thing."

"Have you tried it?"

"Yes."

"With whom?"

"He's dead. We were supposed to have been married."

"Did he love you very much?"

"Of course! Didn't I tell you we were supposed to be married?"

"Well, then, it's different, you see."

"Why?"

"Because I love you very much but you don't love me."

"It takes time, I hardly know you."

He felt disappointed. She hadn't made the slightest sign of surprise or satisfaction at what he said. As if she was used to it. As if he was only one of many. As if it was something that was hers by right. As if he was just any old fool. He felt the need to hurt her.

"Anyway," he said, "you don't have the least confidence in me."

"Why?"

"You've told me a whole batch of lies."

"It's not so! I've always told you the truth."

"Your last name too?"

"What do you mean?" She stiffened, and looked at him with wary, frightened eyes.

"Your name is Anfossi and not Mazza."

"Who told you?"

"What's the difference? Is your name Anfossi or isn't it?"

"Well, what if it is? In the theatre almost everybody uses another name."

"What name do you use at the Scala?"

"Rosanna Mazza. You can see it in the program."

"Why did you want to do it?"

"Tell me instead who told you. Signora Ermelina, I bet."

"What if it was?"

"That hag! I'm glad I've given her up."

"Did you quarrel?"

"What's it to you? I tell you, she's a real horror."

"Still, there must have been a reason."

"There were plenty of reasons! And I know what they are. But I don't have to let my hair down for everybody, do I?"

"What's wrong with you today? Have you got the blues?"

She felt the need to make it up to him. She pouted playfully, raised her eyes to his and fluttered her eyelids with childish coquettry.

"Antonio, come here, I'm cold."

At the very moment that he leaned over to embrace her and put his arms around her naked body, he realized that his splendid assurance of a little while ago was gone; it was utterly untrue that Laide would always be at his beck and call, and that he could always depend on her, for in the gentle passivity with which, responding to his embrace, she put her arm over his shoulder—a cold formal gesture such as women made when they began to dance, even with a stranger, someone who had asked them to dance for the first time—there was that damned separation between them. A little while ago when they were joking about love she had been much nearer to him and more understandable than now when their two bodies were so perfectly joined.

There it was, in a little while this too would be over, she'd go into the bathroom, he'd lie there motionless on the bed, empty and joyless, then she'd come back to get her clothes together, her little gold brace-let, her watch. She'd say: Lord, how late it is, come on, get up, please, there's no more sun on the green carpet, clouds must have come up, she'll say with a gesture of annoyance: what a bitch tomorrow's going to be I don't know how I'll get through it.

"What's tomorrow?" he asked.

"I told you I have to go to Modena."

"You didn't tell me."

"You never remember a thing."

"Modena, to do what?"

"To make pictures, I've told you a hundred times."

"Do they pay you well at least?"

"You can imagine. But if I refuse then I'm out of it."

"How much?"

"Five, seven, sometimes even ten."

"For each picture?"

"Don't make me laugh."

"And your traveling expenses? Your hotel?"

"Well, that's paid for."

"How long will you be away?"

"Two days I think."

"What do you mean you think?"

"You never know with that kind of work."

"And at night what do you do?"

"What do you think I do? At Modena, for God's sake!"

"By the way, don't you have a cousin at Modena?"

"Yes, but he's such a bore."

"Is he in love with you?"

"Out of his mind!"

"Do you go to bed with him?"

"That's all I need. I don't know, you seem to think nobody thinks about anything else but that. He's a nice boy, and he's got great respect for me."

"What? Not even a kiss?"

"He's afraid to lay a finger on me."

"Does he think you're a virgin?"

"Indeed he does! He looks on me as a sister."

"What does he do?"

"Engineer. At an oil works."

"And of course he wants to marry you?"

"*He* does, yes. But I'm not even thinking about it."

"Do you go out together?"

"Sometimes."

"Where? The movies?"

"Mostly."

"Is he good-looking?"

"Not bad."

"You like him?"

"I've told you he doesn't mean anything to me. He's my cousin. I'm fond of him."

"And even if you did go to bed together, I don't know what would be so wrong about it."

"Just I don't want to. And then imagine in a place like Modena. Everybody'd know about it."

"He'd like to, though."

"He? You should know him. He's so shy. In his family they watch him as though he were a schoolboy. Just imagine, when he's in Milan, his father gives him the house key once a week."

"How old is he?"

"Twenty-five, twenty-six, I think."

"What's his name?"

"Marcello is his name. What else do you want to know?"

"Please! Do just as you like, my dear."

"All right then, I've had more than enough of these questions. Understand?"

He kept an angry silence. How he'd like to give her a slap or two. Oh, if only he could!

She was aware of it. "How you fly off the handle, like that, right away. And I was just about to ask you a favor."

"Favor?"

"See how you are? It's better if I don't say anything."

"As you like."

"You see? No, the thing is tomorrow I have to leave at seven and I don't know what to do about a taxi."

"Phone for one."

"There aren't any at that time of the morning."

"At seven there aren't any taxis?"

"Also I can't call because my sister has the phone in her room."

"Can't you wake her up?"

"If you knew her!"

"You want me to take you to the station?"

"At that hour? How would you wake up?"

"I'll wake up, don't worry."

"What will you tell them?"

"Getting up early isn't a crime." He laughed.

"Would you really take me to the station?"

"It's nothing so extraordinary. What time?"

"The train leaves at seven-forty. If you're there at seven-ten, that's plenty of time."

"Where?"

"My house."

"You know I don't know your address."

"Via Squarcia 7."

"Where's that?'

"You know where Vigorelli's is? Near there. You can look it up in the street guide."

"Is seven-ten early enough?"

"We can get to the station in half an hour, I hope, even in that wheel barrow of yours. At seven there isn't much traffic."

To get up early was a martyrdom for Antonio. And it would have been so easy to give a thousand lire to some cab driver, at seven there were always taxis outside his house. But he said nothing. The idea of seeing Laide again even for only a few minutes, having her at his side, entering a little into her private life. The delightful feeling that she needed him. Above all the certainty that this evening at least he would not have to feel the torment of uncertainty and waiting, that he could work or laugh or joke with his friends as in the good old days. A respite. A truce. A sliver of happiness.

"What are you doing tonight?"

"There's a rehearsal at the theatre."

"And afterwards are you going to the Due?"

"When I have to get up with the birds tomorrow? You must be crazy!"

Vaguely he realized that many things did not hang together in the stories she told. The Scala, the photographs, the dance hall, her family, her cousin, Signora Ermelina, so many things didn't quite fit. But then when she talked every doubt vanished. For her way of talking, her manner, was so genuine. No, it was not possible she could be a liar. There'd be something, maybe only the very slightest doubt, or uncertainty, some false note, some hesitation. He always watched her carefully, he scrutinized what she said, tried to figure her out. And he was intelligent, he had an almost unwholesome sensitivity to subtle nuances. A girl like Laide, so uncomplicated psychologically? If she tried to get away with the least little thing, he'd be aware of it at once.

17

BETWEEN Vigorelli's speed track and the Fair grounds there was a large square with a park in the center, closed on the north by closely packed rows of new houses.

Here Antonio at ten minutes to seven parked his Seicento. His being so much ahead of time was absurd. He didn't want her to know, it would have been too clear a confession.

The weather was wet and cold. He lit a cigarette, in spite of the discomfort cigarettes always caused him on an empty stomach.

It was pouring. A furious spring rain beating down on the dark, empty, sleeping city. He was the only one up. Everyone else was asleep. No one else knew.

The truce was ended. In a few minutes he'd see her. Would he really? Maybe it's a joke. Then too, so many things might have happened in the meantime. She might have been taken ill, for example. How would she have let him know?

It's the inhospitable, thankless time of day when all desire is dead. Places of amusement are closed and dark, lovers are sleeping off their bodies' weariness, all lights are out though the light of day is still too weak to see by.

Even the cars of the most desperate night owls have disappeared. All windows are dark. Everyone is still enclosed in the warmth of his bed. Only the garbage wagons roll by now and then. It's a light that isn't light, it's gray, it's sleep, it's skylight, it's absolute indifference.

Unhappy the man who lets himself be caught in a city at this pitiless hour with the rain pouring down like a waterfall and he alone.

He felt like a child unfairly punished to whom no one pays any attention. Everybody was asleep, his brothers, his mother, his friends, those who needed him and those whom he needed. They no longer existed. They were sunk in early morning sleep, so deep, so beneficent in the rain. He was alone. He felt alone, ignored and lost in that hellish sadness of his at which people would have been so ready to laugh if they had known of it. And all around him, in the rain, the great city is still silent but soon it will wake and begin to heave struggle writhe gallop up and down fearfully, to do, undo, sell, make money, seize, dominate, and all this on account of an infinity of mysterious desires and prejudices, things both mean and lofty, work, sacrifice and endless affliction, impulses, the will to destroy, possession and dominion, on, on! and he riveted there in a small car dripping water, desperate for a little white young body with a gleam of a soul inside it—maybe—whose name is Laide and whom no one knows. Curtains of wet gray houses sealed off like lives that meant nothing to him. The world? America and Russia? The domination of the earth?

No. Will she wake in time? Will the alarm clock work? Will she dress quickly enough? Has she already packed? O God, let her bag be packed, let her not be tempted to give the trip up. Is she still asleep? Or is she in the bathroom looking at her face in the mirror, trying to smooth away with a finger the wrinkle that night has left at the corner of her eye? What is she going to do in Modena? Who's waiting for her? What will she be doing tonight? Will she sleep alone? Who'll sleep with her? Never mind. Just let her come. Just let her appear behind the iron grill in Via Squarcia (which he had gone to reconnoitre from the outside last night), let her appear with that haughty step of hers, and at the sight of her all his anxiety will vanish.

At the same time he has the feeling that this rain is dragging him down, an unknown power is separating him little by little from everything that up till then has been his life; more than once he's read about such things in novels and not believed them, ridiculous fairy tales he thought them, and now he's in it and now he no longer even struggles against it, yes sometimes in the evening he rebels in the very exaltation of the night. But not now, now the wild and battering rain carries him off, and he doesn't lift himself out of the whirlpool, he doesn't even lift a hand to ask for help.

Time stands still. His watch says seven-ten but Antonio has the habit of keeping it always a little ahead, it isn't more than two or three minutes past seven. Another cigarette. What if she changed her mind, what if she put off her trip? How long should he wait? His face felt tired. He looked at himself in the rear vision mirror. What a horrible face, the mouth particularly. Now maybe it's time. He starts the car.

Via Squarcia is deserted. There's an iron gate in front of her house and behind it an enormous courtyard with an awning at the end of it. He's parked the car where he can watch the entrance to the house. The porter's glass booth is still empty.

His watch says seventy-twenty, but it's only about ten or eleven past. The rain has let up a bit. Another cigarette. Will she come?

Now she's late. Another five minutes and she'll be too late to make the train. What's happened?

He does nothing but look at his watch, he'd like not to look at it, to wait a little while at least. But the anxiety. Oh at last.

He hears the sound of a glass door closing. Then behind the grating in the darkness he sees a figure.

Inside him something opens, he no longer feels he's suffocating to death, he feels he's coming back to life again. Laide! Laide!

A woman with a shawl over her head comes out. She's at least forty years old. She turns on the light in the porter's booth.

Seven-twenty-three. She hasn't even got up yet. Modena is important to her, he doesn't know why it means so much to her. It's impossible, if she'd got up on time, that she wouldn't be down by now.

He gets out of the car, he goes up the steps to the porter's lodge, there's a man there.

"I beg your pardon, would you be kind enough to inform Signorina Anfossi on the interphone that the car is waiting for her?"

The man discharges his duty reluctantly: "She says she's coming right down."

Right down? It's seven-twenty-five, true enough there won't be many people on the street but if the traffic lights have already been turned on you can't get to the station in a quarter of an hour.

Seven-thirty. What's that wretch doing? Seven-thirty-two. Laide will never turn up, she'll never come down, she'll never telephone again, he'll never see her again. By now she's missed her train.

The lock of the gate clicked. She came toward him, her head straight, her step deliberate and uninterested. In her right hand she carried a leather bag, in her left a large white suitcase.

Dorigo goes to meet her. You'd have said she was almost surprised to see him there. "Can you help me?" He takes her suitcase.

"You'll never make it now."

"The clock didn't go off. If the porter hadn't phoned up..."

"Do you realize it's after seven-thirty? We can't get to the station in five minutes."

"Why five minutes?"

"Didn't you tell me your train leaves at seven forty?"

"There's another at eight-five."

"You might have told me."

"How did I know the alarm clock wasn't going to go off?"

She didn't even say hello to him, she didn't give him a smile, and now that she's sitting beside him in the car she hasn't looked at him once, she's busy trying the lock of her bag that doesn't work right.

She hasn't washed, she hasn't put any make up on, she's wearing a light colored trench coat, she looks gaunt, even a little ugly. But Antonio breathes again, she's sitting next to him in the car, for a few minutes she's his somehow, she grants him her physical presence, for a little while he knows what she's doing, for a little while she's not with anyone else. The trench coat is short, her knees are round and smooth, her stockings are tight.

"What hotel are you going to in Modena?"

"I don't know yet."

"Is he expecting you?"

"Who's he?"

"Your cousin, your little cousin."

"Who knows?"

"How long will you be there?"

"I don't know, it depends on the work."

"Photographs, you said?"

"I've told you a hundred times!" She sounds annoyed, she seems to be aware of his suspicions.

"You'll call me when you get back?"

"Of course I'll call you."

"Will you call me from there?"

"Well, yes, maybe, if I can."

She looked at the street ahead. They were in Via Procaccini, it was still raining a little, her expression was uneasy and tense, like that of a beast at bay, as it had been the day she went to Rome. But he isn't part of it, he has nothing to do with her uneasiness; it's a match, a duel, a game, an intrigue, a conspiracy, something between her and people he doesn't know, people in her world. He's out of it. He's the well-to-do gentleman who pays.

18

WHEN HE got to his office after lunch a few days later he found a note from the telephone operator: "Your niece Laide called from Modena. Wants you to pick her up tomorrow morning early, Hotel Moderno, Modena."

Modena? How many miles is it? Yet never for a second did he consider not going. He thought of his very modest little car, that rather shabby Seicento of his.

He began to plan the journey. Making an early start wouldn't be hard; early risings weren't considered suspicious in his house, only in the evening was it difficult to get away. The important thing was to be back by five, five-thirty at the latest, because of some work he was committed to. It was certainly a tremendous nuisance.

That evening he happened to be dining with Menotti, an old friend of his. Menotti had an open sports car. During dinner he asked him if he could borrow his Spyder the following day. Menotti didn't give the matter a second thought. Certainly, he said, provided Dorigo was back by evening.

The idea of going to get Laide in an open sports car gave Antonio a lift. It was of just such utterly absurd illusions, he reflected, that our lives are composed.

Returning from Corsico's restaurant, along the Naviglio, that scented May evening, at the wheel of a splendid car, with the wind tickling the back of his neck, with a pretty woman alongside him, whose name he didn't even know, who meant nothing to him, with the lights of the street lamps flying past, curious or envious glances of pedestrians, with the thought that on the morrow he would see

Laide again, with the wonderful awareness that Laide for the first time had called him, with the feeling of weightlessness that immersion in the night's blue air gave him, with that intoxicating sense of nakedness one has in open cars, Dorigo felt as he had when he was a child and with the beginning of June stopped wearing knickers and put on shorts and his naked legs gave him a confused sensation of lust and daring and physical enhancement.

The alarm at six, in itself excruciating, filled him with excitement: Laide was waiting for him and he thought of the car he'd be driving. He'd arrive looking like a winner, rich, sporting, at his ease, modern, young, like the hero of some popular film. He'd make a marvellous impression on her. Seeing him at the wheel of a Spyder sport, Laide would no longer think of him as a mere intellectual, a skeleton, a pitiful bourgeois. The car would allow him to enter her world at last, with full rights of citizenship, the world of rich and powerful men who handled girls as they handled cars, maybe even more casually, and the girls look at them intimidated and let them do as they please with them.

He left Milan at six-thirty. The streets were empty. Too bad the sky was gray.

Each time his foot pressed the accelerator down, the distance that separated him from her was one bit less. By habit an almost too careful driver, this morning he flew across the city with houses still sleeping and dark, traffic lights still darting bright yellow glances, a city taken by surprise.

Where he entered the Highway of the Sun, the sun had not yet succeeded in breaking up the mist. The road was deserted.

He'd never driven at seventy-five or eighty miles an hour before. As he accelerated, the white lines drew together. He kept his eyes on them. She'd certainly be sleeping at this hour. Alone? But she was there at the end of the road, on the other side of the horizon, still very far away.

He looked around. No houses, no farms, no gasoline pumps as on ordinary highways. Deserted country. Meadows streaming with mist behind long regular rows of high poplars that lost themselves in the distance. On and on as he drove, from one side and from the other, wheeled the trees, gathering into a thick clump at the far end of the straight road, and thinning out at the sides, while other trees, still further off, ran ever ahead of him into the horizon; it was as though two immense platforms were turning in opposite directions, one to the right, one to the left.

The sun had not yet appeared, it was waiting still behind the curtains of damp and mist, and the immense countryside waited too, with the night's chill on it. As the little white needle of the speedometer rose with quick nervous jumps, the cold air swirled across the back of his neck.

Then it seemed to him that the rows of poplars, as they moved away from the car, were trying to tell him something. Yes, the flight of the trees—a fluid, ever-changing interweaving of perspectives, as far as the eye could reach—had taken on a special intensity of expression as someone does who is about to speak.

He ran, he flew toward love, and likewise the trees as they slipped off the ends of the fields were being carried away by something stronger than they. Each had its own look, its special shape, its different outline. And there were so many of them, thousands and thousands. Yet it was the same force that pulled them into the whirlpool. All the poplars of the broad countryside fled as he did, exactly, wheeling in two enormous curved wings.

In the solitary morning, with the empty road ahead and the empty fields, the countryside was empty. There was not a soul to be seen; it seemed that save for him everyone had forgotten that this bit of world still existed. And she was there, at the end of the road, behind the very last curtain of trees and further still. Probably she was still asleep, with her head sunk in the pillow. Between the slats of the blinds the light of the new day slipped into the room lighting the mass of her black hair as she lay there unmoving. Was she alone?

Then suddenly he saw what it meant, all this natural enchantment. He understood, indeed, what the rows of poplars were trying to say as they moved in procession toward the horizon and seemed to be running away from him at the same moment that they rushed to meet him, then to move away again into the mist, used up, while fresh ranks appeared rushing down inexhaustibly upon him.

Suddenly he understood what they were saying, he understood the meaning of the outward world when it strikes us dumb for a moment and we say, "How beautiful," and a kind of greatness enters our souls. He'd lived all his life without suspecting the cause of it. How often had he stood in admiration before a landscape, a monument, a square, a foreshortened street, a garden, the interior of a church, a cliff, a path, a wilderness. Only now, at last, had he learned the secret.

A very simple secret: Love. Everything in all the inanimate world that fascinates us, forests, plains, mountains, rivers, seas, valleys, steppes, and more, and more, cities, palaces, stones, more, the sky, sunsets, storms, yet more, the snow, still more, the night, the stars, the wind, all these things, empty and indifferent in themselves, were charged with meaning for us because, without our suspecting it, they held a foregleam of love.

How stupid he must have been not to have known it till now. What interest could a cliff have, or a forest, or a ruin, if there was no expectation read into it? And what could the expectation be if not of her, of the creature who has the power to make us happy? What meaning could a romantic valley have, all ruins and strange perspectives, if during a sunset walk among the thin cries of birds our thoughts did not bring her to us? What meaning would the temples of the pharaohs have if in their shadow we were unable to imagine a meeting? What could a corner of a Flemish town mean to us, or a café on the Boulevards, or a souk in Damascus, if we were unable to suppose that some day she too would go there and bring it all to life? And why would the little shrine at the crossroads, with its burning lamp, hold so much pathos for us if no allusion were hidden within it? And to what could it allude if not to her, to the being with the power to make us happy?

He thought of a lonely window lit on a winter's night, of a beach beneath white rocks in the sun's glory, of a wandering, crooked alley in the heart of an old city, of the terraces of some grand hotel on a gala night, of haylofts, of moonlight; he thought of snow trails of an

April noon, of the wake of a white steamer in the lights of a dance, of cemeteries in the mountains, of libraries, lighted fireplaces, stages in empty theatres, Christmas, the gleam of dawn. Everywhere was hidden the unavowed thought of her, and it was so even if we had no idea who she was.

How beggarly if, before some great spectacle of nature, our spiritual exaltation concerned only ourselves and could not be enlarged to include one other being.

Even the mountains that he had so deeply loved, the naked rugged inhospitable rocks, so unloving in their appearance, now took on a different meaning. The challenging of nature in the raw? The overcoming of the self? The conquest of the abyss? The pride of reaching the summit? What a dreadful idiocy it would be if it consisted only in that. Difficulties and dangers would be altogether meaningless. He had long meditated over the problem without finding an answer. Now he knew. In his love for the mountains was hidden another impulse of his soul.

If someone had told him so, when he was a boy and he'd been able to understand it, he'd have said no it wasn't true, out of a kind of shame. And others would still say no, it's idiotic, it's empty rhetoric, it's out-of-date romanticism. Nevertheless, if asked they'd not have an answer as to why a storm at sea so moved them, or a crumbling arch of some Caesar, or a swaying lantern in an alley in the slums. They would never admit that in those separate scenes there lay even for them, the call to a dream of love, despite the disgust such phrases might cause them.

Now the sky began to dissolve into blue and the sun to appear, and the clumps of waiting trees continued to separate slowly into two and then with increasing speed slipped away off to the sides, with a fluid interweaving of perspectives, quickly the nearer rows, slowly and lazily the further ones, in a duplicate rotation of the countryside as far as the eye could see. And when he pressed down on the pedal, the motion of the trees accelerated, and thus it seemed to him that the entire plain was obeying him.

Now into his mind there came the caravans of cackling hens from

America who get down out of their busses in front of museums and cathedrals. Was it possible that even they, in their wanderings from one country to another, were following a glimpse of love? That was it exactly, so pity them. Even in them the call, though unheard, still rang out; sixty, seventy, eighty years old, sober and respectable women, they would be mad with shame if they knew what it was that dragged them up and down the world. And if in their travels there was no such extravagant and improbable gleam, then they'd never move out of their houses. This wandering from frontier to frontier, from hotel to hotel, would become a torture.

And the universal subject of poetry? How did it happen there were so many landscapes, woods, gardens, beaches, rivers, trees, sunsets in poems to the beloved? Because poets more easily than others saw in nature the inevitable reference. Ancient towers, clouds, cataracts, mysterious tombs, sobbing of surf on rocks, bending of branches to the storm, loneliness of gravel banks in the afternoon, it was all a clear statement made to her, to the woman we love, the one who has the power to burn us to ashes. Everything in the world plots with everything else in the world in the wisest conspiracy of all, to bring us to the one we love.

It was an insight so fine and clever that in other circumstances Dorigo would have derived from it considerable satisfaction. But today, just because of its accuracy, it afforded him nothing but pain. The expression of the fleeing trees corresponded, in fact, to the condition of his love, which was both foolish and hopeless. He rushed toward her though he well knew that waiting for him there were only fresh sorrows and humiliations and tears. But all the same he rushed on madly, his foot hard on the pedal, fearful of wasting a minute.

The poplars of the plain, moving processionally, their backs curved, seemed to be saying to him: Stop, man, about face, think no more about her, follow us, stop rushing to your destruction. We'll lead you to the distant paradise of the trees where nothing but happiness dwells, birdsong and peace of mind. Don't be stubborn.

Their argument was so persuasive that at one point, overwhelmed by the inner turmoil, he drove over to the side and stopped. But at that same second all the countryside stopped, all the countryside round him and in front of him as far as the eye could see, to the end of the empty asphalt road. The trees stand tight and motionless, no longer slipping away on one side and the other, the poplars flee no longer, no longer do they say stop, they no longer dare to say anything because they know there is nothing to do. The trees tell him yes it's true, there at the end, in the south, where the road ends, she's waiting to destroy you, but never mind, enough! Enough, the sun is high, and we can't save you.

19

SHE WON'T be there, she'll already have gone, the telephone girl got it wrong, it isn't possible she'd be there, it isn't possible she'd have called him.

He asked for the Hotel Moderno. Just on the other side of the large square, at that moment his damned anxiety began again; he parked the car, entered, with beating heart, a provincial hotel like so many others. On the right was the porter's desk. Signora Anfossi? Whom shall I say? (A quarter-to-nine. Will she have dressed already?) She says to wait, she'll be down in five minutes.

He sat in an armchair; you could see a large room with little tables around the walls, did they dance there in the evenings? Whom would she have danced with?

She appeared suddenly, disheveled, without make up. "How come you got here so early?"

"That's what the girl at the switchboard said. Tomorrow early, it was written that way on the note."

"But I still have to get dressed, I have to pack, then I have to say goodbye to a family that's been so nice to me."

"What time do you want to leave?"

"I don't know. Why? Are you in a rush? Could we leave after twelve?"

"And lunch here in Modena?"

"Listen, have a coffee, and meanwhile I'll go up and get ready."

She said hello familiarly to the waiters, she joked with the girl behind the bar, she seemed to be in her own house, so utterly self-assured was she, with that slightly unscrupulous air of hers, she was pale, her nose more petulant than ever. She was like all brunettes just after they wake, before they've pulled themselves together, that dark transparency of skin, the color of marble, the shadow of night still on their cheeks and around their mouth, that kind of carnal virginity which is renewed every day of the year, that defenseless sincerity of a body taken by surprise, which makes old women seem ugly and young ones less beautiful, but to make up for it the young ones become nuder and stronger, dirtier, wilder, more exciting and familiar. The ugly and the beautiful both stand out, as in Laide—her impudence, her common touch, her little mouth opening and shutting, her two firm little lips, especially the lower one, thrusting themselves out like capricious, impertinent petals of a flower.

As Antonio looked at her, he took unexpected solace in finding her a bit ugly. After all, there were thousands of better looking girls; it wasn't as though every man in the world was running after her, and even to him at that moment she didn't seem terribly important. For an instant he hoped that he had been freed of his obsession, but it was a very short instant. Laide who had sat down and was drinking a coffee grabbed a waiter's arm and said: "Giacomo, be an angel and bring me one of those brioches, you know the kind I like," and Antonio saw that the waiter was a boy of around twenty or twenty-one, with a long heavy nose and a small chin, you might even call him ugly, but he had a kind of drowsy virility, and Antonio wondered if—It was preposterous, it was dreadful, it was extremely simple: perhaps even last night, out of some caprice, he thought, Laide had had him come to her room.

Smiling, Giacomo brought the brioche on a little plate. She took the brioche in her hand, said, "I'm going up to close my bags," and left.

Antonio went with her as far as the stairs. "Can't I come up with you?" he asked.

"Are you crazy?" she said.

He sat down to wait in a wicker armchair that stood in a corner where he could watch the stairway. The porter at his desk could see him. Antonio felt embarrassed and ridiculous. At his age to let himself be led at the end of a leash by a young girl! Her uncle! As if the porter would have swallowed that. It was the classic situation: the old man pays and the girl goes out with her young boy friends. He seemed to see a flash of irony in the glance of the waiter as he passed.

A step on the stairway. No, it was a man's step. A young man in a sweater with a suede jacket over his arm. A sportive type. Maybe training to be a pilot, or a test pilot. Was it because of this boy, Antonio asked himself, that Laide had refused to let him come up to her room? While Laide was drinking coffee with Antonio, had this boy been in her room shaving?

Antonio kept his eyes on him but he went on toward the door without paying the slightest attention to Antonio. He felt calmer. If the boy had been in her room, Laide would have had to give him some reason for going downstairs, she might have told him her uncle had arrived, in which case, out of curiosity if for no other reason, the boy would certainly have had a look at Antonio.

Anyway, it was a ridiculous idea. Laide was so preoccupied with preserving appearances (an absurd preoccupation, he was sure that everybody in the hotel, from the porter to the last client, had already set her down as a tart on business, imagine saying she'd come to model for fashion pictures), Laide would absolutely never have had a young man openly in her room. After making love, she'd have sent him right away.

A flutter of inner rebellion. Was he going into his second childhood? Why this anxious turmoil of jealous suspicions? Was Laide his property? What debt did she owe him? Those fifty thousand lire she'd asked him for (with some story of an obligation taken on when her mother was ill that she'd promised to repay in installments and one installment fell due the very next day) and he'd been only too glad to give them to her, feeling at last that he was binding her to him with a private bond. No, he couldn't honestly feel that those fifty thousand lire imposed on her even the slightest obligation to be faithful. Well then? Couldn't she go wherever the hell she wanted and take on whomever she liked? How could he object?

He looked at his watch. Twenty minutes had gone by, the sun shone brightly into the large room. He rose and went outside to let down the top of the car, he wanted Laide to find it open. Young women liked open cars; they have a sportive, modern, well-to-do look about them. He himself when he was in that car, though it wasn't a de luxe model, felt different, younger, more self-assured, envied; this was the first time he'd ever driven one but already he'd learned that people in the streets kept looking at him, all the women looked at him, especially the young ones.

While he was lowering the top and folding it away into its proper place, a fairly complicated process, he saw that two young employees of the hotel had paused in the doorway and were watching him with that interest all young people have in cars that are out of the ordinary.

He tried to do it all as quickly as he could, worried that Laide might come down. When he got back into the hotel, the porter smiled at him and said, "No, your niece hasn't come down yet."

His niece? He didn't like that business at all: it was almost as though she protested too much: did it never enter her mind that that fifty-year-old gentleman was her lover? as though she'd have felt humiliated if she'd had to admit publicly that she was having a physical relation with a man old enough to be her father. Granted, the fact that Laide invited him there as her uncle proved that she wasn't ashamed of him, maybe she even clung to this fictitious relationship to make people think her family was respectable and that she was the favorite niece of a man both well-known and well-thought-of. Also, of course, this created between them a bond, even though false, far stronger than the usual flimsy link between a call-girl and her client. And this delighted him, Antonio took great pleasure in anything that allowed him, in one way or another, to enter into Laide's life, into that equivocal complicated sinful and terribly Milanese world of hers.

He also understood how well assigning him the role of uncle suited Laide. It was a claim that allowed her to make love with whomever she liked and at the same time be seen in Antonio's company without seeming scandalous. He'd had a mad desire, when the porter at the hotel had spoken to him of his niece, to say, "Niece? That one's never been my niece." But he stopped in time: he'd probably have looked like the old man with the horns being led by the nose. Plus the fact that Laide, if by any chance she heard about it, would have gone out of her mind with anger and was perfectly capable of telling him to go to hell in front of everybody.

So he was thinking as she came down. She was impeccable, well made up and carefully combed, she wore a *plissé* dress and carried a miniature Maltese in her arms. Behind her came a boy with a suitcase, two smaller bags, a beauty case, and a coat of chamois-dressed antelope.

"And is this your famous little dog?"

"Let's put the things in the car right away," she said, and looked around to see if anyone else had heard Antonio's question. Because it would be pretty odd if an uncle had never seen his favorite niece's pet dog.

Laide suddenly quickened her step and when she was some distance from the boy, she said: "Marcello's been keeping him for me since I was last here. If there's one thing I hate it's talking about private affairs in front of strangers."

"What? What did I say?"

"Nothing, nothing," she murmured, because the boy was drawing nearer, "sometimes you men are absolute idiots."

Luckily, however, she brightened when she saw the red Spyder waiting in front of the hotel, sparkling in the May sun.

"Is it yours?"

"No. A friend lent it to me."

"Imagine! When are you going to turn in that rattle-trap of yours?"

They arranged the bags in the luggage compartment, then she said:

"Listen, you're going to have to do me a little favor, so please forgive me."

"What is it?"

"There's still something to pay here at the hotel."

"You mean the bill?"

"See how you are? You always think the worst right away. The bill is paid. Do you suppose I'd have you come from Milan just to pay my hotel bill? You don't think very much of me. It's the porter's bill, four or five thousand lire."

Actually it was five thousand two hundred. He paid. He came back outside. He suggested, as it wasn't noon yet, that they leave right away, because he had to be in his studio in the afternoon. Instead of eating there in Modena, they could perfectly well stop in Parma. In fact there were very good restaurants in Parma.

"Why?" said Laide. "Who's forcing you to leave so early? We can leave after lunch and on the new highway you'll get there in plenty of time. I have to say goodbye to Marcello."

"Who would Marcello be?"

"My cousin! I must have told you a dozen times."

"Haven't you had enough of your cousin these last few days?"

"I saw him once. He's got so much to do there, in the works. He's expecting me to come see him if I can ever find him."

She left Antonio and went to the porter's desk. In order not to be seen looking fretful, he didn't move. He saw her, through the door of the hotel, telephoning. She seemed extremely happy. She was laughing. It looked as though she'd never finish. He lit a cigarette. He watched her as she went on talking, he watched her laugh again.

Laide put down the phone and rejoined him on the sidewalk in the shade of the hotel canopy. She looked happy.

"Well?"

"Well, I don't know if I told you, I absolutely have to go to say goodbye to a family that's been so nice to me. You understand I can't possibly go without saying goodbye to them."

"What time are we going to get around to eating then?"

"Oh I don't care about eating. We can do it this way. Marcello will be here in a minute and he'll take me to see these friends. Meanwhile you can go have your lunch. Then we'll meet at two or two-thirty and leave. That way I won't make you waste any time."

"I come from Milan just to get you and you walk off and leave me to lunch by myself!"

"Oh come, now, don't get mad! Otherwise what do I do about these friends?"

"And this Marcello business doesn't take me in for a minute. He's as much your cousin as I'm your uncle."

Laide's eyes widened in surprise and anger.

"Yes, that's the way it is, as far as you're concerned we're all whores. Isn't it possible to love someone without going to bed with him? I couldn't look him in the face again if he lost his respect for me."

"You're not going to tell me he hasn't even kissed you."

"Son of a bitch!" she cried, exasperated. "I'm not surprised though. You men are all alike. You think we're nothing but whores. If you really want to know, Marcello has never even kissed me. It's as though I was his sister. Can't you get that into your head?"

"I don't think you've got any right to talk to me that way. As far as I'm concerned you're free to do whatever the hell you want."

"I shouldn't talk that way! You call me a whore and I shouldn't talk that way?"

"Who called you a whore?"

"You, if you think I'm with you and going with him at the same time. He might have the right to talk to me that way if he ever found out that you and I. . . ."

Antonio is conquered. Antonio believes her, it's incredible but Antonio believes her, she has such an air of sincerity and wounded pride. To be capable of lying so well she'd have to be a real monster, no it just isn't possible that a girl like her could create so perfect a fiction, she'd have to have the intelligence and the imagination of Shakespeare.

"Well," said Antonio, mollified, "how did you explain me to Marcello?"

"I told him you were my uncle."

"An uncle who turns up out of the clear blue sky?"

"I told him you'd been out of the country, travelling."

"And he believed you?"

"Why shouldn't he believe me? Everybody's not like you. Wait, here he is now."

20

DORIGO looked at him with a kind of fear. But no, Marcello was nobody to frighten even fifty-year-old Antonio. He was riding a motor scooter, he was dressed in moderately bad taste, a patterned tie in yellow and green, a striped suit. But his face? The face was the important thing.

His face fitted Laide's description. He was a tall young man, taller than Antonio, yet already slightly stooped. But his face? The face was the important thing.

The face fitted, fitted exactly. Ugly? No, not ugly. Worse. Inexpressive, lifeless, dumb. But not ugly. His eyes, his eyes above all. Without any flare or sparkle, or any suggestion of them, expressionless. Good-natured, rather clumsy. Yes, it fitted perfectly.

Introductions. Hardly any embarrassment.

"Now listen," said Laide, "you know where the main square is? Straight ahead, maybe two hundred yards, where there's a slope down. You go have your lunch and then we'll meet in the main square."

"What time?"

"What time is it now?"

"Twelve-twenty."

"Let's say two-fifteen."

"So late?"

"Well, you know, these friends of mine don't live right in the middle of town."

"Two-fifteen then but please don't be late."

"Two-fifteen. Are you listening to me?"

"Of course, why?"

"You're talking and you're thinking about something else. Will you do me a favor?"

Antonio looked at Marcello. Marcello seemed not to be there at all, he had a remote, apathetic air.

"What is it?"

"Will you look after Picchi?"

"The dog?"

"How can I take him on the Vespa? Anyway, he's a darling, you'll see."

"Do I have to feed him?"

"No, it doesn't matter, he can eat in Milan. Just a drop of something, a little rice and meat. But remember, only raw meat, and not too much. He's still a little baby, my Picchi."

Laide got onto the small seat at the back of the scooter with the easy air of someone who was thoroughly accustomed to it. Marcello started off. She waved to Antonio. Then she faced ahead, she seemed to be leaning on his shoulders, she didn't turn again to wave. He stood stiffly in the sun, the dog in his arm.

Something inside him said weakly: it isn't right, at your age, she goes off on a motorcycle with a boy of twenty-two, twenty-five, and leaves you standing there like a sucker. With the dog. Can't you see how ridiculous you are? Can't you see what you look like?

He stood in the doorway of the hotel with the dog in his arms; at the entrance to the hotel were the two young uniformed employees, those from before, and they look at him. Neither surprise nor mockery nor irony in their eyes, but they look at him.

He went to the nearest restaurant, a rather famous one. It was hot and he sat down in a small side room that was empty. He put the little dog down, who had, despite his size, fantastic vitality.

He ordered some raw ham which he had no desire to eat; the idea of food made him sick. Alone. A couple sat down two tables away, they must have been foreigners. She was a very pale blond who got interested in the dog right away and tried to call him over. The dog paid no attention to her.

Antonio couldn't get the ham down, he even had trouble chewing.

Where was she now? Trollies loaded with every gift of God circulated through the restaurant, what did he care? It was too much at his age. Suppose somebody he knew came in, he'd have said what on earth are you doing here, whose dog is that? It was too much at his age. He ordered a *paillard*. Maybe he'd be able to get that down. The foreign blond girl was no longer interested in the dog.

He'd never liked going to a restaurant alone, he preferred to skip a meal. They brought him his *paillard*. They brought a plate for the dog. It was hot, there were a lot of people, they ate with gusto—damn them, they were happy. One-thirty. It was hot, another three quarters of an hour to wait. It was an expensive restaurant, waiters kept coming and going, Picchi didn't like his food.

He chose a banana to finish off with, that was the easiest. But the banana wasn't ripe, he left half of it on his plate. A coffee. Disgusted with a customer like him, the waiter brought him the bill at the same time. One-forty-five. Another half hour. He didn't even have a newspaper. He waited a long time for the change, the waiter still hadn't brought it. The dog began to paw the bottoms of his trousers, wanted to get up on his knee. He picked the dog up and began to pet it. He was at home with dogs. And suppose he cut the cord? Suppose he unpacked the bags and left them along with the dog at the hotel and went off? Dimly he realized that a man couldn't have done otherwise, a self-respecting man. But he was no longer a man, he was a beggar, a child—worse than a child, he was a worm, something abject. That too he realized dimly.

With a kind of inward sneer he imagined the scene. She arrives with that little cousin of hers, at the meeting place in the square and she doesn't find him. They wander around the neighboring streets. He's not there, it's two-forty. Is he still in the restaurant? They go to the restaurant. Not there either. Did he go back to the hotel? At the hotel, the minute Laide goes in, the porter looks at her with a smile that might mean a lot of different things. "Signorina, your uncle's gone, he said he had to leave, he's sorry he couldn't wait...." "And my things?" "They're all here, signorina." "And the dog?" "He's here, signorina." She grows white in her anger and with great difficulty she controls herself to save face in front of the porter (as though *that* were still possible). Oh, how she'd like to let fly a volley of curses, how she'd like to give a piece of her mind to that bastard of an uncle. And now what? Not a cent in her pocket. Do you suppose Marcello...? No, she's the one who gives money to him, now and then, in the form of a loan. Her rage. Her humiliation. Her realization that now the porter understands the whole thing; he looks at her with an expression of aloofness and superiority that he's never had before. Now it's clear enough that she's one of those and that her story of posing for fashion pictures is nothing but a childish invention. And so at once, as soon as she says she'll be spending another night at the hotel, the porter announces that her room has already been reserved and that there are no other rooms available. And when she gets upset and begs for a room, the porter with an altogether too obvious smile says, "I don't know, signorina, perhaps as a personal favor...for one night only... we might be able to arrange a bed for you on the top floor.... As a matter of fact, there's a small room empty right next to mine." What a lesson for her, what a blessed lesson for her! He's not the congenital idiot you thought, is he, your uncle Antonio? In love, yes, he's in love with that bitch but he doesn't let even her walk all over him.

Voluptuously Antonio painted in every detail of this glorious fantasy, yet at the same time he knew he'd never be able to make it happen. It was like inventing the most terrible things—catastrophes, an earthquake, a battle, a dreadful illness, total destruction.

Why couldn't he make it happen? Because at the thought of never seeing her again, unlimited anguish took command of him. No. Anything to avoid that fate. What would he do without her? How could he go on? Laide for him was the earth itself, life, blood, sunlight, glory, wealth, the realization of all his dreams. Merely feeling her dog on his knees—luckily the dog was asleep at last—gave him some consolation. The fact that the little thing belonged to Laide meant that Antonio would see Laide again, if only for a minute. Damned bad-tempered dog, querulous, adorable, repository of a miraculous investiture.

The waiter brought the change. It was ten-to-two; conceivably a tire had gone flat while he was in the restaurant. He rose impatiently. He saw himself in a mirror; his face was ugly and drawn. Too bad.

None of the tires was flat. At five past two he was in the square. He got the car out of the parking area. But he couldn't stay in the car, the sun was too hot. He got out with the dog.

There was a little park in the center of the square. You were allowed to walk your pets there if you kept them on a lead. There weren't many people around, but a few stopped to watch, the dog was so little and charming. Ten-past-two, thirteen-past-two. At last! Now, in a minute or two, she'd reappear, she'd come with him, beside him, into the sun, just the two of them on the highway. A trip together for the first time, and with no one to bother them. And he'd speak to her, he had decided to speak to her, he couldn't go on this way any longer, let it cost what it might; he couldn't continue with this constant turmoil, this seeing her only now and then, this not being able to phone her, this measuring out of love at twenty thousand lire a time. Once they were in the car there'd be no one to get in the way, neither that peculiar cousin Marcello, nor her family, nor the boys at the Due that she danced with at night, nor the madams. They'd be alone, in the immensity of the plain. He'd never been able to talk to a girl and tell her what his heart wanted to say, never. He was always hopeless at it, but now something had overflowed, now unless he spoke he'd crack up; it was a question of life or death, he could no longer go on this way.

The sun was so hot he took the dog in his arms and went over to the side of the road, where the house fronts cast a bit of shade. Two-seventeen. In a minute or two. At his age, with an absurd little dog in his arms, to stand there waiting for a call-girl who, while he was lunching in the restaurant, had probably gone to bed with her true love, and with her true love she'd laughed long and loud at him, the imbecile who'd swallowed every insult she'd been able to invent. And maybe at that very moment she was still laughing at him, as she straddled the bidet, while her true love wiped off the sweat from the ride. But maybe not. It could all be true, it had to be true, she'd never have that much nerve, a girl like her. It was true. Of course it was true. But why make him wait like that in the middle of the street

with a dog in his arms? Did she think so little of him? Why humiliate him that way? If his partners knew, if his friends could see him.
It was that stinking little dog that made the situation so utterly ridiculous. Two-twenty-five, ten minutes late. Why? He was a man of
nearly fifty, serious, well-thought-of, respected, almost a man of importance. He was a child, he was lonely, he was badly treated, he was
humiliated. No one knew his trouble, no one in the world even if
they knew would feel sorry for him. The dog was a nuisance; bored
with being carried, it wanted to get down. How could anyone in the
world have pity for his idiotic predicament? They'd laugh at him,
even his oldest friends would burst into loud guffaws.

It was at that moment that Marcello's motor scooter reappeared
with Laide on the little seat behind.

"It's twenty to three," said Antonio.

"All right, I'm here," she replied, very sure of herself.

21

MARCELLO accompanied them on his motor scooter as far as the gates of the city. Antonio, anxious to be free of him, pressed down on the accelerator, and where the traffic thinned Marcello was soon outdistanced.

Laide got up and knelt on the seat so as to be able to look back and wave goodbye. If she'd been leaving for China, she couldn't have made more of it. If she was never going to see him again, she couldn't have been more agitated.

Did Antonio realize, or didn't he, that these were so many slaps in the face? How could he still believe in that timid, respectful, virginal cousin?

Finally Laide sat down again but for a good while continued to turn and wave goodbye.

"Well, have you finished?"

"With what?"

"Saying farewell to your true love."

"True love my hat! How many times must I tell you that there's never been anything between us? You want to know something, I'm getting sick of it."

"All right, don't get in an uproar."

"No, I know you pretty well by now, when you get something into your head that's the way it is and that's that. By your rules and regulations I've never told you a lie."

"And when you lied to me about your name?"

"What about my name?"

"You told me your name was Mazza instead of Anfossi."

"That wasn't a lie. At the Scala I used the name of Mazza."

He was silent. Laide's assurances that there was nothing wrong in what she did, that she didn't go to Signora Ermelina's any more, that the Due was a family place, that Marcello had never dared to touch her, that she went to Modena for her "work," that everything in her life was tidy and respectable, all her inventions down to the very last fraction of an inch had the extraordinary effect of calming him, and he allowed himself to be persuaded they were true, despite the continuous and crucial objections of good sense, as though he had taken a love potion.

Meanwhile he was eager to propose to Laide the agreement that he had long been thinking about. This agreement was of fundamental importance for Antonio and might indeed be his salvation.

Whence rose his torment, his disquiet, his anguish, his inability to work, to eat, to sleep? Why was Antonio no longer himself but rather a trembling slave incapable of all reaction?

The answer was clear enough. It was because, obviously, in order to go on living he needed Laide, but Laide in no way belonged to him. She came and went, telephoned or not. Up until now it was true she'd been as good as her word, but suppose she took to not telephoning? or to saying she'd phone and then not? She was, in a word, an uncertain, changeable possession, on which he couldn't count. And from this uncertainty came his torment and his anxiety.

He entered the turn-off for the highway and then the wide upper sweep of the approach. There was a wonderful sun, the time was three-fifteen. To drive an open red car beside a pretty and exciting and very up-to-date girl knowledgeable in all the matters that very up-to-date girls need to know, but more than that: beside the beloved, the beloved herself, the most desirable woman in the word—obsession incubus fate mystery vice secrecy fashion evil perdition love—she beside him with a blue kerchief with white dots tied under her chin, an enticing haughty peasant girl; to ride this way in an open car was wonderful, too bad there were no people around, no one who could appreciate his good luck in driving a red Spyder on a May afternoon with a wonderful girl beside him, a girl and not a girl, child and woman both, flower and sin and all that was easy to see a glance was enough; oh to go on like this forever and not have to go back to work, let the sun never set and the road never end and her not have to return to Milan. Obviously she wasn't in any hurry but tonight she said she had to go to dinner with an aunt and he didn't make a point of it but everybody knows what aunts mean for broadminded reckless girls who love money. He didn't question her about it, it would have been like a slap in the face, punctilious as she was, but he would have sworn she had a job to do that night.

Maybe Signora Ermelina phoned her from Milan yesterday just for that; a wonderful opportunity: a gentleman from Biella up to his ears in cash, respectable, reserved—one of those who when they find what they like don't worry about a ten more or less, and maybe it would work out into something more permanent; he'd come from Biella a couple of times a week and for the rest she'd be free as a bird. That's why she called Laide and not one of the others, because Laide, when she wanted to, knew what to do all right, and in a case where the client, an educated respectable gentleman it goes without saying, favored certain little caprices, well, naturally, why not? after all is there anything wrong in it? She was an intelligent child who took in the situation at a glance, not like that pretentious old bag Nietta (look at me but don't touch me) who the other day disappointed a flower of industry with a Mercedes and a chauffeur, a fine-looking man to boot, he'll never show up again at Ermelina's you can bet on that.

No, no, that's enough. Once again Antonio has forced himself to feel the pricks of those jealous fantasies constructed out of nothing maybe, but why not? Laide had come to him to take her back to Milan, with weapons, bags and dog, in time to reach home in the afternoon and get ready for the evening—to wash and perfume herself and change her linen and take on a new client. No, no, that's enough.

The dog meanwhile had slipped onto his knees and was in the way, the long straight road began, numbed by sun Laide leaned her head back against the seat and seemed ready to sleep. Maybe, he thought, it's the languid, delicious after-effect of having made love a little while ago with Marcello, while he waited in the restaurant; everybody knows how wanton and furious goodbye caresses can be before a long separation. But if she went to sleep now, maybe he'd lose the courage he needed in order to make his proposal. And so, with a tremendous effort of will, he said: "Laide."

"What?"

"Listen, I want to tell you something."

"Tell me."

"I need you, I admit it, I need to see you."

"Don't we see each other?"

"Yes, but.... I'd like it to be different.... Well, I want to make you a proposition. You think about it.... and then maybe tomorrow, the day after tomorrow, whenever you want, you can give me your answer."

She was silent.

"I'll give you fifty thousand lire a week and you promise me we'll meet two or three times a week. For the rest of the time don't worry, I'll leave you free. I don't even want to know what you're doing, and if one day you can't you tell me and if another day you have to go out of town you tell me. But this way, you see, at least I'll know that we'll certainly see each other, and we don't have to make love every time. It'll be fun to go to the movies or the theatre or have dinner together... otherwise you'll be free. Naturally if you stop going to Signora Ermelina's and all that I'd prefer it, you can understand that. I've told you I love you very much, I really do. So...well, you think about it, now we'll talk about something else, and if you want to take a nap, go ahead."

At once, with a steady, sure gesture, she turned her head to look at him.

"I don't need any time to think about it," she said. "Of course I accept."

Life coursed through his veins again, he felt a sudden liberation, his anxiety was ended, the world was back on its old axis, his pleasure in his work, in art, nature, beauty was reborn. So powerful, so overwhelming was the relief Antonio himself felt bewildered. Was his hell derived, in that case, from so little?

Yes, the situation had been suddenly reversed. Now he was on top, now he was master. Nor did he consider whether it was abject to have won the duel of love with the weapon of money. His happiness was so great that how it was attained no longer had any importance.

22

YET THE moment he put her down in front of her house in Milan with suitcases, bags and dog and she disappeared behind the gate, and he, supposing himself free of his possessive jealousy, turned his thoughts to the rest of his life—to work, family, mother, friends, and the city with all of its day-by-day distractions—the moment he hoped once again to relish the taste of the days as he had before, to experience again that total and perhaps ordinary tranquillity of mind, of being sure of each day as it passed and as he, with middle-class satisfaction, continued along the now smooth road that had brought him to ever-increasing pleasure in his success—at that very moment he felt himself alone.

Alone, and no one was able to help him, much less to understand him, not even perhaps to pity him. Work, family, friends, evenings in company, none of it any longer said anything to him, everything around him was empty and senseless. He hadn't been freed, that was it, he hadn't been freed at all. Thought of her, torment, disquiet, anxiety, entire unhappiness took hold of him as before.

Even worse than before because his agreement with Laide—even if he tried to deny it—now gave him a sliver of a claim over her. As of that afternoon he was no longer the sometime friend and affectionate client; he was something more, a kind of official lover, or protector (after all, if he was being honest, he'd have to admit that he'd offered her a weekly sum with the intention in mind that she'd become at least partly his, so he could demand a more constant attendance from her than before. Yes, it was the very same claim that ordinary insensitive business men make on their mistresses, there was no point in his trying to tell himself that his own case was different, that he was leaving her free, that he was asking only to see her a little oftener with the assurance that she wouldn't disappear from one day to another as before she might have. No, he, the artist, Antonio Dorigo, the man without prejudices, he had become like the others and had assumed the miserable role that to him had always seemed synonymous with mediocrity and impotence).

Worse than before, because now his embryonic claim made Laide's freedom of action even more unbearable, and it sharpened his own jealousy. Basically, up until now, his meetings with the girl had seemed to him a kind of wonderful concession on her part, a privilege. Till now he'd been excluded from her world. There was a kind of wall that hid her life and its attendant mysteries and he had never presumed to know them: her family, her first love affairs, her boy friends, her engagements with the madams, evenings at the Due, the doubtful business of the Scala. Only now and then did she come out of that world for her meetings with him. He waited anxiously outside, and every time that Laide actually did appear was, for him, a moment of inexpressible relief. When she returned to her own world again, he no longer knew anything about her and gave up hope.

But now a small door had opened in that wall, just a crack, and he'd got in, a step or two, only it was so dark there he could see nothing, less in fact than before when he was outside. Yet he'd gone in all the same, and got involved a bit, a very little bit, in her life and now he's happy about it. He thinks of it as a step forward, as a victory, yet all the same it's worse than before, now he's no longer a stranger, in a certain sense he has the right to know yet doesn't know. He can't even ask or make investigations for fear of spoiling everything (how awful if Laide got the idea that for those miserable fifty thousand lire a week he believed he had the right to order her around. Didn't he himself tell her he was leaving her free?).

So now more than ever the few things Laide has told him about herself crowd about him and torture him, some of them quite terrible things that filled him with a kind of fiery feeling difficult to explain, in which pity was mixed with jealousy, anger, and lust, and which rekindled his love. Shameful, equivocal bits and pieces, either true or false, maybe she invented them out of some instinctually subtle cunning, with the idea of exciting him, making herself more interesting, showing how self-assured she was, beyond good and evil, a mixture of unblushing defiance, with a chaotic craving for life, a desire to make up for her unfortunate fate, the pride of the proletarian, the candor of a child. For example:

She tells how she was entered at the Scala as a little girl hardly four. She was the youngest of all. Her mother wanted her to do it, and at the dancing school everyone called her Mouse. Erna Allasio, who at that time was director of the school, had got to be very fond of her. And little by little she became quite good. She did a *pas de deux* with considerable success, and sometimes even danced alone like a prima ballerina. But the dancing was very hard on her. Sometimes she felt very unwell and with great difficulty managed to go on. Finally one night—they were giving *Old Milan*—she fell suddenly. They had to carry her off; the doctor who came diagnosed it as heart trouble. Nevertheless she insisted on continuing with her career, although it got to be harder and harder for her, and now her heart is damaged; for instance, she can't go up into the mountains, at three or four thousand feet she begins to feel terrible. That was another reason she decided to give up dancing. But when Antonio questioned her, she was evasive. It wasn't clear whether she'd left the Scala definitively, when she left it, or whether she was still there. Every now and then she said, "This morning I went for my exercises," or "This afternoon there's a rehearsal," or "Tonight I'm working."

He checked with the program but it almost never corresponded. If he insisted, she grew peevish. Her entire life as a dancer, in fact, was covered by a thick fog. There seemed to be no doubt that she had been a dancer, she knew so much about the Scala, names, customs, shoemakers, suppliers of tights. But Dorigo got the idea that for some time Laide hasn't been at the Scala. And he doesn't like the thought that she's not a ballerina any more—it's really a shame, being a ballerina at the Scala would heighten her, make her more important, draw her out of that hopeless troupe of call-girls, make an artist of her instead of a nobody without arts or parts, place her to the best advantage in the Milanese scene, of which she seemed to be the very incarnation, a graceful little flag fluttering over the endless stage set of roofs, chimneys, churches, factories, hidden courtyards, old gardens, folk tales, superstitions, sorrows, sounds, crimes, festivals.

Yet the contradictions and the omissions are too numerous. Among others, was it possible that the corps de ballet of the Scala, famous in all the world, would have a dancer who did a number every night in a fairly infamous dance hall? By now Antonio was even doubtful that he actually had seen her on the stage during the rehearsal of *Evening Star*. At the time he had no doubt it was Laide. But could it not have been auto-suggestion? It was so easy to mistake one girl for another, just a change of hair-do or make-up or costume was enough. And there at the rehearsal they were all done up so oddly. And how for that matter can you explain the inexplicable fact that Laide, if it really was Laide, hadn't even deigned him a glance, as though he weren't there at all? How explain the fact that they called this presumed Laide, Mazza, while Laide's name was Anfossi? How explain the fact that Laide, if Signora Ermelina was telling the truth, went to Ermelina's at four the very day they were rehearsing, and at the very time he saw her or thought he saw her on the stage dancing the ring-around-the-rosy of the goblins? And another thing: after the performance, he got a photograph from the Scala of the nine goblins in costume but he couldn't pick out Laide: of course, in that costume, and with that make-up, it wouldn't have been easy. There were in fact at least two who could have been Laide. The funniest thing was some time later when he showed the picture to Laide and said: Can you tell me which one you are? she pretended to be offended with him, crying, "So that's how you love me, is it? You can't even recognize me."

These queer little things, that Laide explained away instantly without the least embarrassment but with rather ridiculous stories, now seemed to him additional proof that she was no longer at the Scala. One sole enigma remained unexplained: how on earth, after the production of the ballet, when Antonio telephoned Signora Ermelina to make a date with Laide, could Ermelina have said, so playfully:

"Congratulations! Laide tells me she saw you in a box, a stage box actually, and you were all alone." And that was absolutely true, the manager having given him permission to use this box at a time when no one else was there. On the other hand you couldn't exclude the fact that Laide might have been present that evening in another box or in the orchestra; but you also had to bear in mind that Antonio, by nature timid, had kept a bit back so that only from the stage or one of the few boxes directly opposite could you have seen him. Or among the dancers at the Scala did Laide have a friend who kept her informed of everything that happened? To satisfy his curiosity Antonio could have asked the ballet school directly; they certainly wouldn't have refused to answer. But now that there were no more performances of the ballet, he no longer had any reason to go backstage or to the school. To go there just for that would have seemed a bit strange; and in his heart he already knew the answer: they'd have told him there was no dancer named Adelaide Anfossi. Or they might even have said: Be careful of that one, she was asked to leave three years ago for reasons best not discussed. Yes, for sure, they'd have said something like that. And that, for Dorigo, would have been worse still. Better not go into it, better leave one's mind in peace. Anyway, Laide would have thought up some fresh yarn, there was never an end to that.

She recounted being on tour with the Scala in Germany, England, South Africa, Egypt, Mexico, and while they were in New York she had had a part in a film. But if you asked for details she didn't remember a thing, if you ask where she stayed she doesn't remember. On the other hand she knows all about the great hotels of Italy; she always seems to have stayed at the most luxurious hotels. How did that happen? Did the Scala treat its dancers that well? "Of course not, I went on my own and paid the difference." And she knows the hotels on the Riviera. She says that at the Bristol in Santa Margherita, or some such name, the rooms are so terribly nice, and all with bath of course. Two rooms, two connecting rooms. Naturally he doesn't ask whom she was with. She'd answer, as always, that she'd been on a holiday with her mother, or her grandmother, or some other elderly and innocuous relative. Antonio however thinks of spicy week-ends with sons of millionaires or elderly industrialists overloaded with years and work, who get their clothes at Caraceni, very *soignés*, advised on the state of their heart by a weekly electrocardiogram, but with heavy, hairy, sweaty hands which, as the panting grows louder and deeper, squeeze those childish small breasts.

Shortly after Laide had her quarrel with Signora Ermelina, they went to the house of a friend of Laide's, someone named Flora who had a little apartment near Piazza Napoli. Antonio already knew Flora, he'd been with her two or three times. She was a slim girl—pity her face was too long, her body however was marvellous—who said she was a law student. When Antonio and Laide went to make love in her house, Flora wasn't there and they began to talk about her. Laide knew perfectly well that Antonio had been with Flora and did not care. She told how Flora had had somebody who kept her at the Hotel Gallia and handed her half a million a month; yet she, through some utter imbecility, had pulled a boner and let the whole thing go down the drain.

"If anything like that happened to me, I'd hold onto it, believe me, I wouldn't let it fly away."

"What happened? Did she let him find her in bed with someone else?"

"Not even. At least I don't think so. Just some nonsense or other, I don't remember now."

"Who was it? An old man?"

She laughed: "Well, he wouldn't be a twenty-year-old if he was giving her half a million a month."

"And if somebody like that offered you the same you'd accept?"

"Look at you, right away you start.... I wouldn't want to put myself in a class with that whore, I can tell you. I've never seen anyone carry on the way she does."

Meanwhile Laide was taking off the bedcover and folding it carefully; you could see she wanted to do everything right to keep on the good side of Flora; she even took a pile of records from a chair and replaced them in the record rack, hung up a dressing gown that had fallen to the floor, emptied the ash trays.

"But she told me she was going to the university," said Antonio.

"Yes, Intercourse University. She's such a pig. She even likes women."

"Really? Did she try it with you too?"

"Well, I thought she was just doing it as part of the exhibition, you men get so excited watching certain things, but instead...."

"You two went together with some man?"

"Only once, I swear it, Signora Ermelina insisted so."

"Who was the man?"

"*I* should remember!"

"And Flora really meant it?"

"If you'd seen her when she began to kiss me, she looked as though she was going out of her mind."

"And you played along with her?"

"You think? It made me sick."

Their tone was playful but at every word a knot around Antonio's heart grew tighter, desecration, shame, jealousy all the bitterer for the spiteful candor with which Laide recounted the exploit. "How much does Flora make?" "She makes plenty, there's no question of that. But she's got her family to think about, everyone's always trying to get money out of her. So she's always broke. Right now she owes me fifteen thousand." "How come? Did she get someone for you? Is she a madam too?" "It was ages ago. Before we ever met, you and I. Anyway, it wasn't anything bad. It was for a trip." "A trip that ended in bed, I suppose?" "There you go! Nothing like. Just a trip, that's all. She made an engagement and then couldn't keep it, so she asked me." "If somebody was paying, he wouldn't have paid money for nothing, I imagine." "You're really not very nice, you know... always trying to hurt people." "I beg your pardon, but you don't have to be evil-minded to imagine—" "Imagine my foot! Do you think everybody's like you? Take Furio Sebasti for instance...." "Who's this Furio Sebasti?" "Haven't you ever heard of him? He has a factory where they make bathroom fittings." "Rich?" "You should be so rich! On his yacht at Portofino he can have thirty guests." "Have you ever been aboard?" "Me, no. But he calls me every now and then, takes me out to dinner, then maybe to the theatre, and every time he gives me twenty thousand." "That much? Just to go out with him?" "Well, I lose a whole evening, don't I?" "Does he call you often?" "I haven't seen him in months now. He's on a world tour." "How does it happen he can phone you and I can't?" "He's a friend of my brother's. And you want to know something, you're a pain in the neck with all those questions of yours. What else would you like to know?"

He said nothing. A trip! The introductions when she appeared for the appointment. Two men and two women for sure. "Ah, you're Flora's friend. Not bad. Congratulations." They got in the car. "I'm not sorry Flora couldn't make it. You're just the kind of doll I like. I don't like those great big amazons. But you...let's feel it.... Hey, wait a minute, you're not going to make trouble, I hope. If you're a friend of Flora's.... As long as nobody sees us.... Oh good, that's good...now while I'm driving put that little hand of yours there." Fury, angry helplessness takes hold of Antonio while his imagination reconstructs the scene. But Laide notices it: "May I ask why you're making that face? What are you thinking about?"

The first time Antonio took her to Corsini's house, Laide showed him bruises on her arms and legs. "How did you get those?" "Doing my number at the Due," she answered, with a hint of pride in her voice. "At a certain point in the dance he pushes me and I roll over on the floor. You have to take some punishment if you want to dance the blues."

"Were you there last night too?" "Yes, why, Oh, and listen, do me a favor. When we leave, take me over to the Fair Grounds, will you? It's only two steps away." "What do you have to do there?" "A friend of mine, one of those boys that's always at the Due, he took me home last night, and I left my bracelet and my watch in the car." "How come?" "I was in a hurry to get dressed and get out. I had them in my hand and left them on the seat." "It sounds a little peculiar to me." "You're certainly always ready to think the worst. He's just a good friend, and when I say a good friend that's what I mean and nothing else."

He doesn't go on, they don't discuss the matter any further, but when they leave he doesn't resist the temptation to stay with her a little longer, never mind if he's late for the office. Nor is he held back by the shame of taking her to meet a man who probably last night in the dark in his car.... ("No, baby, not here, not tonight.... I don't like it in a car. Take it easy or you'll tear my skirt.... Well, wait a minute till I take off my bracelet....")

They find him sitting at a stand advertising household electrical equipment. He gets up and comes over; he's about thirty, not very prepossessing.

"But I left the car at the entrance in Via Domodossola, it's a bit far."

"Are you coming too?" says Laide to Antonio.

"No, it's late, I'd better go."

"So long then. Maybe later I'll stop by the studio to say hello. 'Bye again. And thanks."

The man and Laide go off. He continues on alone, his distress and his exasperation mount dangerously, like water in a drain that was closed off but now the cover's been removed and the pressure from below shoots it out. Why does Laide expose him to such humiliating situations? Does she do it deliberately? Does it amuse her to torture him? Or does she do it quite innocently, not seeing anything wrong in it? And meanwhile he feels himself sinking ever lower and lower; into his mind comes Professor Unrat of *The Blue Angel*. Oh how much truth there was in that story. When he saw the picture, in those good old youthful carefree days, it seemed to him unbelievable. A respected teacher in a school to degrade himself to such a degree. Now he understands. Love? It's a curse on your head and heart and you can't escape it.

She told him about how her mother had never loved her. When she was a child, her mother made marvellous dresses for her, gave her wonderful toys, but only so she'd look good in the eyes of the neighbors. She never loved her. For absolutely no reason she'd bang her on the head with her knuckles, hurting her something awful, and from that day to this Laide has always suffered from terrible headaches. Her mother never loved her, in fact hated her. She also hated the boy who was Laide's fiancé, a really wonderful young man. And the day he was killed in an accident, her mother found out first and right away called Laide at the Scala. "Good news," she said. "Out of God's mercy your boy friend's been smashed to bits on his motorcycle. Dead as a herring. I can't tell you how pleased I am." Then Laide went into one of the toilets and with a pen knife cut her wrist, then so nobody would find out she bandaged it and left in a hurry. But the blood was gushing out and right in the middle of the Galleria she fell down in a faint. They took her to the hospital and there she stayed for months.

"But why?" he said. "Why did she hate you so? Wasn't she ever good to you at all?"

"Do you want to know when she was good to me? When I brought money home."

"Didn't she ask you where you got it?"

"She never looked under the carpet. Whether it came from here or from there, it was all the same to her, as long as it came from somewhere. Then, yes, then she'd be as sweet as pie. Little Laide here, little Laide there. Oh, how disgusting!"

"But didn't she ever suspect the kind of life you were leading?"

"She knew, she knew it better than me. What did she care? As long as I brought home the bacon."

She told him that as her married sister was now expecting a baby, she was going to have to find a place of her own. And of course, though she didn't say so, she was depending on him, Antonio, for help. He asked around, and one of the men in his office offered him his apartment, a small *garconnière*, that he was giving up the following month. Antonio and Laide went to look at it but she fled at once. "For heaven's sake, don't even think about it! I know this house all too well. You know who lives on the top floor? Matilde."

"And who is Matilde?" "But I've told you about her!" (Although in fact she hadn't.) "One of *those* houses." "And you went there often?" "She had a specialty, that one. All her clients came in the morning, around ten or eleven." "Why on earth? Business men from the provinces?" "No, no, they were real gentlemen, early birds if you know what I mean. There was one I remember, young, not bad, who had the hots for me every morning, do you understand? ten days in a row.

By that time I had enough of it." There was a kind of candid pride in Laide's words, like a little girl recounting her triumphs at school.

"And just imagine," she added, "the last time, I got out half an hour before the police came. Think what would have happened, a minor like me."

"What did happen?"

"To me, nothing. Matilde got six or seven months, it was in all the papers."

"Does she still live there?"

"I don't know exactly because I haven't had any more connections with her, but I imagine so. Just think if I lived in the same building, though."

One day they were in the car. Laide asked him to stop at a news stand and buy a copy of a fashion magazine. She took the magazine from him and showed him the cover: two girls on a beach, one standing, one lying on the sand.

"What? Don't you recognize me?"

"Which one? The one standing?"

"Of course! Can't you see that's me?"

Antonio feels uncertain: the girl resembles her, there's no doubt of it, but Laide's nose is more pronounced and her lips are thinner. "But look at those lips, they aren't like yours."

"Of course they're not, you don't know how much make-up they put on before they take the pictures. And then you've got to hold your mouth in a certain way. The fact is, you'd hardly know me."

"Could be."

"What do you mean, could be? Who do you think it is if it isn't me?"

Later on, when he leaves her in front of her house, Laide gets the magazine from the back seat, shows him the cover again, and exclaims, with a radiant smile, What a cute little thing you are! He's ready to swear that the beautiful bather isn't Laide, looking again he sees that even the shape of the ears is different but he doesn't dare to say anything more. On the contrary, he actually begins to believe her. Because it's impossible that she'd lie about it. If she were lying she'd have spoken in a different tone of voice, she wouldn't have sounded so peremptory, so sure of herself. Or could it be that Laide herself, though never having posed for the picture, had ended up persuading herself that she was indeed the beautiful bathing girl?

She told him one day that Fabrizio Asnenghi, the youngest of the sons of Count Asnenghi, had a weakness for her. He's very rich, she says, he has a delicious little apartment around the Via Venti Settembre. A very distinguished fellow, very nice, good looking too, though rather boring. When she goes over to his place, before they get down to business, she has to sit there for an hour at least listening to records while he smokes his pipe and drinks whiskey. Then he takes her home in his Flaminia Sport and slips into her purse a check for fifty thousand. And then sometimes Fabrizio gives big parties, lots of people, all of them drunk, everything happens.

"So you go in for orgies too, do you?" says Antonio breathlessly.

"Like mad."

"All the girls are naked, I suppose."

"Sure, some of them do a strip tease, girls of the highest society too. But not me! Do you know what I do? I go to the bar and I stay there and mix drinks. I don't even dare to dance. I go to the bar and no one gets me to move, even if they make fun of me I don't care."

These were the few fragments of a portrait that Antonio failed to put together. Sad things, pathetic things, maybe even abject things. Thinking about them, there emerged only a squalid, mean figure, clinging hungrily to impoverished illusions taken from the cheapest magazines. Was she kind? Was she generous? Was she bright? No, the more Antonio burned his strength away thinking about her, the more she seemed an unsolvable problem.

Stretched out in bed, hour after hour, he would fix his eyes on the ceiling, where there were two cracks in the plaster in the form of a 7, both strangely alike. In these two irregular shapes were concentrated his obsession and his torment. Her words, her gestures, the expressions that moved across her face came back to him while he watched the two thin motionless cracks above him, they seemed full of mockery and evil, and of philosophy too. He repeated, word for word, everything she said to him, her exclamations, her stupidities and banalities, her jokes, her memories of her childhood. Everything conspired to make her seem a hopeless little wretch lost in the powerful tide of the city that day after day drags both men and women away to devour them. God, why did he love her so? Why couldn't he give her up? What did she have to offer him? Everything seemed to say that for him Laide could be nothing but humiliation and anger, that disaster waited there for him with doors opened wide.

Yet in that proud and shameless girl there shone a beauty that he was never able quite to characterize to himself, a beauty different from that of all the other girls like her, who sat around waiting to answer the phone when it rang. The others, by comparison, were dead. But in Laide lived the city, tough, determined, presumptuous, shameless, proud, insolent. In the degradation of both mind and body, among ambiguous sounds and lights, in the bleak shade of apartment buildings, among walls of cement and plaster, in frenzied desolation, a kind of flower.

23

CORSINI'S apartment, afternoon. Laide is sitting naked on the edge of the bed and, using a mirror she's arranged on a beside table, is plucking her eyebrows with a pair of tweezers. Undressing, parading naked through the house, that sort of thing she does with the greatest of ease. Her lack of modesty is so whole-hearted as to be quite without ulterior motive. Antonio is naked too. Squatting on the bed by her shoulders, he follows impatiently. She's been at it for over half an hour, Beginning at the center and working out, she plucks the hairs one by one, so as to widen the distance between her eyebrows; then she thins them out. Her forehead, that way, seems wider.

She concentrates wholly on what she's doing, she doesn't care how unhappy Antonio is. It isn't lust that goads; it's her indifference that exasperates him.

"Laide, how much longer are you going to be?"

"I've just started. What's wrong? Afraid you're going to miss making love today?"

He watches her face in the mirror, fascinated. He follows the precise movements of her hands, her tongue caught between her lips in her concentration. Though Laide's back is a little curved, her breasts are up beautifully straight and erect, her belly is smooth.

Antonio has a hard time keeping hold of himself. It's not desire, it's fury. He thinks: Is she doing it deliberately? Does it amuse her to excite me and humiliate me? Or is it just that she doesn't give a damn about me? Or all together? It would be so easy in this position to put my arms around her from behind and take her breasts in my hands. Better not. How annoyed she'd be. And here I am like a complete fool watching her. If I went over to the chair and began to read, at least she'd feel a little less fascinating, maybe she'd even come over to me. But I can't.

"I've almost finished one," she says.

"One what?"

"One eyebrow. I guess you're glad of that. The right one goes faster."

"Why faster?"

"I don't know, but I work better on that side."

He thinks: What evil thing have I done that this should happen to me? He's never before found himself in a mess like this. He's never found himself naked on a bed, eyes wide, watching a girl thirty years younger than himself, a cocky little whore without the least semblance of affection for him. He's never found himself head over heels in love with a girl who doesn't give a damn about him, who doesn't even need him inasmuch as she could find a dozen just like him, who goes with him only because for the moment it seems convenient to her. A man as discriminating and intelligent as he to ruin himself over a creature like that! Yet it isn't that simple either. Because she's got something he hasn't found in anybody else. He still hasn't succeeded in figuring it out. Coarse as she is, there's something clean and healthy and fine about her. What is it? Is it nothing but a literary fantasy? Is it the sad and naked truth that, approaching old age, he clings to Laide as his last chance at lost youth? This something clean, and healthy and fine—could it be no more than her age, her long black hair, her childish breasts, her narrow Degas-like hips, her long legs of a dancer? Has he been lying to himself?

Someone told him once about having lost his head over a girl who liked to tease and he was almost out of his mind till one morning, when he woke up, he realized she no longer meant a thing to him. Between evening and morning he'd been completely and finally cured. Oh if only the same thing would happen to him! She'd phone him and he'd say sorry, he couldn't today nor tomorrow either, so goodbye. Then he'd like to see whether she'd spend hours plucking her eyebrows while he waited impatiently to make love.

"There. All done. Do you like it?" Laide turned her face toward his. Then she rose, put the little table back, hung the mirror up in the bathroom, put her tweezers into her bag. She had a mania for tidiness. Then, instead of going back to bed (Antonio was lying there, waiting to take her into his arms), she moved the telephone from the living room to the bed room, put it on the night table, plugged it in, got the *Corriere*, opened it to the classified advertisements, folded it carefully, and began to read the listings.

"May I ask what you're doing now?"

"Oh, nothing. But I've got to be on my toes if I want to find an apartment. There are two or three things here. Let me try them."

"Can't you do it later?"

"No, maybe later it'll be too late and nobody will answer."

"Come on, I've been waiting over an hour."

"For heaven's sake, the sky won't fall in if you get to the studio half an hour late!"

"It's not that."

"Then what is it?"

"Can't you possibly understand—"

"That I'm a numskull? Yes, I understand it very well. We can't all have your intelligence. But instead of talking about it I could already have made two phone calls."

Why was she such a bitch? He thought of rising, getting dressed, and leaving without a word, it would have been a splendid and salutary lesson for her. But it was only the shadow of a thought. He'd never be able to do it. He stayed there, stretched out on the bed, with his arm around her waist; and she, in her kindness, permitted it, as she began to make her phone calls.

"Hello? I'm calling about that advertisement.... Oh, yes?... Very nice.... And where is it?... On the third floor you said?... Yes, I could come in a little while.... will you be in your office, doctor?" Her voice sounded polite and well-bred with just the slightest hint of flirtatiousness underneath.

"Hello? I'm calling about that advertisement in the newspaper, I was wondering.... What? Yes.... Are you Signor Tamburini of the accounting firm?... July would be all right.... Three rooms?... I'm afraid that sounds a little large for me.... That's true, you never know.... Yes, I'd like to see it.... No, I'm alone.... No, I work at the Scala.... The theatre, yes, I'm a dancer.... Oh, please...." A burst of laughter. "Yes, tomorrow morning.... Thank you so much, Signor Tamburini."

Like a fool he said: "And what remark did you find so amusing?"

"Oh, nothing. What idiots men are! Just because someone's a dancer, right away they think.... As though that one's going to see *me* tomorrow morning!"

"Why? Aren't you going?"

"Not me, I don't like that type. Too complimentary. Plus the fact that he's from the south. But he did have a nice voice, I must admit."

Antonio's eyes were importunate. "Come on now, Laide, that's enough. It's not so warm today either. I'll catch a chill without any clothes on."

"Just wait!" Her voice sounded peevish. She called a third number.

She called a third number, and a fourth, and a fifth, her voice flutier each time, her "r" more accentuated than usual; and at the other end of the line they seemed to be all witty and gallant young men who had put advertisements in the newspaper solely in order to ambush artless young girls with no roof over their heads and in need of protection. By now it was obvious that she was going on with the calls solely in order to tease Antonio and with those absurd telephonic flirtations to make him jealous.

Suddenly his anger overwhelmed him, he himself was taken by surprise. He grabbed the newspaper out of her hands, tearing it as he did so, and threw it down onto the floor. "All right now, that's enough!"

She reacted like an offended child, jumped to her feet, ran to the chair where she'd left her clothes, took her brassiere, and began to put it on.

"Very well." She sounded as though she were about to cry. "I'm going now. You'll never see me again. It doesn't matter to you, I can sleep under the bridge." She had fastened the clasp of her brassiere. "I'm going I'm going I'm going! Understand?"

Antonio was routed. The fear that she really might go, and go forever, was stronger than any surviving trace of dignity. He jumped out of bed, went over to her, put his arms around her, and in a trembling voice implored her: "For heaven's sake, don't talk like that, Laide, please, I beg you not to...."

She allowed him to go on a little longer, then, mollified, sat down on the edge of the bed again and picked up the receiver to make another call. Getting the newspaper up from the floor was Antonio's job.

24

"Do we see each other tonight?"

"Yes, but we'll have to make it late, my sister's coming back from the rest home tonight, and I have to clean the house. I want her to find everything in order."

"But you've got all afternoon."

"Pardon me, but when I do something I do it right, and besides I've got to go out this afternoon. I've got an appointment with my foot doctor."

"What time then? Eight-thirty, quarter to nine?"

"Not before nine-thirty...."

"All right, I'll be there at nine-thirty."

At nine-thirty the street is almost deserted, only a few cars parked there, mostly small. He parks so as to be able to keep his eye on her windows. There are two french windows that give onto a large balcony. It's a modern building, five stories high. She's on the fourth floor.

Although it's relatively late, quite a few people are still coming and going through the downstairs gate. Once inside, the house becomes a kind of huge barracks, there must be several dozen families.

Antonio looks up, one of her windows has its shutters closed, the other is lit up. It's hot. After five minutes he gets out of the car and lights a cigarette, he paces up and down the sidewalk. There aren't many people. The sidewalk is bordered by a long railing and on the other side is a huge yard surrounded by sheds. It must be the warehouse or storeroom of some factory. At the bottom of the yard, on the right, is a private gas pump and nearby under a roof burns a small blue lamp like the kind they used during the war. Under the roof is a bench.

On the bench a man is sitting who seems to be asleep. There's no other sign of animate life.

Nine-forty. Antonio feels the usual tenseness beginning to mount. It's a disquiet that penetrates every part of his body, an uneasiness that mounts and mounts. This unbearable misery overwhelms him each time, though he tells himself: She's always come before, she's never broken a promise, Laide might come twenty minutes late but she always comes. If only he were sure she'd come, he'd be willing to wait hours, if only he could be absolutely sure waiting would be a delight. But there is no certainty. Precedents aren't enough. Each time, once ten minutes have gone by, obsession begins to take hold of him: Tonight Laide won't come Laide won't come Laide won't come and tomorrow she won't telephone Laide won't come because she's already left Milan she's found someone better than you younger more amusing richer and she's left you forever. Or else: Twelve minutes have gone by now, last time she was ten minutes late, she's never been more than sixteen minutes late, so there's still an available margin, let's say not until after twenty minutes will I resign myself to the fact that tonight she's not coming. Besides, she said she had to clean the house maybe she miscalculated the time, she's so meticulous she can polish then repolish a windowpane six seven times, tonight she may make me wait more than twenty minutes. It's terrible for me, she won't do it out of ill will she'll do it absent-mindedly without thinking but it's terrible for me. Each time I admit it's my fault I admit I'm a nut it's a kind of mental state but what can I do? No I can't go on this way any longer I don't work any more I don't eat any more I don't sleep any more, people talk to me and I don't hear them, I'm like a dummy I'm not myself any more I'm killing myself I've got to get rid of her. Come on man pull the damned tooth out get yourself another girl for a few months two three other girls, spend the money you've put aside, you couldn't spend it more wisely, I'm fed up I can't take any more.

That's enough now, take your courage in your hand and get out. If you can't do any better, wait another fifteen minutes maximum then get out. Let her be surprised. Yes, everybody I talked to, too many people, if I'm with someone a quarter of an hour I start telling them the whole story and they listen to me. They listen to me, it must be very funny to see how loony somebody can get—my problems must be a great comfort to whoever hears about them that's why they listen to me, they even seem to be so interested, anyway they all tell me the same thing: pretend you don't care stop paying so much attention to her, when you have a date with her never wait more than ten minutes, it's infallible, the world's always been the same way if you want to win the war with women pretend to be indifferent. Sure sure it's easy to say but if I go and if she drops out of my life and if she doesn't phone me again it's just too bad. Laide's so tough her pride is something I can just see her running after me, no I'd better wait but now sixteen more minutes have passed I've had enough and there's a woman on the ground floor watching me, not that she's parked herself right there on the window sill to look at me, no she's inside and she's turned out the light but every once in a while I see her going near the window just to look out and she looks out she always looks out in my direction she's probably laughing at me maybe she's called over some other people and they're all together in there giggling at a fifty-year-old man waiting for that, that what? well better skip it, that, well that one on the fourth floor who at the age of twenty has done better than Bertoldo in France. Fifty years old? After all, if I compare myself with people my age I can console myself at least I don't have a belly and I'm spry. My face yes that damned face of mine some days it's got a few wrinkles not so many wrinkles but it sags a bit it's a thin face but some days it sags—it's not true that only fat faces sag—but on the whole people don't think I'm older than forty-five forty-six. The hell with it. Can I knock a girl up or can't I? so? in that case I could go to bed with a fourteen-year-old girl and there wouldn't be anything funny about it, what hypocrisy what disgusting hypocrisy. Damn, it's already ten minutes to ten, twenty minutes are too long and suppose I went to the porter and asked him to call up to her? yes, it would look a little peculiar maybe, he'd certainly get the idea, but who cares if he knows whether Laide goes around with men or not? Anyhow, let's wait five minutes more, more than five minutes no, because then he'll close the gate, at least I'll know whether she's at home because it's very possible that business of her sister coming back from the rest home is just a lie to explain why she isn't going to keep the date with me. Actually maybe she's out to dinner with somebody, maybe with that count of hers, the devil take him, the one that plays Bach for her before he gets into her. Damn, now it's five to ten and if I don't decide right away he'll close the gate.

He gets out a banknote for five hundred lire—a tip of five hundred is more than generous but it's better to give too much, you never know—and goes through the gateway up the four steps to the porter's room, raps a knuckle on the glass because he doesn't see anyone inside. A fifty-year-old man appears: "I beg your pardon, could you call Signorina Anfossi?" and he holds out the five hundred.

First the porter says no but then he takes the money and gets her on the phone right away. Antonio hears her voice, her drawl, her mysterious I-don't-give-a-damn voice.

"Well, are you coming?" She gets mad right away: "I'm not finished yet." "How much longer then? You could at least tell me how much longer you're going to be." "I don't know I can't possibly tell you." "Well, should I wait or should I go?" "Do whatever you like. If you want to wait, wait," and she puts down the receiver.

He goes outside, once again up and down the sidewalk. Very odd that man still asleep under the covering, but is he really asleep? Looking more closely Antonio realizes that it's not a man at all, it's a trestle, some wooden affair, a dark shadow that had the shape of a man but it wasn't a man at all. The yard is completely deserted, the street's deserted too, even the one on the ground floor that was watching has closed her shutters. Now there are lights only behind two windows on the first floor and her window on the fourth floor. He lights one cigarette then another. It's ten past ten, but is Laide up there cleaning the house or is she with another man? it could perfectly well be that her sister's away, but it could also perfectly well be that she's taken advantage of it to have somebody come, somebody young maybe, she's having a very good time thinking about him waiting down in the street. Maybe the two of them are up there behind the shutters looking at him, maybe they're both undressed and he's holding her tight and she's telling him how that one waiting down there in the street has lost his head over her and she goes with him for the cash, and anyway she doesn't have to do anything in return because it doesn't bother him and he's satisfied taking her out to dinner and the movies but could anybody be more of a horse's ass than that?

And now those corrosive fantasies start up again that poison his life, that make his life a hell. Yes, it serves him right, the intellectual who used to wonder that novelists never wrote about anything but love and songs and everything else all about love, the hypocrite who used to say it wasn't so. There are so many things in the world more important than women, aren't there? a hypocrite and nothing else because it wasn't that he didn't understand, he understood all right but he refused to admit it. A Tartuffe like all the rest.

But now he knows how important a woman can be in a man's life, now he knows how much a man can want a pretty girl, now he thinks and thinks some more about how false the world is when it pretends that the desires of the body don't exist and doesn't talk about them while in reality if a man's honest with himself he'll admit that when he sees a girl in the street, an unknown girl, the first thing he thinks is: Do I want her? would I like to go to bed with her? And the second, equally inevitable question is: How could I arrange it? Right away, even in the very highest society, even in church, when a man sees a young and pretty girl, right away he begins to wonder what she's like under her clothes, if her breasts stand firm without any help, if she's got a narrow waist. Antonio for example always wonders whether she's shaved or not, because one of the things that excites him most are armpits without any hair, above all if they're young and plump and fleshy. When a girl raises her arms her opened armpits are the most appetizing aspect of her body. And then of course everybody wonders what the thighs are like, or the behind, there are even some who like the behind best and all of them, all of them, when they see a girl or even a child maybe, right away they think about the same thing, but no one says so, no one has the courage to say so, no one dares to admit it because they're all a lot of hypocrites.

It's enough to make you sick, and they live and talk and behave as though above all they loved making money, position in society, children, their own house, but just remember that everything, all one's efforts, all one's secret thoughts are focussed on that one thing, but it's a forbidden thing and no one dares speak about it and so when somebody gives a friend a present, no matter how generous he is, he gives him maybe an art object an automobile a yacht but he never gives him a chance to have a beautiful little whore. No he doesn't offer the most acceptable gift of all and even millionaires when they invite their friends to their town houses or their villas in the country, they offer them exquisite foods liquors champagne by the bucket, they spend hundreds of thousands of lire to make them happy but they don't even dream of sending to their room some pretty little doll ready to do whatever they want though that's everybody's chief desire. Especially toward evening everybody thinks about it but nobody really knows it they're born they grow up they get old they die as though the love of the body was something pleasant, yes, but not so terribly important while actually it's the most important thing of all and he was a fool and a hypocrite not to have realized it until now.

But now he knows because now he's been burnt, he's seen how a girl like Laide gets looked at in the street and how they whistle at her. Once she came to his studio dressed like a nymphette with a short balloon skirt and she'd pulled her hair back into a pony tail and that pert little face of hers looked fifteen or sixteen at the most and the two of them went out and the young masons who were sitting down on the ground across the street eating their lunch began to suck in their breath loudly when they saw her and she began to wiggle her hips in an absolutely indecent way, very amused, and he too enjoyed the incident. After all when you're fifty years old and have at your disposal a girl like that—whether it's for money or not what's the difference? the fact is she goes to bed with him—let all the rest drop dead with envy. They envy him, they all envy him and now he's atoning for his pleasure because the envy in this case is only the desire to possess Laide; the others like her too and why shouldn't they like her, she's a very exciting type, not a sensual type to be sure but exciting which is something else of course. He continues to look at his watch; it's twenty past ten. He's been waiting fifty minutes. Not even when he was a student had he ever waited that long. If I went now she couldn't complain, actually it's my duty to myself to go, if I wait any longer it would really be unworthy. She's not counting on it any more for sure, she's convinced for sure that I'll have gone however crazy I am about her. There are limits after all, but suppose she does come?

His torment was so great it seemed to him years and years of his life were being drained away; by now he was like an automaton, an automaton run down. Suddenly she was there with her imperious walk undaunted by the fact that it was now ten-forty-five.

"Do you realize you've made me wait an hour and a quarter?"

"If you want to know," she said, smiling, "once I made Marcello wait in the Piazza San Babila an hour and forty-five minutes and you should have seen how it was raining."

Unfortunately for him he couldn't take these things with a laugh, he was in love and so he lacked all sense of humor. He realized it but there was nothing he could do about it.

"Then admit you did it on purpose."

"On purpose? I've still got the hall to do!"

"Then why were you up there looking at television?"

"Television? Me?"

"I could see from here. You turned out the light in the room and then right away a little blue light went on down below on the left like the light from a TV screen."

"You're dreaming! Do you think I'd waste my time on that political stuff?"

"How did you know it was political?"

"Because they announced it yesterday. It was supposed to have been the Music Makers but they postponed it to a quarter to eleven."

"Too bad, then you can't hear the Music Makers tonight, can you?"

"Why?"

"Where are you going to find a restaurant with television?"

"We'll go over to the dairy around the corner. I've gone there before."

"A dairy?"

"Why, are you ashamed or something?"

"What about eating?"

"We'll eat afterwards."

25

"LISTEN," she said—they were in the car crossing the ramparts of Porta Venezia on their way to Corsini's apartment; it was a sunny day but muggy and heavy like most summer days in Milan—"listen I've got to ask you to do me a favor and I'm begging you from the bottom of my heart so please don't say no."

"If I can of course I'll do it."

"You can and it's terribly important to me. You know I'm going away now for a little holiday. I really need it, the air of Milan has always been bad for me."

"Near Sassuolo you told me, didn't you?"

"Yes, Rocca di Fonterana."

"Ever been there before?"

"Four years running. My mother always took me."

"Well, what's the favor?"

"Drive me there, will you? You really must because if you don't how will I ever manage with the suitcases and everything and the dog."

"Naturally Marcello will be there too, your beloved Marcello."

"Will you stop calling him my beloved? You know better than me he's like my brother and anyway he's working on the other side of Modena. It'll be a lot if in the two weeks I'm there he gets down to see me two or three times."

"You've got to admit it's a very peculiar business, a boy of twenty-five doesn't go after a girl just to read her poetry. After all, I don't suppose he's impotent."

"Peculiar my foot! If you don't want to believe me don't. Really it's no good being honest with you. If you really want to know the truth since we started seeing each other I haven't once been to Signora Ermelina's and the other night she actually called me because there was a German gentleman who's been wanting to go with me for months and she made an appointment and I didn't even keep it."

"An appointment where?"

"He was supposed to pick me up at the Contibar."

"Didn't you let him know?"

"Who cares? And if you don't want to take me, don't. I'll find somebody who will."

"I didn't say I wouldn't take you."

"No, because you drive me crazy with all that talk about Marcello, when honestly you ought to be grateful when I go with somebody and don't do anything bad."

"When do you want to leave?"

"Monday."

"Why Monday? Wouldn't it be more convenient to go on Sunday?"

"Sunday there's one of those excursions."

"Where are you going, to a hotel?"

"A new hotel, it's supposed to be very good and not expensive."

Monday morning was cloudy and gray and Laide felt sick to her stomach. She hadn't closed her eyes all night she said, and up to Lodi she was half asleep. At Lodi she asked him to stop at a bar where she had a coffee with three brioches, and then towards the east the sky began to clear.

On the other side of Parma Laide started to sing. The sun was out, she tied a handkerchief around her head which made her look like a country girl and began to sing. Not popular songs, these were songs that had come out of the far distant depths of the people, crude and coarse, neither nostalgic nor maudlin, songs of barracks rooms and public houses full of double meanings, authentic and sharp.

As she sang she seemed not vulgar but free, not malevolent but keen, a little tough of a girl who suddenly found within herself the music of the streets and the courtyards of her childhood, of the time they had made war whole-heartedly, one kid gang against another, of the time when, as a joke, she used to bite the legs of old ladies sitting in the garden, of the time when she'd go down into cellars looking for friendly rats and once brought one home that weighed at least half a kilo and that stayed happily in her arms and even licked her hand.

Antonio remembered how one night in Milan, around two in the morning, he was awakened by the sound of singing, with a sharply marked rhythm. It must have been a gang of boys riding up and down on their bicycles, and at first Antonio didn't know what it was. Then he recognized the old song of the chimney sweeps; he'd heard it a hundred times; the peasants also sang it in the country where he used to go as a child. He himself perhaps had sung it in the mountains and it had always seemed coarse to him, but that night the anonymous little boys transformed it into something very beautiful and powerful, a ballad of anger and regret that issued out of the very guts of Milan. They weren't trained choristers obviously; they were boys of the people who had stayed out late and maybe they had got a bit drunk, although you couldn't tell because of the precision, the force, the measure that made their unselfconscious surrender to the music so perfect. Sung in that way, the old vulgar jokes became a hymn, a secret pledge, a mysterious challenge.

Antonio realized, astonished, that Laide was singing in exactly the same way, with the same hammer-like rhythm, the same vitality as if in those songs she could rediscover the best of herself, the true meaning of her life.

He kept turning to look at her for never had he seen her so beautiful, with a moving purity, a joy of living in the world, and stupidly Antonio felt proud of her; no, she wasn't like so many of those girls, frantic and shameless, she was a human being in the fullest sense of the words. She was something important.

"Please sing it again."

She laughed and began over, and then, without a pause, continued on to other songs of soldiers and whores, but once again she transformed them in some mysterious fashion into something old and noble, reminiscent, through the pages of Manzoni, of bivouacs of lancers and soldiers of fortune.

Then suddenly she fell silent, like a threatened animal seized by one of those frequent attacks she had of tension and anxiety. And when he begged her to go on with *Urca uei*, she said, "You know, you're an awful bore." In an instant she had become a different being entirely.

Meanwhile they'd left the highway and were winding into the hills among meadows and beautiful and lonely trees.

"Not bad here," he said, just to be saying something, feeling that idiotic embarrassment he always felt when alone with a woman he hadn't known very long.

"Haven't you ever been here?"

"It's the first time," he said, "and probably the last."

"Why?" she asked, with lightning-swift insight, turning to look at him.

"Because, dear Laide, you're a very delightful girl, and I love you deeply, but ours is bound to be an unhappy story. Every day I see it more clearly. Apart from the help I give you what can I possibly mean to you? At some point or other one has got to find the courage to look facts in the face. Think only of the difference in our ages."

Where had he found the strength to say these things to her, things he'd decided a hundred times to say but had never yet dared to? Now what end did he hope to reach? He himself could not have said, in fact hardly had he finished speaking when he began to regret it. Maybe it was a mistake, maybe she'd take him at his word. Suppose she said yes, he was right, it would be better if they parted? At that thought he felt in the region of his stomach something terrible, like an attack of nausea.

But Laide didn't say yes. With her eyes on the road ahead, she said softly, "No, I'll tell you, without me you couldn't go on living."

At that moment Antonio understood that everything was useless and that he was as good as lost. She looked ahead at the road that wound gently among the fields. She didn't look at him seated beside her driving the car, a modest Seicento, a poor little car unworthy of her badly dressed as she was, without make-up, uncombed. But for her at that moment nothing would do but a Ferrari or a Daimler with bumpers of silver and gold so well polished you could see them glisten and shimmer from afar, from hill to hill. With her woman's awareness, so astonishing at her age, she had said, *"No, I'll tell you, without me you couldn't go on living."*

And he made no reply. He might have answered with a hundred phrases, dignified or sarcastic or witty, but no, he said nothing. Once again he'd failed, she'd defeated him. She held him in her hands, in her frail gentle terrible hands, but she didn't press tight, just a tiny contraction to make him understand that if she had pressed tight she would have broken him in two. But she didn't. She didn't even smile. It was such a natural simple thing for her to do, not a game, not a duel; for her it was the most natural thing in the world, an ordinary moment in her life which rose from irresistible feminine power.

It was a beautiful splendid sunny day; the countryside was green, smiling, and empty. The clouds, too, were very beautiful. It would have been easy to be happy sitting beside her but instead she had said: *"No, I'll tell you, without me you couldn't go on living,"* and it was true, the sacred and the cruel truth. That was why he kept silent. Yes, he was old, an old man held, he and all his world, in the warm soft hollow of her hands. Yet a tremendous power held him up though he was old—old in years yes, but young in spirit, younger even than he thought—and this power was not evil even though, in order to manifest itself, it made use of money. It was something rather foolish, unselfish, crazy that somehow had burst out of a man like Dorigo. It was the long blare of a trumpet, it was a beam of light, it was the wild whistling flight of a body falling straight down into an abyss where at the bottom it will crash into a thousand pieces, but until then alive, alive—mercy of God, it was love.

But there was the hotel, it was new and fairly attractive. Antonio helped Laide bring in the bags. They'd given her a corner room with two beds. "I always take a room with two beds. Sometimes I like to change off and by now it's a habit."

"It might also be a convenience," he said, knowing perfectly well she'd be offended but unable to resist.

"What kind of convenience? Are we beginning all over again? In any case understand I've never in my life spent a whole night with a man. That's one reason it doesn't suit me to get married."

He was aware that Laide would have preferred, while she unpacked and put her things away, for him to wait downstairs. She wasn't quite ready to assign him the role of lover, but she herself realized that that would have been just a little too pretentious. In order to prove, therefore, that between her and him there was nothing, she left the door wide open. Dresses, linen, shoes were all arranged in the suitcases with geometric precision, everything in its plastic envelope. From her beauty case she brought out such a battery of jars and little bottles that one might have thought she was a movie star. She lined them up carefully on the dressing table in two semicircular rows. Then she arranged the little rug for the dog, the plastic bowl for his water, and the other dish for his food.

She seemed to take pleasure in making the operation last as long as possible, endlessly smoothing and folding her linen, changing it from one drawer to another, one might have thought she intended to spend the rest of her life in that hotel. He looked at his watch; he'd have liked to get back to Milan by five.

Every once in a while Laide turned to the balcony to look out, was she waiting for Marcello to come? But Marcello didn't appear. Finally at one-thirty she was ready and they went downstairs. She said she'd rather lunch in Modena and Antonio had the impression she wanted to be seen with him as little as possible there in the hotel. Why? Was she ashamed of the difference in their ages? But as she passed him off as her uncle anyway, what did it matter? Or did she want to keep the field virgin, so to speak, for Marcello's arrival? What would Marcello's official role be? Cousin? Fiancé? The uncle business was a continuous source of annoyance and humiliation for Antonio, but he lacked the courage to rebel. All he had to do was say: "I warn you that if you call me uncle in front of strangers, whoever they are, I'm going to say in a loud voice that I am not and never have been your uncle." Yes, and maybe she'd have gone along with it, but at what cost? Was it worth the trouble to contradict her, to upset the artless plans she was always making, a girl alone, in the hope of saving her face at any cost?

They went to Modena to eat, it was a dreary lunch with few words spoken on either side. Now that the moment of separation approached, Antonio felt the return of his disquiet and the increase of his suspicions.

It was nearly three o'clock when they got out of the restaurant and very hot. "Well, I'd better go," said Antonio.

"Drop me at a movie near by," she said.

"A movie now?"

"Yes, that way I'll kill time till five. At five-thirty I'm meeting Marcello in the Piazza."

They got into the car, Antonio felt fretful; the dog climbed onto his knees and began to nibble the buttons of his coat.

Halfway there Laide changed her mind, or did she change it? Perhaps she'd had the idea from the first but hadn't dared to say so. "Would you mind turning here to the left?"

"Why?"

"Now stop here at the corner."

"You want to get out?"

"No, listen, be an angel, the first or second street on the right is Via Cipressi, number six is where Marcello stays. It wouldn't be any trouble for you to go over and ask if by any chance he's at home. You see, it's a boarding house, it's run by some woman, I'd rather not let her see me."

"So I'm the one who has to go?"

"What's wrong? It's not even fifty yards away."

Now's the time to show you're a man thought Antonio, rebel, tell her to ask you to do anything but not to play the pimp. But Laide was in a bad mood; if he'd started anything, she was quite capable of walking off and leaving him then and there and disappear from his life forever. He got out of the car and walked to Via Cipressi. At Number 6 he asked for Marcello. Some boy said Marcello was at the yard, working.

"Who's looking for him?"

"Signorina Anfossi is outside."

"Laide?"

"Yes."

"I'll come right away."

The boy accompanied Antonio to the car; he and Laide greeted each other happily. They seemed on intimate terms. Then Laide introduced them. "Peppino, I'm sorry I've forgotten your last name . . . this is my uncle." They shook hands. Peppino went back to the house.

The movie was very near. Antonio couldn't hold back any longer; it seemed to him that he'd been much too patient.

"Listen now, Laide, I can't understand why you don't realize that there are certain things that are in the worst possible taste, not to say. . . ."

"Not to say what?"

"Not to say coarse and crude, if you really want to hear it. To ask me to go to that house looking for your—"

"For my what?"

"All right, let it go."

"I won't let it go!" she cried in a loud voice. "Always calling me a whore! I've had enough of it!" With her right arm folded, she made a swinging movement as though chopping off a beard. "It's enough to drive a person crazy, that one who never even touches me and you who make love to me anytime you want and you're the one who's jealous! I've told you so many times, with all your fine airs and your education you certainly know how to hurt people! You want to soil the finest feelings, you can't admit that a man and a woman could like each other very much without having to go to bed. You're cheap, that's what you are. It's very easy to see you've never had anything to do with a decent girl, only with bitches, and as far as you're concerned everybody's a whore and there's nothing in the world but whores!"

They had paused in a large square. Two women, hearing her angry voice, turned around to look at them.

"Keep your voice down, at least? Do you want everybody to hear you?"

"Let them hear me, I don't care, I'm sick of these stories of yours."

Antonio was silent, once again vanquished. She too had finished. After a moment or two, he said, in a cold voice:

"Well, I'm going. It's late."

"Bye. I'll call you, probably the day after tomorrow I'll have to go to Milan, if I do I'll come by the studio."

"As you like," he said and threw the car into gear, and the poison coursed through his veins.

26

TWO WEEKS apart. For two weeks Antonio ceaselessly examined the illness that held him captive. In his not having to wait anxiously, day after day, for Laide's phone call there was certainly a kind of peace. But, to make up for that, the distance between them multiplied his sick fantasies. Stretched out on the bed, of an evening, his eyes fixed on the two cracks in the ceiling in the form of a 7, he would circle, for hours and hours, indefatigably, his pain and his sorrow. She phoned him every two or three days. Actually she was unusually punctual. It was a small consolation but he wanted others.

He prayed God to release him from his hell. Maybe one morning he'd wake altogether changed, free and weightless. What a wonderful thing it would be. It's almost two in the morning now, tomorrow she's to call me at the studio. Will she? This terrible wasting-away. The burning in his stomach. Whom is she with now? Is she alone? Is she dancing somewhere? But those aren't the important things. Today is Friday, since Monday so many things might have happened, a new interest might have come into her life. And now the only thing she remembers about me, maybe, is that I'm supposed to send her money. I must be very ill, these tranquilizers are no more use than water. I can't stand sitting, I can't stand lying in bed. Where is she now? The dreadful thing is there is no hope: even if she phones me, even if I see her again. Why shouldn't I see her again? I've decided to tell her everything. So at least she'll know. So there shouldn't be misunderstanding between us. Then let her do what she thinks best. I'll write her the whole thing. A final no, with the wrench, and the pain, and the long period of melancholy, would be better than this constant unbearable anxiety. To sleep, to sleep would be my only salvation.

But then, when he woke, as the last traces of the dream that he'd been dreaming vanished, once again the anguish came and the sense of guilt and desolation. At once he asks himself: Why? Why? Laide! His heart begins to beat, his mind is flooded by his obsession, it overwhelms his entire consciousness and leaves no means of escape. Whatever you think about, or rather try to think about, she's always there, right in the middle, barring the way. He tells himself it's absurd, she's not worth the trouble, she is contemptible, and yes, they're all excellent arguments. But the day he renounces her, gives her up, exchanges his anxiety for the burning pain, what will there be left for him that day? Emptiness, loneliness, the prospect of a future ever drearier and dead. O God, help me!

He kept thinking about the letter he wanted to send her, no treaty of peace ever took so much hard work. For he had to write simply, to use down-to-earth words, or she'd never understand, and he had to make her understand that he'd come to a decision. Yet he didn't want to go too far, he wanted to tell her the naked truth but without offending her, without endangering that strange dignity to which she clung so firmly, and at the same time to seem sympathetic and affectionate.

The following day he finally got it written down:

Dear Laide, don't be frightened by this letter. Read it calmly, when you're lying out in the sun maybe or before going to sleep, there's no hurry. But these are things that concern you and that I feel I ought to tell you. As you're on a holiday you'll be able to think them over. Here is what it's all about.

I don't know whether you're aware of it or not but I, though I love you more all the time, am not entirely happy. There's no point saying what's good and what's bad between us. You're woman enough to guess and intelligent enough to understand that coldness and rudeness can do more harm than a true and proper betrayal.

It seems to me you've asked too much of me, and I don't mean money. Let's not discuss the difficulty of phoning you, finding you, seeing you, being together a little while, though God only knows how much I've suffered on that account in the past. I'm referring to many other things that I think you know about, such as the unpleasant part you make me play with Marcello, and I'm not going into the question of what your true relations with him are. I think sometimes you go too far. After three months, in which you've had time to realize how much I love you and the sacrifices I'm willing to make in order to prove it, your only return is coldness, boredom, and fatigue. You've told me often that between a man and a woman there always has to be a time of breaking-in. But this breaking-in is going on, I think, for a hundred thousand miles. Yes, you're very dependable so far as little daily obligations go, telephoning, keeping appointments, and so on. But never any warmth from you, never a sign of affection or kindness!

The danger is that if you continue to go on this way, I'll end up in such a state of crushing humiliation that I'll no longer be able to bear it.

I don't want you to mistake my love, dear Laide, for unlimited weakness. There comes a time when a man must be able to open his eyes, even though he may be in love, and face reality, cost him what it might.

I hope this won't happen to us. But if that's to be the case both of us will have to do the hoping. That's why I'm writing you, dear Laide. So that you'll realize our affair as it is now can't go on.

You'll ask me what I want. I want you to respect me as a man and not ask me to play only the part of the uncle that pays the bills, a kind of uncle-of-all-work. I want you to act toward me as all women do toward the man they're attached to, whether out of affection or for their own advantage.

I don't think I'm asking very much, when you come down to it, after everything I've done and am doing for you. And would like to continue to do in the future. That, my dear, depends entirely on you.

Now go on with your holiday and have a good time. But try to think a little bit about this affair of ours that began as such a simple little thing and that has gradually become a matter of very great pain for me.

I don't know how it will end. See if you can make it work. Love, or affection, between two people, or just the habit of seeing each other, even when there is no passion, has got to have in it at least something of human kindness and well-wishing.

Don't be too overwhelmed by this unexpected letter of mine. I wanted to tell you everything I found in my heart. And I don't want you, one day, to be surprised by anything that might happen.

That's enough now, have fun, get beautifully dark, let me hear from you. I hold you tight.

That, after a couple of tries, was the third version. He jotted it down, then copied it off on the typewriter, then decided it would be more polite and perhaps even more effective if it were written by hand, so he copied it once again with his fountain pen, writing in very clear letters. He read it, reread it, put it in an envelope, addressed it. Then he thought about it some more, opened the envelope, read the letter once again, and decided it was absolutely odious, unctuous, hypocritical, cowardly, and, worst of all, ridiculous. Begging for a little sweetness and kindness just because he donated fifty a week! Even a traveling salesman would have done it better. He decided therefore not to send the letter, he'd tell her the same things personally when he went to Fonterana to pick her up. Yes, a lot of things can more easily be said than written, and he could temper his words at once depending on her mood and her initial reactions.

But when he went to Fonterana, after two weeks, to call for her, he couldn't speak to her as he'd hoped to because Marcello was there too.

She was waiting for him in front of the hotel, she came immediately to the car to meet him:

"Lord," she said, "you're going to be mad at me but it's not my fault. That nuisance! He's beginning to be a real pain in the neck."

"Who? Marcello?"

"Who do you think? He knew I was leaving so he came to say goodbye to me and now I don't know how to get rid of him."

"What does that mean? That he's going to have lunch with us?"

"I don't know. But I can't be rude to him, he's always been nice to me. Well anyway come up a minute you'll want to freshen up with all this heat."

Antonio evidently must have looked annoyed. With that "Come up a minute" of hers, she hoped to calm him down: a gesture of intimacy right under the eyes of Marcello who was waiting in the lobby. Solicitude unheard-of.

Antonio had no desire to freshen up but nevertheless he followed her upstairs. Her bags were ready. Everything was in perfect order.

"You'll have to admit that this business of Marcello is really pretty much of a nuisance."

"Of course it is!"

"Why did he come, did you say?"

"I told you in the beginning, didn't I? But after all ... if there was anything between me and him I'd understand."

"Did you see him every day?"

"What do you mean, every day? In the whole two weeks we saw each other three times. He's got a lot of work to do ... Oh, do you want to hear something funny? But if I tell you, you mustn't get mad afterwards, just so you'll realize what gossips people are.... Do you know who they think you are here in the hotel? Just after having seen you here that one time. They think you're his father."

"Whose father?"

"Marcello's."

"That's wonderful. And who do they think Marcello is? Your husband?"

"You're kidding. To the few I introduced him to I said he was my cousin."

Antonio looked at the two beds side by side though separate, each with its own linen and covers. One looked absolutely untouched as though no one had even sat down on it. He remembered how Laide, before he brought her to Fonterana, had asked him to write the hotel putting "signora" and not "signorina." "If hotel people know you're married," she said, "they have much more respect for you. That's why I always wear my poor mother's ring." At the time he didn't think anything more about it: some silly whim of hers. But suppose instead it was a very smart trick? That way Marcello could come to sleep with her in the hotel without anybody having anything to say. If that's the way it was, however, his staying overnight would have to be marked on the bill. She'd already have paid it. He wanted to see it. (But the bill hadn't been paid already, he paid it, and on it he found nothing suspicious. Which made him feel a little calmer. Although you couldn't exclude the fact that some hotels wink an eye at things like that. Or did the price they quoted give her the right to use both beds?)

They went downstairs. Marcello greeted Antonio deferentially. The more Antonio thought about him the more his suspicions tended to diminish. Physically he was an attractive boy, but with such a sleepy look, almost apathetic, lifeless. His way of speaking was so sluggish. When the time came to leave—they were to lunch in Modena—Marcello didn't ask any questions. It was as though he and she had already arranged it between them.

Marcello went first on the motor scooter. Antonio and Laide followed in the car. On the way into the city they found Marcello beside the road, he'd punctured a tire. He left the scooter in a garage and got into the car, finding room as best he could in the back among all the suitcases and bags.

The agony of that lunch for three. Antonio wanted to seem witty and agreeable, even at the cost of playing the role of the indulgent cuckold. It wasn't easy, however, to find mutual topics of conversation.

Then Laide, at a certain point, probably acting out a comedy whose intention was to reassure Antonio, began to tease Marcello.

"Last night being Saturday what did you do? I'll bet you went to look for a woman as usual."

"Of course," said Marcello, on a playful note.

"Well, tell me, who did you find? That blonde I saw you with last time?"

"What do you mean, a blonde?"

"A brunette then? Who? I'll bet you I can guess."

"Who was it then?"

"Will you give me a thousand lire if I guess right?"

"I will."

"The girl in the leather shop in the arcade."

"You're cold as ice."

"Then you went with Sabina. You told me you don't know any others."

"That bobby-soxer? I haven't seen her in a month."

"A new conquest then?"

"Well, maybe."

"Nice?"

"Not as nice as you," he said smiling, "but not too bad."

"I hope it wasn't a whore—"

"Stop!" Marcello quickly put his hand over her mouth. "Censored." He looked around to see if anyone at a nearby table had overheard her. But he saw that nobody had turned.

Antonio sat there with increasing discomfort. It seemed as though the lunch would never end.

After lunch Laide had one of her sudden whims. Before leaving for Milan she wanted to go to the movies to see a picture, some American comedian. She'd seen it once before at Milan and had loved it. When she liked a film she could happily go to see it a dozen times.

Unfortunately it was Sunday. There was no reason in the world why Antonio had to be back by five. Marcello too, naturally, was free.

They got in the car again and started off toward the movie Laide had wanted to see, While they were on the way, she glimpsed, on the other side of a square, the advertisements for another movie. "Wait a minute," she said, "what are they showing?" "Not that one," said Marcello. "It'll be full of stinking soldiers." Antonio continued on.

"But what were they playing?"

"I don't know," said Marcello. "I think I saw the word 'kiss.'"

"Kiss what?"

"The mouth I imagine." He smiled disagreeably. "Or would you prefer it somewhere else?"

"Cut it out!" said Laide in a hard voice. "You know that kind of joke gives me a pain."

They got to the right movie house, left the car in the shade so the dog wouldn't feel the heat too much, and went inside. Hardly a soul was there. They sat in the balcony, with Laide in the middle. It was a color film, and for Antonio a film of unbearable stupidity, but even a masterpiece, under the circumstances, would have been so much gall.

Laide however was ecstatic. She laughed at everything, in an exaggerated way, her bursts of laughter sounding almost hysterical. Then Antonio became aware of the fact that Laide had taken Marcello's right hand in her left and was pressing it, as lovers do. Did she imagine Antonio hadn't noticed? Meanwhile she went on looking at the screen, with continual bursts of laughter. It was the story of a young man who finds himself obliged to look after three impossible brats, not his own children, and to play nursemaid to them. A series of kindergarten jokes. The two joined hands now rested in Laide's lap. Worse: Laide had quietly shifted so as to lean against Marcello's shoulder.

The effrontery of the manoeuvre was such that Antonio felt paralyzed. It should have been easy to say: have fun, then go outside, unload her bags, and leave forever. He knew almost any man would have done it. But he couldn't. The greater the humiliation, the more unbearable seemed the idea of losing Laide.

He stared at her continuously, his face clearly turned toward her. But Laide appeared unaware of it. Only, at one point, still without looking at him, she reached her right hand over to take Antonio's hand. He whispered into her ear: "Not enough?"

"Oh no," she replied, pretending she hadn't understood, "I'm having a wonderful time. It's so terribly funny."

27

THEN AT last, one morning, the great moment came. It happened this way: he'd hardly awakened when he began, as he always did, to think about Laide, and he discovered he felt no pain. He touched the wound and the wound didn't hurt any more. He tried two or three times more to think about her, thought about her hard, challenged his anguish to return, but his challenge wasn't accepted. It was an indescribable sensation. A miracle. They were right when they told him.... He got out of bed and began to hop around the room. He positively jumped with joy, like a mad man. With, however, that rather apprehensive temperament of his, he stayed on guard. He washed and dressed with open eyes and ears lest the enemy return unexpectedly, but during the night the enemy seemed to have mysteriously fled the field. He thought about Laide, he pictured her in bed at that very moment with some guy or other doing those things she did. He even pictured her doing something worse; nastily he went into all the details. But his anguish failed to come back. Then he left the house and began to walk. He'd lost the habit of walking, but now he walked like a free man, like a civilized man, while before, he hadn't really walked. It was more accurate to say he crept, he ran, he fled trembling. Now he wanted to do something he hadn't done in months, a silly thing yet a symbol of his cure; he wanted to walk across the gardens. Though it was hot now—an hour had gone by since he'd awakened—by now he could be sure, now he was eager to get to the studio. He anticipated the satisfaction of looking unmoved, even contemptuously at the telephone. Let it ring as long as it wanted! He'd let it ring seven or eight times before he lifted the receiver, and maybe he wouldn't lift the receiver at all. That wouldn't bother him either. He felt like discussing work with his partners, felt like laughing. Oh what a wonderful thing life was!

But as he walked past the cement track for roller skaters, empty at that hour, as he walked with long strides, lit squarely by the sun, he felt a hint of something inside him. No, he told himself, it's only the last echo of the illness, inevitable, a feint, not real, nothing. Now I know I can think about Laide stretched out in bed with a young man in her arms and her tongue in his mouth. I can think about even worse things than that and they won't bother me any more than a stock market report or the difficulty of parking a car.

But he didn't have time to construct that disgusting scene because his illness instead of having disappeared now invaded all his gut, and suddenly, for no reason in the world, Antonio was utterly and completely unhappy. He kept trying, he tried two or three times to turn about, to bring himself back to how he'd felt a few minutes before. But his sublime sense of liberation was gone; it had been a mirage. It was incredible, one of those things you read about in books which simply aren't true. The cruel leap from freedom back to prison again made the illness that held him in its grip seem more painful still. He stopped walking; once again he began to limp, trembling, along the day that was just beginning. The yoke had fallen once again across his shoulders and now cut ever more deeply into his flesh. Then, for the first time, he experienced actual fear. He felt himself growing ever more cowardly and contemptible, abject, like a terrified rabbit. The little work he succeeded in doing these days cost him an immense effort, but he held on because he knew that once he let his work slide he'd no longer have the money he needed for Laide.

He'd often heard about ruined men, characters of fiction, who, to someone so thoroughly bourgeois as Antonio, were quite incredible beings. He'd read about Count Muffat reduced to poverty and despair by Nana. Stories. Easy inventions by novelists, ridiculously foolish situations. Never in his well-protected world could catastrophes of that sort occur. So he had once thought, but now Antonio wondered if he hadn't already set foot on that famous road. And he glimpsed the ghastly future. An old *délabré*, dragging himself around the clubs and restaurants of the intellectuals, hoping to get fifty thousand lire out of some annoyed colleague, reduced to a furnished room, cold-shouldered, lonely as a dog, while Laide, living under the protection of some big industrialist, would pass in front of him, in her Jaguar, plump, covered with diamonds, wrapped in mink.

How could he go on? He was in constantly increasing need of money. Laide had rented a small apartment, not bad at all, in a modern building in Via Schiasseri, near University City. Long arguments had followed because she didn't want him to have a key to the apartment, and in order to win out Antonio had had to threaten, in a fit of anger, to leave her forever. She hadn't of course believed him but what did she lose after all? Even when he had the key, she could always lock herself in and, if he rang, pretend not to have heard the bell or to be out.

Confusedly Antonio realized that the tighter and more intimate his relations with Laide became, the more he'd have cause to feel hurt and jealous, the more, in other words, he'd be dragged onward toward a fate he was quite incapable of imagining. Even his friends, in whom he had felt desperate need to confide, had by now given up trying to restrain him. If he was going to go mad, let him destroy himself with his own hands.

In the evening, for instance, after they got back from the movies or the theatre, instead of leaving her in front of the house, Antonio would have liked to go up, not to do anything, just to watch her undress and get into bed. But on that point she was immovable. To keep her company at night she had a friend, she said, a girl named Fausta, a little waif from the south whom Laide had introduced him to one day in the street. In fact you could see there were lights on in the apartment.

Even making love with her—and Antonio certainly made no great demands in that direction—had grown more difficult. It was all too clear that Laide hadn't the slightest desire to go to bed with him. She was always trying to find some excuse or other: either she was having her period or she had a sore throat or her head hurt. And when she did agree, she did it with such ill grace that there was no pleasure in it at all.

She wouldn't even discuss his spending a night there. "I've never slept all night with a man in my life, if I'm not alone in bed I can't sleep," was her refrain. Only after great insistence did Antonio succeed in extracting her promise to let him stay with her the night of the mid-August holiday. When the night came, she kept her promise, but before they went in, she warned him that that night she couldn't bear the thought of even being touched. The whole night through she slept on her side of the bed, her back turned to him. Was this love then? Against that wall of indifference broke the wave of dreams, the divine fire!

From time to time Antonio felt astonished at himself. How could he put up with so much? Once it would have seemed impossible. Luckily, one can get used to hard knocks, too. Luckily or unluckily? Was it anything but a symbol of moral decay? Rebellion, however, was unthinkable. The idea of losing Laide filled him with the usual dread.

A man, a proud man, intelligent, successful, once self-confident, dragged down by a girl out of hell, not because she is a wicked girl who wants to destroy him, but only because he's lost his head over her and she finds that fact terribly annoying. Or is it his own fault, is it because he doesn't know how to manage things, because he's losing his mind and makes one mistake after another? When and where will it end? Will the longed-for weariness come? or resignation at least? He's alone now, he's got to get out of it himself. There's no one who can help him; little by little he's lost the release that confession to his friends had formerly provided. Now he would have to confess such shameful degradation that his friends would refuse to believe him. He no longer has the courage to confess.

And then one Sunday they had agreed to meet and go for a drive. He went to his studio to call her so that he could speak to her freely.

"I'm sorry," she said, "I'm really terribly sorry but I can't see you today. Marcello's coming, poor thing. His family's still in the country and he'd be all alone. How can I just leave him like that?"

"Didn't you have a date with me?"

"But we meet every day! Don't be so selfish, he's my only friend and he's such a nice boy, too. I told you he's like a brother to me."

"All right, do just as you like." (He remembered that sentence spoken in front of the movie house in Modena: "A kiss on the mouth I imagine. Or would you prefer it somewhere else?" Unhappily the situation with Marcello is one he has already more or less accepted. If he made a fuss now, she'd be right, to a certain degree, to complain.)

When one-thirty came around, Laide phoned him. "Listen, honey, are you going out?"

"No, why?"

"Because you've got to do me a great favor. I don't have anything for Picchi to eat. You'll just have to go to some restaurant and get half a pound of chopped meat, today's Sunday all the shops are shut."

It was horrible, infamous, but the very idea of seeing her, even if only for a few minutes, made him feel better. "All right, I'll go right away."

It wasn't two yet when Antonio rang at Laide's door with the little package of meat in his hand. Before the door opened he heard, from the other side, a man's voice. Laide faced him uneasily: "I'm terribly sorry, I really am, I didn't know you'd get here so soon."

He had to go in. Marcello, sitting in the kitchen, got up and said hello with an air of deference, to Antonio he seemed so listless and vapid, it was not after all impossible that he and Laide should be nothing but good friends.

"I've got to go now," said Antonio.

"Don't you want to stay for a minute?"

"No, they're waiting for me. What are you going to do?"

"Well, we'll go out as soon as Picchi's eaten. We're going to a movie." Laide went with him to the elevator.

"At least you'll have dinner with me, I hope."

"Well yes, maybe dinner."

"Why maybe?"

"Are you going to the studio today?"

"It's Sunday but...."

"Yes, let's do it this way, I'll call you at the studio at six-thirty."

He left with an odd feeling of uncleanliness, of injustice. The two of them alone in the house. They'd gossip about this and that, play with the dog, joke in the most innocent way: what else would a handsome girl of twenty and a husky young man of twenty-five be doing? And yet, quite sincerely, he did believe it. If he didn't believe it, he couldn't bear it. His sincerity was his salvation. Other people, yes, ordinary people, people who were incapable of understanding certain things, would split their sides laughing.

At six-thirty promptly she telephoned. "Now please don't get angry with me but I really don't know what to do. Poor boy, he's going to France and he'll be away months and months, how can I walk out on him? His train doesn't leave till eleven-thirty."

"But I told you—"

"Please don't start again. Please! You know there's nothing wrong. And anyway, I repeat again, he's leaving for abroad tonight."

Abroad! A rage so overwhelming that it dazed him. He was like an automaton at dinner with his friends; by now they no longer paid any attention to him. And after that the nightmare of the lonely night: eyes fixed on the two cracks in the ceiling, cars passing outside, voices of prostitutes. Where were the two of them now? Did Marcello really go, or was he instead in that double bed in Via Schiasseri, granting a dividend on the afternoon's love?

By eight o'clock in the morning Antonio still hadn't slept. Wild-eyed, he got up, dressed, went to the garage.

This time, at the first ring, Laide opened the door.

"What's the matter?"

"The matter is I've had enough of it. Being treated like a donkey! Can't you realize—"

"This is no time to be preaching me a sermon, you ought to be grateful to me instead."

"Grateful?"

"I got rid of him last night. I told him, if you'll excuse the expression, to drop dead."

"Your beloved friend?"

"Beloved friend my ass! A pig like the rest, that's all he is. And me, what a fool I am, I thought he was a nice boy."

"What happened?"

"What happened is only that after dinner he brought me home. I said all right he could come up for a minute and when we got up here he tried to go to bed with me."

"What did he do? Put his arms around you? Kiss you?"

"I thought he was kidding at first but when he tried to paw me I gave him such a slap! I gave him a slap he'll remember the rest of his natural life. Then I got him out the door before he knew what was happening. And now you come and try to start something with me instead of being pleased the way you ought to be. But one way or another I'm going to convince you, by Christ, that I don't lie to you!"

28

HE HAS the telephone receiver still in his hand, undecided whether (his face is haggard and drawn, his face has aged, four months have gone by, today is the first of January but he still has the receiver in his hand) undecided whether to telephone her or not. The stream carries him on in the same wild way; he can't get to the side, on the contrary he's always right in the middle where the current is swiftest. Here the largest rocks spring from the river bed and he's hurled against them with savage shocks that tear him apart inside. He would like to gain the river bank but he's afraid because if he reached the bank, the river would carry him no further and in that same river, just a little ahead, flies Laide lightly through the water. The rocks do not ravage her; she sees them in time, or it's as though she sees them and slips around them just so Antonio as he follows her is struck by them with terrible force. But maybe she isn't thinking about it. She's not evil, not even she. It's only that she's like a porcupine with its quills always out. In fact one day during a quarrel, when he reproached her with the humiliating experiences she'd made him suffer, Laide said: You'd better understand me. No one has ever really loved me. It seems to me that everybody in the world is my enemy—that they want to cheat me and make use of me. It's not my fault if life has taught me to mistrust everybody. Yes, I'm always in a state of alarm, I'm all thorns, I try to protect myself, and so maybe it's true I haven't always been very nice to you, but you've got to understand: it isn't all my fault.

As a boy once, in the Dolomites, he slipped down a small snowfield and it had been a strange experience. The surface wasn't smooth but full of little holes, perhaps because of the thaw. As he slid down with ever-increasing speed, he was thrown hard against the sides of the hollows and was badly tossed about: he felt as if—he remembered perfectly well—as if an enormous giant were slapping him with enormous hands, and he was quite unable to protect himself in any way. There was only the hope that the slope would level off in some basin or plateau—which was in fact what happened, luckily, or he'd have been smashed against the great boulders in the moraine at the bottom. He had felt at the mercy of a savage force infinitely stronger than he, one that made him a frail, defenseless baby again. Well, it was this same feeling that his adventure with Laide aroused in him. But this time there was no invisible giant sprung out of the mountain side, this time it was a girl of flesh and blood who dragged him along after her and he was banged everywhere against the walls while she ran on with the anxious frenzy of her twenty years. Maybe she didn't know or care what the man hanging onto her long black hair was suffering, dragged along over the cobblestones, open-mouthed, gasping for air, through the dust and filth. Was it her fault if he clung to her so stubbornly? And perhaps the weight of that tall gray-haired man was a terrible hardship for her, and maybe if only he'd let go of her she'd stop, turn and come to his aid, but as long as he held onto her that way it was impossible.

Four months went by but in those four months there was no change in her: punctual always about her telephone calls and her engagements, kind and even considerate, in her way, but always with that hard core of absolute indifference. Marcello, true, had disappeared over the horizon, and there was no reason to suppose that Laide continued to live the life she once did. There was even a kind of long pause when she fell ill of an intestinal infection which was complicated by her heart trouble and had to spend two months in the hospital. Under these conditions, obviously, he no longer felt that utterly unreasonable anxiety that Laide might from one moment to the next vanish forever, never to be found again. But even in the hospital she found ways of keeping him on tenterhooks and humiliating him. There was that loathsome business of being called uncle in front of the doctors and the nurses. Also, she flirted shamelessly with all the doctors, especially on days when she had one of her attacks. For example, he'd be standing at the foot of the bed and then she, seized by an attack of breathlessness, would press the hand of some young and attractive doctor as though only from him could she hope for help and love. And one evening he went to bring her a dressing gown—naturally he'd bought it at the best shop in Milan—the room was in darkness, with the nurse reading in a corner by the light of a small lamp, so before going he leaned over to kiss her goodnight. Laide pushed him away with such angry violence you might have thought he'd tried to rape her. Because of such actions there was no one who didn't realize exactly what kind of uncle he really was.

And then there was her strange desire to stay on at the hospital as long as possible. Every time the doctors spoke of releasing her in a couple of days, for she seemed much better, she'd have another heart attack. So on cue did they come that Antonio decided she must be bringing the attacks on herself, making use of some tablets she'd had him buy one day. She had told him they were for her friend Fausta, who was broke. He had no idea what kind of medicine it was, but the very day after Laide had her first violent attack he questioned Fausta who looked surprised and said she'd never asked Laide to buy her any tablets; she hadn't an idea what they were for. So, with constant disquiet, several weeks passed. At last, when she did leave the hospital, fearing further attacks, she kept a nurse by her all night.

It was in the company of this nurse that Antonio and Laide spent New Year's Eve, and a dreary affair it was: Laide in her dressing gown with a headache, the nurse silent and apathetic, he with the feeling that it was something compulsory to which Laide was reluctantly submitting. He'd bought meat pies from one of the best shops and two bottles of champagne, but the whole evening was spent in front of the television set. When midnight sounded Laide went on looking at the screen where they were showing a gala night at one of the large hotels. She hardly tasted the champagne, saying she didn't care for it much, that as a matter of fact she knew a bit about champagne. And she told him how in this house or that, friends of the family, they always drank either Dom Pérignon or Monopole.

But Antonio decided not to mind last night, last night Laide hadn't felt very well, but today Antonio hoped to go out to dinner with her, for today was New Year's Day—to such fatuous and sham pleasures did he cling merely in order to spend a little time with her. Last night she had agreed to go and so he had spent a fairly comfortable morning. By now he no longer wondered how this affair was going to end; tomorrow or the day after was as far as his furthest thoughts went; there was no reason to think beyond the day after tomorrow, for Laide might at the last moment change her mind.

She did in fact change her mind that day as well. He called her at two: she was terribly sorry, last night she had completely forgot that today was New Year's Day. New Year's Day she always ate with her family. In addition to which, her uncle and aunt would also be at her sister and brother-in-law's house. It was absolutely unthinkable that she shouldn't be there.

What could he say? Actually he felt almost relieved because today at least he knew she'd be with her family, and tomorrow, certainly, having put him off today, she'd go out to dinner with him.

Then his mind began to turn. Wasn't it strange, he thought, that Laide who was always so punctilious about her appointments, with a quite astonishing memory for all the small details of life, should have forgotten last night that today was New Year's Day? Was it not, rather, an excuse to go out with someone else?

Whenever he entertained suspicions of this sort, the idea of going into action and investigating them made him feel a little sick. It seemed to him such a vile thing, disloyal and dirty. But perhaps that was not the real reason. The real reason he did nothing was very likely fear, fear of finding her out, of confirming the lie and the betrayal, of seeing himself obliged at last to give her up. No matter how despicable he seemed to himself, a final assurance upheld him: if he once had proof that Laide had lied to him and betrayed him, he'd break with her finally and forever.

This time, as a matter of fact, it would be easy. All he had to do was telephone around dinner-time at her sister's house on some pretext or other. Laide almost certainly wouldn't have warned her sister or her brother-in-law. Unquestionably they'd tell him whether they were expecting Laide to dinner or not.

It took a lot to make that decision to call. All afternoon in his studio he thought over the possibilities, the risks, the complications. No, he finally decided, there was really no danger at all. Around six, as usual, she called him in the office, begging him once again to forgive her, promising to go out with him tomorrow. She said she felt better, she sounded happy, indeed downright affectionate. "Bye, baby," she said, "and don't you go out with another girl tonight!"

But how long an afternoon can be! He couldn't possibly call before eight-fifteen or eight-thirty, and time refused to move. He kept looking at his watch. It wasn't boredom, it was anger that made the hours pass so slowly. As though the imminent crisis he'd been living with for months had now decided to move backwards, and beneath the motionless minutes was a device made of wheels turning in the wrong direction which kept time from moving on. It was enough to drive him out of his mind.

He was already worn out by the time the clock in the studio made its nervous little click at ten to eight. He realized how wild-eyed he must look. He ran outside—had a tire by any chance gone flat? No, the tires were all right. He started to his mother's house and arrived there at five past eight. God, another ten minutes of waiting.

Dinner was ready but how could he eat? However, he didn't want the others to notice anything, so he forced himself to swallow a few spoons of soup and said nothing. His mother watched him with a kind of sorrow that had now become habitual; he kept his eyes on his watch.

"Aren't you going to eat your cutlet? You used to have a passion for cutlet à la milanese."

"Well, I'll eat a bit of it, I don't know why, I don't have any appetite tonight."

Eight-thirteen.

Somewhere he found the strength to wait till eight-seventeen. Actually if he were to telephone at nine, it would be time enough. It might even be better; Laide might get there late. But he was quite unable to wait any longer.

"I'm sorry, I forgot, I've got to make a phone call."

He went in the other room, dialed the number, the line luckily was not busy. But nobody answered. Was no one there? Laide told him once that the phone was in her sister's bedroom, but even so, couldn't they hear it? Maybe that would be best: if no one answered there'd be nothing to do about it. A truce if nothing else. Tonight, at least, he would not be required to make the fatal decision.

No, someone was answering—a man's voice, it must be her brother-in-law. "I'm sorry, this is Dorigo, would you mind calling Laide to the phone for a minute?"

"But Laide's not here."

"Oh? She's not dining with you?"

"No, we don't expect her tonight."

"I'm sorry. Good night."

And now a damnable thing inside his breast: palpitation, breath-lessness, devastation, fiery spades digging into him. By God he had been right to be suspicious.

What if he tried phoning Laide? What if she were still at home? It would cost nothing to try.

That tired, diffident, impassive voice that meant so much to him answered at once.

"This is me," he said. "You told me you were going to your sister's but it isn't true."

"What do you mean it isn't true? I'm leaving this very minute."

"I just telephoned your sister's house. They told me they weren't expecting you."

"That's because I changed my mind."

"Where are you going then?"

"I'm going out to eat alone. And now please let me go because the taxi's waiting."

"Eat with me."

"No." The no was hard and firm.

"Why?"

"Because I don't want to. And I don't want to discuss it either. Taxis don't wait forever."

"I'm telling you to come out with me."

"And I'm telling you no."

"Then I'll wait for you in the apartment."

"No, I don't want you to." A hint of apprehension. She put down the receiver.

Had she gone crazy? She'd never before acted or spoken like that. There must be something new. This time there must be someone new in her life. And on account of this someone she was ready to break with him. She was willing to give up almost half a million lire a month, what with one thing and another.

But it was better this way, Antonio said foolishly to himself, so much better. It had to happen some time anyway. However, it was very odd. She was always so punctilious, so preoccupied with money. She must have fallen for somebody—or has she met someone a great deal richer?

His disquiet and his nervousness had now been transformed into something else—a curious new feeling, tumultuous, dynamic, decisive. He was like someone who, for the first time, after having thought about it so long, lets himself loose from the mountain ledge where the double rope is anchored and drops out into the void. It was as when a battle begins and one thinks at last about nothing else, and in the fever of the battle loses even one's fear of death. What will happen afterwards? It doesn't matter, whatever happens must happen, there is no longer any choice. After so much careful handling and diplomacy and deception, the cards were at last all on the table. Antonio felt, for the moment at any rate, almost relieved.

He went to Laide's house at around ten to ten and rang the bell. "Who is it?" It was the nurse's voice. "Antonio." the door opened. So much the better.

Teresa, the nurse, did not seem surprised. She was a girl from the mountains, about thirty, who appeared totally uninterested in everything.

"I hope you're not going to get me in trouble," she said. "Signora Laide told me not to answer the phone or open the door to anybody. Are you going to stay?"

"I'll wait for her."

"Will it bother you if I look at the television?"

"Of course not."

He went into the kitchen and tried to read a copy of a comic book that he had found on the bookshelf. There was a whole pile of them. But something other than Donald Duck was needed. These were the endless hours. The fact that a girl had gone out to dine with a man in one of Milan's many restaurants the evening of New Year's day might be of absolutely no importance to the world at large, but to him, to Antonio, it was the end of everything.

From somewhere there came into his head the idea of phoning his mother.

"Sorry to bother you, Mamma, did anyone call?"

"Yes, a little while ago, it must have been . . . well, I suppose you know who I mean."

"All right, never mind. Bye, Mamma."

She telephoned. She was hoping maybe he wouldn't go to her house. Obviously she was worried. In a little while, without question, she'd be calling here to find out.

In fact, less than ten minutes later, she did telephone. Two rings, then silence. The signal agreed on to let Teresa know it was she. Teresa went to answer in her dressing gown. He whispered: Don't tell her I'm here. Teresa said: No signora, nothing so far, no, nobody phoned. Although the house was completely silent, Antonio could not hear the other end of the conversation.

"What did she say?"

"Nothing. Just if you'd come."

"Nothing else?"

"No, she only told me again not to let anybody in."

Oh, the bitch! Now she'd like to kick him out, would she? After all he'd done for her. Yes, this was certainly the last time. But at least he meant to tell her a thing or two; he'd wait for her if he had to wait till tomorrow morning.

It was the last time. The alarm clock on the *étagère* said five to eleven. He sat on the couch in the breakfast room, the light on. Above the *étagère* stood an enormous cloth gosling, a toy Antonio had bought for her when she was in the hospital. Silence, with only the sound of cars passing. In the other room the television was on, they were giving Goldoni's *La Bottega del Caffè*. Teresa watched it sluggishly. The minutes pass slowly and, to Antonio, every minute was one slap more, one more snub. The refrigerator began to hum. It was now five past eleven. Antonio stared at the furniture, at the dolls, at the childish things he'd never have to see again. On the table was a Christmas candle, surmounting a pedestal of pine combs tied with ribbons. Still she didn't come. Against the refrigerator was a dark straw basket with a little toy dog inside—another silly present he'd brought to the hospital to cheer her. All that love thrown away for nothing. She'd never been serious; she'd understood nothing. Over the door was gilded mistletoe. When would she be back?

The telephone rang, this time without the signal. Teresa answered. It wasn't Laide. "No, the signora is out. No, I don't believe we'll need it tomorrow."

"Who was that?"

"A man from the phone company, the one that has the alarm service. He was wondering whether the signora wanted to be called tomorrow."

"That sounds odd. What's it all about?"

"I don't know. I think it's someone the signora knows."

So. She even flirted with the telephone company. Maybe she'd worked something out with this man too. He went back to the kitchen, took up the magazine again. He heard Teresa turn off the television set.

"Signore," she said, in the doorway, "I'm going to bed now."

Midnight. Twelve-forty-five. Where could she be? If she'd gone to the movies, that mania of hers, she'd have been back by now. Don't be naïve, he told himself. It was something other than the movies. Maybe she'd be out the whole night. Never mind. If he dropped dead he'd drop dead, but he swore he was going to stay there till that whore got home. Laide, his love, what had she done to him?

At one-fifteen the telephone rang again. It was Laide.

"No, signora," said Teresa, who strangely enough hadn't undressed yet. "Yes. But what could I do?... All right. Good night, signora."

"What did she say?" he asked at once.

"She said she was on her way back when she saw your car downstairs."

"So she's not coming?"

"She says she's going to sleep in a hotel."

What a fool! Couldn't he have thought of it? He went downstairs at once to put the car in a side street, then went back up. He'd wait, by God he'd wait. But what was the good of waiting if she'd gone to a hotel? Did he disgust her so that to avoid him she'd go to a hotel without even a piece of soap in her bag? Or was it fear of him?

Teresa looked at him without speaking.

"Teresa, after all this time, haven't you figured out who I am?"

"What?"

"Who did she tell you I am?"

"She always says you're her uncle."

"Uncle! It doesn't take much to figure out I'm not, does it?"

Desperation. Who is Teresa? what can Teresa tell him? Nothing, but he feels the need to talk, to let loose.

"While I ... all I've done for her ... look what an unlucky wretch I am.... To fall in love with a ... a ..."

He was a child again, a child unfairly punished. He threw himself down on her bed, his face in her pillow, his body wracked with sobs.

"Control yourself, signore."

He got up, realizing with shame how squalid the scene must be.

"I'm sorry. Sometimes it's too much, that's all."

"Oh, signore, it can happen to anybody."

"Come on, off to bed with you."

"Will you go on waiting?"

"No, but I want to leave a note for her."

In the kitchen he found a sheet of paper and took it into the living room to write the note on a little table with a glass top.

"Laide," he wrote, "after what has happened, it's quite clear that everything between us is over. I think I've always been kind and patient with you. But beyond a certain point a man can't go. I hope you find—"

The telephone. It was one-thirty. Like a wild beast, he grabbed the telephone out of Teresa's hands.

"Hello, this is me."

There was a click. Laide had broken the connection.

If she telephoned, that meant she was still undecided, didn't know what to do. It might mean she didn't have the money to go to a hotel.

Almost at once the telephone rang again. Teresa answered but once again Antonio grabbed the phone from her.

At the other end was a voice that sounded almost happy. "All right, I'm coming home now."

"I'll wait."

Two. Two-fifteen. Teresa had gone to sleep, fewer and fewer cars passed. Antonio had not finished the letter. There was no longer any need to. He'd tell her what he wanted to say. Yes, he knew, it would be far better if he were to go now, without leaving even a note. If only he could! But he had to see her. If only for half a minute, he had to see her once more.

At ten to three a car stopped below. Then, in the sleeping house, came the sound of the gate opening and closing, the click of the elevator door, the hum of the elevator coming up.

He was standing in front of the door. He knew what his duty was: two slaps across the face, at least.

And if she made a scene? what if she had another heart attack? what if he had to call the doctor?

She came in, pale, her eyes round and wide, with the look of a haunted, hunted beast.

"Hi," she said.

At this moment he felt tired to death. Something within him broke. He felt only exhaustion, a hopeless indifference.

"Who were you with?"

"A girl friend."

"Where have you been till now?"

"At her house."

"Do you think I'm fool enough to believe you?"

"Do just as you like. Where is Teresa?"

"How should I know. Asleep, I suppose."

He was unable to find the right words, the words that might save his face. This way lay emptiness, an abyss, an admission of defeat.

Laide went into the living room and saw at once the partly written page. Without reading it she crumpled it into a ball and threw it into the kitchen.

"Read it. Read it, it will do you good to read it."

Without answering she went into the bathroom and, leaving the door open, began to pee.

What more was Antonio waiting for? Did he want her to give him a slap or two? As though she hadn't already shown him contempt enough? Or was he waiting for some word of repentance from her? did he hope she'd beg his pardon?

Pardon for what? She'd been out with her friend, she had done nothing wrong. He was the one in the wrong—what woman could put up with a man as boring as he was?

He said goodbye. He might have said see you later, but he didn't. Did Laide notice it, however? Laide was sleepy, and tomorrow morning at nine she had an appointment with her hairdresser.

29

HE WAITED a day, sure that Laide would get in touch him. If he died of it he wouldn't phone her, he swore he wouldn't phone. It would be the final degradation, it would be like saying: Look, here I am, spit on me. Anyway she'd certainly have read the letter he had begun and left on the table. Laide had made the gesture of throwing it away in front of him, but did he suppose the minute he left, she hadn't run back to the kitchen to read it? Not that Antonio's letters were of any great interest to her, but this time she must have been a little afraid. After all, she must have realized that this time she'd gone a bit too far.

He waited two days, she was evidently playing the offended party, as though Antonio in going to her house to wait for her had been wanting in respect. And then too, everyone knew that the best tactic when you've been in the wrong is to pretend to be offended. Naturally the fact that Laide hadn't yet phoned made him uneasy. It was obvious to him that this was only a skirmish; he'd never for one moment considered the possibility that this might be an out-and-out break. But what if, on the other hand, she took Antonio's letter seriously? what if she was aware of having gone too far, what if she was convinced that Antonio, however weak however in love, had no choice now but to walk out on her? But what made him think Laide was afraid of that? Probably by now she'd forgotten all about him. Yes? and where was she going to go to find half a million lire a month?

He waited three days. Beginning to feel terrible, he was still convinced she'd turn up. Not that she'd ask his forgiveness or say she was sorry; she'd just reappear with her little tough girl air as though nothing had happened, she'll certainly reappear. There was nothing like cutting the string and pretending to be indifferent to make women run after you. But still it was odd all the same—though at the moment he knew she was not badly off for money because of a legacy of half a million she had got from her mother, severance pay from the company where her mother'd been working that Laide had collected only a little while before.

He waited four days. By then every time the phone rang in his office it was like an electric needle going into his back. The shock went through his whole body and he couldn't breathe. Yes, he thought, with all the money she had on hand now she could hold out a long time. She was so sure of having him at her beck and call whenever she wanted. Without doubt she was laughing at the pain he was suffering. No matter what hour of the night she woke, he was sure she said to herself: At this very moment he's thinking about me. How pleased she must be with herself. How she must rub her hands together in glee and laugh at him with her girl friends! No, maybe not that, because the only girl friend she had was Fausta, and Laide knew what Fausta was like and she'd trust her up to a certain point and no further. But rubbing her hands together she certainly was and saying: So that one wants to play the offended party, does he? all right I'll show him, I won't phone him for at least a month. So long as I've got money. And at the end of a month I'll find him there at my feet, good as a little dog, better trained than before. That is the treatment. Maybe he thinks that for the few pennies he gives me I should adore him day and night. But I'm twenty years old, I've got to breathe, I need a little liberty of action, and that's what he refuses to get into his head. Well, I can drive him crazy with jealousy. I know what he's thinking. My dear little uncle pictures me going from one man to another without stopping, and he grows pale and he lights one cigarette after another, and maybe in his frenzy he goes looking for girls, hoping to find one he'll like and who will make him forget Laide for an hour or two. But instead, it's worse for him because, first of all, there aren't many around like Laide, and even if he finds one that's prettier than Laide—it wouldn't be easy but even if he did—her beauty her face her mouth her legs her breasts would only make him remember Laide's face her mouth her legs her breasts more clearly. Not that they're so much more beautiful but they're unique, and it's that particular face that mouth those legs he needs, and all the others even if they're more beautiful—though it wouldn't be easy—would turn his stomach at once.

Thus Antonio reconstructs Laide's train of thought and he hates her because he knows it's all true. In fact the truth is worse because Laide, in her strategy, relies heavily on her physical qualities and doesn't realize how important to Antonio are the way she carries herself and walks and speaks, the way she moves her mouth when she laughs and grimaces, her way of kissing, her enchanting Milanese accent with that strange aristocratic "r."

He waited five days with no word from her. By now it was clear Laide had decided to play for the big stakes. She had nothing to lose: even if she turned up after a month, she still wouldn't be the one who gave in. She'd still be the gracious sovereign who at last granted her long-awaited favor, giving back to her impertinent slave the light of life. But suppose when she called in a month he put down the phone? suppose in a month his illness had been cured? suppose Laide was no more than a disagreeable memory? Suppose in a month he'd found another girl just as attractive as Laide, but kinder, sweeter, more considerate and maybe even a better player in the game of love? A dream, a utopia, a miracle. Antonio knew that for him there could be only Laide, only Laide could give him peace whether a year from now or two years from now.

He waited six days. That morning he couldn't hold out any longer; he had at least to know whether she was in Milan or not. Perhaps she was off on a trip with somebody. So he asked one of the men in his office to call her number and ask for Professor Romani. A woman's voice answered.

"What kind of voice was it?"

"A woman's voice."

"Young?"

"I'd say so."

"Did she have the Milanese 'r'?"

"Ah, yes, yes I think she did."

"How did she sound? Happy?"

"Yes, I'd say she sounded happy enough."

"What exactly did she say?"

"Nothing. She said I'm afraid you've got the wrong number. What did you expect her to say?"

So he made himself appear even more ridiculous, as if the story of his love affair hadn't already become the talk of all his friends. And he must be an idiot as well if he hadn't realized that Laide would know at once he'd arranged that phone call just to spy out the land. What a triumph for her to know that Antonio couldn't hold out any longer! Though he didn't dare phone himself, still he was at the end of his strength. Anger, disquiet and jealousy had knocked him out; another two or three days and he'd be throwing himself at her feet, begging her pardon. What an idiot. Laide must now see herself in a still stronger position; she would be in no hurry to let him hear from her. She'd put off that phone call till God knew when.

He waited seven days. With the hope of getting a little information he went to Signora Ermelina's. In an effort to appear indifferent, he asked if she had a really first-class girl for him, but Signora Ermelina saw through him and asked at once for news of Laide.

"I haven't seen her recently. Have you?" Antonio said.

"Not since April. I called her once—I didn't know, I swear it, she was with you—I wanted to introduce her to a very nice gentleman, and she gave him an appointment and then didn't keep it. I never tried again because in the meanwhile I learned that you were interested in her, and in cases like that, you understand, I always step aside."

"Who told you?"

"I don't remember, but things like that, you know, you can't keep them a secret, the girls talk. I don't remember now whether it was Flora or Titti. But how is it that you don't see her any more?"

"No special reason. She played her little game once too often, that's all."

"The usual. You spoiled her and she took advantage. They're stupid girls, when they do have a bit of luck they do everything they can to spoil it. A man like you! I'm not just making compliments but any girl, even nicer than Laide, would have done anything she could to hold on to you, a man like you. Not that she's a bad girl, she isn't. No, I must say, as far as I can see, she's a good girl but you know what happens? Some girl friend or other will be jealous and give her bad advice.... Self-assured, yes, maybe even a little too sure of herself... and of course with you ... well, if you knew...."

"What?"

"Oh, I don't have anything bad to tell you. One day when she had a date with you, I imagine it must have been the third or fourth time, certainly it wasn't any later than that, after you left we started talking ... nothing important ... about a suit she'd got from me. No, now I remember, it wasn't a suit, it was a wool *princesse* dove-colored—"

"Yes, I remember the dress."

"Good, now you know I'm not making up a story. Anyway, she still owed me fifteen thousand ... and she claimed she ... well, it's not important, is it? I remember my sister-in-law was there too, and after a while to put an end to it I said to my sister-in-law, 'Well, all it means when Signor Dorigo calls, we'll have to get somebody else for him, now we know what he likes.... Believe it or not, Laide raised her fist like this, and she said,' Signor Dorigo? Don't make me laugh! I've got Signor Dorigo right here, I can make him do whatever I like.' I tell you, we really felt.... Do you know what I mean? She'd hardly seen you three or four times and already it had gone to her head."

"The last few days hasn't she turned up here?"

"Not so far as I know. Unless she phoned when nobody was here.... But don't worry.... You won't get rid of that one so easily. I know them. They think they're God knows who but when they need something.... But you've got to stand firm. You know that. Don't even dream of phoning her. Stand firm. She'll come back, you'll see, crawling like a worm."

He waited eight days. A gleam of hope. That morning the phone in the office rang, he answered at once but no one spoke at the other end, although he could tell somebody was listening; then the connection was broken. He asked the girl at the switchboard if the call had come from a man or a woman: a woman, she said. It must have been Laide. Maybe she had thought she'd won, the try-out on the phone the other day must have given her the idea she had victory in the palm of her hand. But with another couple of days gone by even she'd begun to worry.

He waited nine days. Still nothing. Save for unavoidable interruptions, he thought about nothing but Laide. The more time passed, the greater his humiliation became. After all the love he'd shown her! His anger with himself at not having behaved like a man was aggravated. New Year's night, when she came home at three in the morning, why hadn't he given her the beating up she deserved? Not just a slap or two, but a couple of haymakers that would have knocked her flat on her face, then let her make a scene if she wanted to. He'd feel like a different man today if he'd given her the lesson she needed. Even at the risk of her never turning up again. But now he was the conquered one, and if she didn't come back he would have to spend the rest of his life eating crow. She would always have the right to despise him, to make fun of him before the whole world, to prefer husky self-assured clodhoppers who were capable of knocking a bitch's face in when the need arose.

He waited ten days. He made an appointment at Signora Ermelina's for the afternoon. Happily Signora Ermelina promised to introduce him to a little brunette "who looks like Laide's sister." Actually Antonio went only in the hope of getting some news. Through her network of girls Ermelina always had information at hand. Laide's "sister" was a rather dreary, shabby girl named Luisella, not too bad-looking but dull in bed. When Antonio reappeared in the parlor, Ermelina said to him:

"I hear that Laide was at the Due the other night. They say she looked very nice. She was wearing a little red dress. She danced all night. Is it true she's got a little red dress?"

"Yes, she bought it three months ago. Have you heard anything else?"

"No, nothing. Oh, wait a minute . . . Luisella! Luisella!"

"Coming!" cried the girl from the bathroom and in a few minutes appeared dressed.

"Listen a minute, Luisella. Have you ever by any chance known a girl named Laide?"

"Laide? Dark? With long hair?"

"The very one. Is she a friend of yours?"

"Please! I only knew her at Iris's house."

"The one in Via Moscova? The one they put inside for a while?"

"That's the one."

"How could you, Luisella, a girl like you, go to Iris's? That wasn't a good house at all. They tell me . . . they used to say it was a regular pigsty . . . I'm not surprised they locked her up."

"Well, I only went a couple of times, then I saw what it was like. You're right, signora, it was worse than any house I ever saw. Coming and going all the time."

"And you say Laide used to go there?"

"She was there all the time, from one in the afternoon till late at night."

"How many did she take on?"

"How do I know? Judging by the activity, I'd say at least nine or ten a day. And then there was Iris's son, I remember, she took a fancy to him, and every day before the clients began coming, she had to have him too as a kind of appetizer. Oh, she kept busy, that one. . . . But why do you ask?" Luisella looked at Antonio. Antonio was pale.

"Where was this Laide from?" he asked, with one lone surviving hope.

"I don't know, maybe Naples or Calabria," Luisella answered. They used to call her Terroncina."

"That's something anyway," said Antonio. "I didn't think it was possible that—"

"No, it couldn't be the same one," said Signora Ermelina, who was proud of the quality of her merchandise. "I knew right away. I couldn't have been so mistaken. Besides, Laide isn't the type to throw herself away like that."

He waited eleven days. By now he felt he'd shown he was capable of holding out, he could phone her now without losing face: so he began to reason. Then he realized that, on the contrary, it would be even worse. The more time went by, the graver, the more catastrophic, would be his capitulation if he were the one to give in first. It would be throwing away the reward of his long punishment? Signora Ermelina, who was so wise in these matters, had advised him to hold out. But how difficult it was! There stood the telephone, a couple of feet away. All he had to do was lift the receiver and dial the number. Her voice would answer. "Hello." It seemed to him that he could hear the word now as she pronounced it, with that melange of diffidence, laziness, boredom, lack of concern, that dear voice, that wonderful sound, was he ever to hear it again?

He waited twelve days. By this time she should have got in touch with him if only for the money. By this time there was no longer any doubt. She'd found someone else, someone who gave her more money, who perhaps lived outside Milan and came in once or twice a week, but otherwise left her completely free. There couldn't be any other explanation. One of these days he'd see her very smartly dressed at the wheel of a Giulietta Sprint, she'd look at him, but she wouldn't even say hello to him.

He waited thirteen days and still no news. He went back to Signora Ermelina's. There he had the impression of being nearer the front lines, of getting whatever news there was at first hand. Signora Ermelina had found him a young girl from the country near Rome, splendid looking and magnificently trained but so crude and rough she was like an animal. Once the ceremonies were over, he went into the parlor where he found another girl, a young woman who had got married a short while before. "Doesn't she look like Laide?" He said yes, to be obliging, but it wasn't true. Crouched on the divan, looking sad and bored, the girl let him see her firm fleshy legs, so disproportionate to her build. She looked at him disinterestedly: this gentleman, it was clear, wasn't for her. The two girls left.

"Tell me, Signora, have you heard any news by chance?"

"Of Laide?"

"Yes, of Laide."

"No, I haven't heard a thing."

"I want you to promise me something, Signora."

"Gladly, if I can."

"Should Laide call you, will you let me know right away?"

"Of course! Right away. But she won't call."

"Maybe it wouldn't be a bad idea to make a date for me as though I were somebody she didn't know. Then I'd come in and find her in bed, undressed. What a shock that that would be, eh?"

"No, I couldn't do that. If Laide calls me, I'll let you know right away, I promise, but that's all I can do. You're a friend of mine. But I won't have her in my house again after what happened."

"I thought she was one of the girls who always did so well for you." Antonio had the desire to hurt himself, to prod the aching tooth.

"I can't say no to that. Between her and Flora and Cristina we had a good season last year."

"But the last time she was here it was with me?"

"It was."

"The day she left for Rome?"

"Look how you remember! The very day! But only God knows if she went to Rome."

"I took her to the station."

"And would you like to know where she went afterwards?"

"What do you mean afterwards?"

"After you left her at the station."

"Didn't she take the train?"

"She left her suitcases in the baggage room and then she rushed off to Ersilia's place. Ersilia's a friend of mine, I think you know her, don't you? A very quick worker."

"How did you find out?"

"Ersilia told me. I haven't got to the best part, though. About four-thirty she calls me. I thought you were supposed to leave, I say. I'm going tonight, she answers, but right now I want to come over, I've got somebody with me. Come along, I tell her; that day I wasn't expecting anybody. Well, in less than ten minutes I see her coming in with somebody to make your hair stand on end. A really repulsive old number, sixty years old at least, a belly out to here, no teeth. God knows where she found him, maybe in the Piazza Fontana where they have the market. It upset me so I took her off to one side. What's the matter with you, Laide, I say to her, have you lost your mind? I know, she says, it's enough to turn your stomach, but what can I do? I need the money. Well, I swear to you, Signor Tonino, if somebody said to me, here's a million for you if you go to bed with that man, I swear to you I wouldn't have done it. Whereas that one, for five thousand, maybe ten ..."

He waited fourteen days. The ghastly things Ermelina told him hadn't turned him from her, they were old stories of a time when to Laide he had been only another client. He also reasoned that the fact that she hadn't gone back to Ermelina's proved she'd been faithful to him. A lot of others, even if they had a rich friend who supported them well, would continue to go to the call houses. Or if they had a car, they'd go out cruising in the evening. And then who knew if all those stories Ermelina told were true? Women were past masters at the art of making up filth. Or perhaps the stories were true but not about Laide. It would be easy to change one name to another. Also he didn't forget it was to Signora Ermelina's interest to get him away from Laide if she could. With that hail-fellow-well-met air of hers, she was probably doing every thing she could to break it up. After all, Laide had taken one of the best clients away from her. What a fool he was to believe all that filth! But now fourteen days had gone by, he no longer had the strength to struggle. Sometimes he felt as though he was living through some horrible nightmare, a kind of madness, a disorder of the mind. Sometimes he felt that Laide existed no longer, that she'd never existed, that he would never see her again. Yet he had to, he needed her, he could not go on living without her. Without her the world was empty and senseless. Like an automaton he went to his studio. God only knew how he was going to get on with his work; one of these days he would have to admit he was finished.

He opened the studio door. Strangely enough the light was turned on. Antonio saw her sitting at his desk waiting for him, her eyes wide and frightened. She was pale, haggard, unkempt.

"I'm here," she said.

"And how's it going?" he asked with the tiny bit of breath that was left in him.

"How do you think? Badly."

30

THEY RESUMED seeing each other as though nothing had happened. Stubbornly she refused to acknowledge her fault New Year's night. She really had been with a girl friend, she kept repeating, and if she hadn't wanted to go out with Antonio, it was only because Antonio still didn't trust her, which was something she couldn't bear. Hadn't he got it through his head yet that she had never told him a lie?

They resumed seeing each other as before, oftener in fact; nevertheless Antonio, facing himself, could see no way out. Along with his customary sense of disquiet there grew from day to day, a dark presentiment as though an end, a conclusion, a catastrophe was drawing ever nearer. More than ever he realized that his only salvation lay in an act of will, in a final and complete renunciation. But he knew himself to be incapable of it. His obsession was painful, she was never out of his thoughts: What was she doing, where was she, whom was she with, what new tricks was she thinking up?

As a man on a raft in the center of a wide river, though unable to make out the shape of the banks in the darkness, realizes that the quickening current is carrying him toward an unseen chasm, so Antonio, without quite understanding why, knew that nearer and nearer now came the inevitable termination that he had so long, and with such rash obstinacy tried to put off. That whirlpool in which he had allowed himself to be caught almost a year ago was now swirling faster and faster; its walls were now almost perpendicular. It seemed to him that Laide sometimes looked at him now with a kind of apprehension, as though she were thinking: Yes, Antonio, at heart you're a good fellow, I don't like what's happening, I don't like to lose your help, but I can't change, it's not my fault.

Now there came a fresh complication. One of Laide's aunts—the only person in her family, she said, who truly loved her—went into hospital with cancer. As she was extremely ill and there were very few night nurses at this hospital, the family took turns going to stay with her over night. Every three or four nights it was Laide's turn. The hospital was far away, near the Porta Nuova; it was not a real hospital, more like a home for sick old women. The aunt had a room to herself but there was no other bed in it, so whoever stayed overnight had to be satisfied with a wicker armchair. Sometimes, if the aunt looked as though she were going to have a peaceful night, Laide would go home around one or one-thirty. Sometimes she had to stay till dawn.

Antonio could hardly object, nor was he seriously disturbed that this story might be only another trick. Aside from everything else, it would be easy to check on it, but Laide supplied such precise details of her aunt's illness, the symptoms, the surgery she had to undergo, the names of the doctors, the favors the aunt asked of her, her instructions about her funeral and her tombstone, that he really had no reason to suspect her. And more than that, after one of those wakeful nights when Laide stopped by the studio she looked like someone who had indeed not slept a wink, muffled in two or three old sweaters, thin, pale, with deep dark rings under her eyes.

But there was one curious incident. One evening, after they'd been out to dinner together, Laide surprisingly suggested going home. The nurse had left a week ago, there was no one there, they'd be able to make love. Then, around eleven-thirty she'd have to pick up her sister and go with her to the hospital to see the aunt. But she hoped to be able to come home around one or two.

Laide had been rather depressed but that evening in bed she was more affectionate than she'd been in months. Although she hadn't had anything to drink at dinner, she seemed actually excited. A happy, agreeable evening at last.

At a quarter-past-eleven she got ready to go out.

"Why are you putting on your new dress? Just to spend the night in a hospital?"

"Yes, but I wanted to show it to my aunt. She's still so interested in everything. She wants to know all about me, even what I eat at lunch or dinner. And then I told you, tonight I hope to be able to get away and come home to sleep. I can't tell you what it's like to spend a whole night in that damned armchair."

"Want me to drive you to your sister's?"

"Oh no, Antonio, you've got to stay here."

"Why?"

"You know that girl friend of mine from Venice? Well, she's supposed to be coming to Milan and she said she'd call long distance around midnight. It's possible she won't call at all, but I heard from her only yesterday, so if she does call how would it look if I weren't here?"

"But what am I supposed to say?"

"If she calls, tell her that my aunt's in the hospital and I'm terribly busy these days. However, if she wants to come anyway, she's to tell you whether I'm to get her a room at some hotel."

"Couldn't you wait here until midnight?"

"No because then we'd get to the hospital too late, and they always make such a fuss when you come in late."

She left him there alone thinking how strange the whole story was. Why did Laide have to go to the hospital tonight with her sister? And why did she have to go to get her? And why did she refuse to let him drive her there? Didn't that phone call sound rather unconvincing?

No one did, in fact, telephone and at twelve-fifteen Antonio went home. At one Laide phoned him, wanting to know if her friend had called. She was still at the hospital she said and had gone down just for a minute to the bar on the corner to telephone, she'd got there just in time because they were about to close. Now she was going back to her aunt's, her aunt seemed easier tonight and she hoped to be able to go home to sleep. "I'll call you tomorrow morning at the studio. Bye."

Now why did Laide call him at home? Did she really need to? Odd: it was as though she wanted to be absolutely sure Antonio had gone home.

Doubts. The more Antonio thought about it, the more implausible Laide's behavior seemed. Too many complications, too many explanations, too many telephone calls. If she'd wanted to be free to go out and meet somebody and then bring him home, what would she have worked out? Exactly what she did work out tonight. First, lull Antonio's suspicions by displaying out-of-the-ordinary warmth in bed. That way he'd be in a relaxed unsuspicious mood. Next, announce the visit to the aunt so she'd be able to get away before midnight. Then invent a phone call from Venice to keep him from going with her. Finally, call Antonio around one to be sure he had actually gone home.

Antonio stretched out in bed, with the lamp turned on, tense with ever-mounting anxiety turned it all over in his mind. On the ceiling the two cracks that were shaped like a 7 seemed to be some sort of enigmatic warning, a graphic symbol of his distress. It was after three when all of a sudden the details of her trickery were revealed to him with glaring clarity. Try phoning her? That wouldn't do any good. She'd say she just got home. Go to her apartment? Wouldn't it be better to wait until morning? If there were someone with her, he'd still be in bed at eight-thirty in the morning, after a night of love. And it wouldn't seem quite so strange—he'd think of some reason for going there. He might, for instance, say that his work was taking him out to University City and as he was passing anyway he stopped to say hello to her. No more than a kind impulse after all.

A horrible night, the clock stood still and sleep would not come. At seven-thirty Antonio was up, by eight already on the way. However impossible it seemed to Antonio, life went on as usual: a weak sun issued listlessly from the mist; people came and went, into houses, offices, cafés; men and women walked as always with tense faces on their way to work, to their daily occupations; at the corner two construction workers joked with each other; cars and trucks hurtled past. Nowhere was there the slightest warning. Evidently no one was thinking about Laide, no one guessed that within a few minutes the whole world might fall apart.

It was a quarter-past-eight when he parked the car in front of her house and looked up. The shutters were closed. He went in. From her little office the porter saw him and waved at him lazily. He took the elevator to the third floor and listened for a minute in the hall, thinking perhaps to hear voices coming from inside. But all was silent.

In a moment he pressed the bell. He could open the door with his own key but this way seemed more correct. No one answered.

His breast became a hell again, his heart beat like a hammer. He rang again, longer, much longer. Nothing.

He pressed the bell all the way in. Surely the other tenants were going to complain. The bell echoed powerfully, the entire building seemed to vibrate with it.

When at last he tried the key, he knew already that it was going to be useless: Laide had left her own key in the lock. Antonio's key made hardly a half turn.

He rang a fourth time and thought he heard from the apartment next door voices of protest.

Like a madman he went downstairs. Not stopping to question the porter, he ran to a nearby bar, put a token into the telephone. It was easy to guess there would be no answer. If Laide answered, she'd have to open the door. But Antonio was still too near; the man with her wouldn't have time to leave. Probably he was still in bed, naked in bed.

What could he do? Was he to be defeated once again? Laide would certainly provide the most innocent of explanations. At this very moment, maybe, just as he came out of the bar, she was looking at him through the shutters, victorious. (And from the bed would come a sleepy voice: "Did the old boy go? Be a good girl then, come on back here where it's hot.")

He might have known. When he called again, a quarter of an hour later, from the studio Laide finally answered.

"May I ask why you didn't let me in? I must have rung at least ten minutes."

"Did you? I thought I heard something but I was so sleepy. And then I had the bedroom door closed and I decided they were ringing the apartment next door."

"You must have heard it."

"If I'd heard it, I'd have opened the door, wouldn't I? I swear to you I didn't hear a thing. My head feels like a rubber ball. I'm even surprised I heard the telephone. I'm stuffed with Gardenal. I had such a headache last night when I got home. I took three tablets all at once. But why did you happen to come?"

"And what's this business of locking yourself in with a key? What's the good of my having a key in that case?"

"Honey, you'll have to be patient with me. Since the nurse left, I feel a little afraid alone in the house."

Were the explanations sufficient, believable? No. Yet every word of hers was miraculous balsam soothing his anguish. Her voice sounded sincere and honest. It simply was not possible she could be lying. Not even a devil could lie that well.

And then too, and then too, it was so pleasant to believe her. Lovely cowardice. Maybe some day Antonio would have to stop believing her, would have to make the frightful decision. But for the moment no, not yet, everything was still safe; officially; everything could go on as before.

31

No, everything could not go on as before. He had to know. A friend introduced him to a certain Imbriani, once a lieutenant in the police, now a private detective. Imbriani came to his studio—a man of about thirty-five, with a pleasant, open face.

"A kind of home for old ladies?" he asked where Antonio stopped talking. "Do you know the exact name?"

"Asilo Elena, she told me. In Via Sormani. It must be a very modest sort of place."

"Via Sormani, via Sormani.... I don't remember it."

"Near Porta Nuova, at least, so she said."

Imbriani put away his notebook.

"Well," he said, "from the looks of it, it shouldn't be too difficult. In fact, fairly easy, I'd say. Unless difficulties arise. But I'll tell you right away, I've had a lot of experience with affairs like this. I'll tell you right away that almost certainly the investigation will be useless—"

"Why useless?"

"We won't find anything. Everything, I suspect, will be exactly as the young lady says."

"How can you tell?"

"My dear sir, this is a case that's altogether too easy to check up on. If she had something to hide, it seems to me, the young lady would have invented a more complicated story. Let's put it that way: it's not very hard to ascertain whether there's a certain patient in a particular home and who goes to see her, especially at night."

"When do you think I'll hear from you?"

"By tomorrow, the day after tomorrow at the latest.
That is unless difficulties arise."

"What kind of difficulties?"

"I can't imagine. But it's always best, at least in my business, to anticipate all possible obstacles."

Lieutenant Imbriani left. Antonio sat alone. It was late and the studio was painfully quiet. Lieutenant Imbriani was right: it was impossible that Laide would have invented a story so naïve if she were trying to conceal nocturnal adventures. On the other hand, Antonio knew Laide knew how much she counted on his own naïveté. The minute Lieutenant Imbriani left his office, Antonio realized that he had at last opened the forbidden door. What exactly lay behind the door was still unknown, but certainly some new anxiety would come out of it. Fresh humiliations, the latest falsehood. He would find himself face to face with it, and no matter how much he'd like to he would not be able to look some other way, pretending he hadn't seen it. The hour would strike, the hour that all these months he's feared. It would be his death warrant.

As good as her word, within five minutes Laide was on the phone, full of reassuringly exact details, like a considerate little wife of unblemished innocence. But already Antonio felt the distance between them widening. This fresh little creature, bold, impertinent, genuine, was already turning into an improbable memory, a character in fiction. She had risen for a brief moment in time out of her world, her common, dissolute, mysterious world, and he had deceived himself into believing he could bring her into his, his middle-class, respectable, honest world, the world that at bottom he despised and to which he belonged with all the power of the blood that flowed through his veins. No, love had not been enough. Little by little she was drawing away from him, out of his house and his life. Now she was about to set out fearlessly toward the secret heart of her city, a heart that was seldom seen. Laide was withdrawing from him, into a city squalid yet moving, with peeling smoking courtyards dripping with rain, into the caverns of ancient houses, down interminable passages with linoleum floors, into dark corners in foul cellars. A city alive with the squealing of tires, the turning of lathes, howls, moans of sorrow, and bursts of laughter, the bustle of tireless and tired men, hurried kisses, shadows of adventures against the light, green smocks of surgeons, appointments by telephone—it was all a lunatic stirring of desire, energy, and illusion that burned confusedly in the crowd which came went mingled pressed broke apart and disappeared while another identical crowd was hurled into the whirlpool where it sank.

From the buildings around him he felt it drawing away, that hidden Milan unknown to both history and guide books. And its houses, its tattered roofs, its overcharged streets were shut softly away amid shadowy gulfs and dark reverberations of crime, receding from Antonio and carrying away forever his Laide.

Once again he felt he'd entered into the wrong dream, one not meant for him, and a power far stronger than his will or his convictions was dragging him off as if he were just any wretch and not a man of fifty years with a respected position in the world. He was like some haughty prince who by order of the king is suddenly stripped, publicly beaten and chained to a bench in a galley. The king makes no explanation, and so he doesn't know why all this has happened to him but he understands in some confused way that there must be good reason for it.

32

ANTONIO looked up Via Sormani in the street guide. "Corso Garibaldi third on the right," he read, "through Vicolo del Fossetto." Strange,
it was exactly there he had seen that striking girl who looked so Spanish disappear into an alley one evening two years before. Later he had
thought it was Laide, but Laide had assured him she'd never been there.

It was a quarter-past-eleven and Laide had told him that this evening
around ten she was going to visit her aunt. He felt the need to know,
the need to see for himself. Perhaps he'd drunk a bit too much, but
he was no longer frightened by what a couple of hours ago might have
dismayed him—going personally to the home and asking for her, at
the risk of finding himself in some horribly embarrassing situation,
or of enraging Laide, for the thing that she hated most, he knew, was
his wanting to stick his nose into her private business, to investigate
her affairs, and thus to demonstrate his total lack of confidence in her.

He decided to go, all the anger stored up in so many months of
worrying and waiting—yes, he must be drunk, even his own street
seemed somehow changed, with houses that in all those years he'd
never noticed, and his car moved on with a curious *souplesse*, it seems
to anticipate his desires as it slowed down and turned corners.

He left his car in the Piazza San Simpliciano and continued on
foot. There were only a few people about, and Antonio suddenly felt
he was walking absurdly fast. He slowed down, lit a cigarette. There
was the corner, an old alley made its way darkly among ancient houses
with heavy brick breccias that clung to the scaling plaster.

There was a street lamp where the alley widened into a kind of small square where a man was busy locking up a rolling shutter. Another leaned against the corner of a house, smoking.

Antonio went toward a woman wearing a dark dress and carrying a market bag. "I beg your pardon, signora, could you tell me where the Asilo Elena is?"

The woman stopped, looked at him and shook her head.

"Pensione Elena? Don't ask me, I'm not the one to ask."

She went on, as though irritated.

What did her words mean? And the way she acted? Antonio looked around. Luckily the alcohol he'd drunk sustained him, he felt strangely excited. Via Sormani must be over there on the right. There was a street sign but in the darkness he couldn't read it.

"Excuse me," he said to the man who was smoking, "do you know where Via Sormani is?"

He was a young man, and strangely enough a few minutes before Antonio had thought him to be about fifty or fifty-five, but actually the man was young, with an ironic good-natured face.

"Looking for someone?" he asked, as though Antonio were one of his serfs and he had the right to know.

"Via Sormani. The Asilo Elena."

"Ah! The Asilo Elena!" He smiled and exhaled a mouthful of smoke. "Pensione Elena!"

"Is it here?" asked Antonio, feeling now somewhat bewildered.

"Over there, over there," said the young man, jerking his thumb toward the little street, "a yellow house, you can't miss it, there's a light over the doorway."

"Thanks very much."

"Not at all." He smiled again.

The little street is badly lit. A cat. The distant sound of a piano. A piano or a radio? To the left a dark courtyard. Antonio turned, the young man was still standing at the corner, still watching him.

By the dim light of the street lamp he continued on another fifty yards, but the yellow house with the light over the door wasn't there. Then Antonio noticed in front of one of the doorways a prostitute waiting. She was smoking, her hair was raven black. She looked at him with a sickly sweet smile, and Antonio said:

"I beg your pardon, signorina, could you direct me to the Asilo Elena?"

When she opened her mouth a gold tooth glittered.

"Are you asking me, sir, *me?*" She burst into laughter. "Over there, honey, that yellow house over there."

She pointed, he turned, she'd pointed back to the street he had come from. Yes, now he saw the little yellow house a bit further on. It had a small doorway and right above it a tiny wrought iron lantern with red frosted glass. The lantern was lighted. How strange, he must have passed right in front of it without seeing it, really incomprehensible.

"Thank you," said Antonio and headed toward the yellow house. The door was closed.

Antonio looked up. It was a two-story house in good condition, but old. Its shutters were closed but through one pair filtered a bit of light. What a strange sort of hospice, he thought, not even a sign out. Then he decided to ring the bell.

There was the click of a lock on the other side of the door, quick step of sandals with high heels. The door was opened by a woman of about thirty; heavily made up around the eyes and lips, her wide thin mouth looked extremely common.

"What do you want?" she asked with a silly smile.

She wasn't thirty, she was old. Antonio decided she must be at least sixty.

"Is this the Asilo Elena?"

"Yes. Who do you want?"

"I was looking . . . I was looking for Signorina Laide Anfossi."

"Ah, Laide!" cried the old woman and nodded her head quickly as though she were aware of everything. "Just go on up, the first floor. Ring, you'll find your Laide."

A flight of stairs with a dark red strip of carpet, a triple door with stained glass, a copper plate: "Elena Pistoni." He felt tempted to run away but his finger had already pressed the bell.

Light went on, steps, a shadow. The door opened. A thin woman dressed in black stood there, rather distinguished looking.

"Sir?" she said in rather a suspicious tone of voice.

"Is this the Asilo Elena?"

The woman laughed. "Well, that's what we call it. But you, excuse me...who sent you?"

"I beg your pardon," said Antonio. "I was looking for Signorina Anfossi, Laide Anfossi. She told me she was coming here tonight to stay with her aunt who's ill."

"Oh." An expression of agreeable surprise lightened the sympathetic face of the woman. "That's how it is, is it? Well, all right, come in. But Laide, I beg your pardon, Signorina Anfossi, is occupied at the moment, I believe."

"Could you call her?"

"Oh yes, of course. You might have to wait a minute or two, though. Do come in."

She showed him into a small parlor, with modern furniture in horrible taste, an imitation tapestry, television, a tea set in silvered porcelain. On the walls were three crude copies of Millet.

"Do sit down. If you'll excuse me.... There are cigarettes in the box. Five minutes, no more. The moment Laide's ready I'll send her in to you."

"What does 'ready' mean?" Antonio wondered. Now he began to see how imprudent he had been to come.

"Is her aunt in there?" he asked, with one last ray of hope.

The woman looks at him for a moment, unbelieving. Then: "Of course."

She nodded her head at every word as though repeating a formula. "Naturally. Her dear little aunt isn't so well tonight."

She left on a snicker of laughter.

Antonio, alone, sat down in a little gilded armchair, twentieth century style. The woman had left behind her a sickening scent of perfume with musk in it. She had drawn closed a curtain from the other side of which every now and then came subdued voices and laughter.

In the little space between the door jamb and the curtain, a silent figure suddenly appeared. Someone was peering into the room.

He felt terribly uncomfortable, had a desperate desire to run away.

He got up just as the curtain was slowly drawn back. A dishevelled girl in a dressing gown was standing there, dark, with a beautiful, tired, apathetic face.

"Are you the gentleman," she said in a voice of astonishing slowness, "are you the gentleman who's waiting for Laide?"

"Yes."

"And who . . . are you?"

"I . . . I'm a friend."

The girl looked at him in silence. Then in a very low voice, she said: "If I were in your shoes . . . I'd . . ." and she makes a gesture as though suggesting that he leave.

"Why? Is she worse tonight? Her aunt?"

"What?"

"I say, Laide's aunt. She's being looked after here, hasn't she?"

"Sure," said the girl, with the same expression the woman had worn earlier. "Her aunt."

Once again she fell silent, peered at him as though trying to figure something out. At last she said:

"Her aunt. . . . Her aunt. . . . If only you knew how ill her aunt is tonight."

"You say she's very ill—"

"Her dear little aunt. . . . Luckily Laide's here to help. . . . The poor aunt. . . . Come on! I'll show you, no one will ever find out."

She took his hand

"But I. . . ."

"Come on, I say. Don't you want to see Laide? Busy with her good works? Come on then. But walk softly, don't make any noise."

Only then did Antonio realize that the girl was barefoot.

She led him into a narrow dark hallway, opened a door, and they entered a room which was also dark. But on the left, through a stained glass door covered with a flowered curtain, a little light filtered from the room next door.

"Come here. Be still. . . . Do you hear her?"

From the room next door came a man's voice, then the voice of a woman with a Milanese accent, with the Milanese "r."

No, no, why torture oneself this way, Antonio tried to leave but the girl held onto him.

"There's Laide! Isn't it interesting? Her poor sick aunt!"

Now he listened. Through the glass door the voices sounded unbelievably clear, as though they were in the same room.

"Very nice," a man's voice said. "Congratulations. Small but very nice. Let's see...."

"Come on.... Get undressed, will you?"

"A little kiss first."

Silence.

"Tell me one thing, baby," he said then. "How do you live?"

"What do you mean?"

"What I say. Do you live only on...fun and games like this?"

"I...I have a friend."

"Ah? Does he come across with plenty?"

"I can't complain."

"Old?"

"Not old, no, but he certainly isn't a boy either."

"Do you love him?"

"What a question!"

"Does he let you have your freedom?"

"I should say not! He's insanely jealous."

"How do you manage then? To get here, for instance, how do you work it?"

"Oh, I tell him I've got a sick aunt and at night I've got to come here and look after her."

"A sick aunt! Oh, that's wonderful! And he swallows it?"

"He swallows everything."

"Just tell me one thing—"

"What? If only you'd get undressed instead...."

"If he gives you enough money, why do you come here?"

"There's never enough money, my grandfather used to say." A burst of laughter. "Aren't you undressed yet? Hurry up, I'm cold."

The girl with Antonio whispered to him: "Would you like to watch?"

He shook his head no.

"Come on, it's worth it. Look up there, there's a nice little hole in the wood. Wait, I'll bring you a stool."

"Tell me, honey," said the man, "who's in the room next door?"

"Nobody. Can't you see it's all dark? Come on, now, madam told me to hurry."

"Why? After me have you got another dear little aunt to look after?"

"No, this way! Let me breathe. My God, you're heavy!"

"Don't be afraid, I won't kill you."

Carefully Antonio got up on the stool. The unknown girl steadied him. Actually there was a hole through which he could see.

And there it was, the ghastly scene, the one he'd imagined so many times, like an inferno, the end of his whole life, there it was:

The white, muscular body of a young man kneeling on the bed. He straddles her, she's lying flat. Her face isn't visible. Antonio can see only her naked legs spread apart. Are they kissing?

Suddenly the man gets up, as though she had rejected him. Now she in her turn sits up, leaning against the pillows. He can see her face.

But it isn't hers. It's Flora's face, it's the face of his secretary at the studio, it's the painted face of the old woman who opened the door to him a minute ago. But it isn't her face. It's a horrible woman. It's the wide swollen face of a mastiff. Opening her disgusting lips, she fixes her eye on Antonio through the tiny hole in the door and she laughs, she laughs, she opens her mouth wide in savage laughter.

Antonio jumped up, surprised at having fallen asleep in an armchair in his bedroom. God, what a dream.

Then wasn't it true, was the truth then something altogether different?

But the evil shadow of the incubus was within him, it filled the room, hung like a pall over the world.

33

THEN EVERYTHING happened quickly and quietly as when some long-feared misfortune suddenly overtakes a man, but in a form so meagre and with such banality his soul is hardly able to conceive it.

Lieutenant Imbriani phoned Antonio at the office the next morning. He sounded rather crestfallen, perhaps because of the prognostications that he'd made which actuality had disproved.

The little rest home was there, and Laide's aunt was there too, ill, but the head nurse excluded in no uncertain terms any possibility of night-nursing by relatives. No member of the family was allowed in the home at night. A girl who fitted the description given came a couple of times with an older woman in the afternoon, during visiting hours. That was all. "Shall I go on with the investigation?" "No, thank you. Now I know what I need to know."

The crack-up did not take place; instead a kind of tense exaltation kept Antonio going. The almost unbelievable exaltation of love, especially unhappy love, was so strong that from the very first moment he struggled against the catastrophe with a kind of fury. He felt almost liberated. Much the same thing had happened, Antonio recalled, when they opened fire during the war; then the waiting and the fearing were transformed into energy, into taut, unemotional energy.

Laide phoned him at eleven. She spent another night with her aunt, she said, and she was terribly tired. She was going to try to rest for a couple of hours, then she was going to lunch with her sister.

"Then we don't see each other today either?"

"Well, I don't know. Could you call for me in Via Squarcia?"

"What time?"

"Two-thirty."

"But please don't keep me waiting as you usually do."

That damned Via Squarcia, that anxious walking up and down on the sidewalk opposite, he'd never forget it as long as he lived.

But now he said nothing. He waited impatiently for the meeting wanting to hurl in her face what he knew and see her unmasked at last. He hated her, he'd like to see her dead. He'd strangle her happily, his thumbs on her smooth white throat, with her little mouth, showing all her pretty little teeth, opened wide for the death rattle.

But an hour later Laide telephoned again. Unfortunately they can't meet at two-thirty. She had to rush to the hospital, her aunt was worse. Antonio would have to be patient with her. It was harder on her, after all, at the hospital day and night.

"All right, but I think you're going too far now."

"What do you mean too far? I'd like to see you alone in a hospital like a dog."

"No, going too far with me. It seems to me—"

"Antonio, don't talk to me that way! I'm dead tired, and I feel as though my head's about to split, and if you're going to start—"

"But the fact is we're not going to see each other today either."

"No, listen, be a good boy, do me a favor, will you? Could you come to my house around three-thirty? Picchi hasn't had a thing to eat since yesterday. There's a package of chopped meat in the fridge. Wait for me there. At four o'clock I'll either come or I'll phone."

"I can see you coming."

"If I can, I will, I promise. . . . You don't know how she depends on me!"

At three-thirty he was in Laide's apartment. The dog was eating. It was one of the first nice days, you couldn't call it spring because there was no spring in Milan, but even if it were the most radiant spring day in the world, Antonio wouldn't have been aware of it. However, winter was over.

He wandered through the apartment looking at the little things, the sweet and silly things that reminded him of days lost forever:

little dolls and big dolls, figurines, bottles of perfume, the yellow and orange dress, the green flowered dress, the red dress.

He opened the cupboard, lifted the sleeve of the yellow and orange dress, touched it, smelled it, kissed it, no one was watching him. Yes, this was certainly the last time. This couldn't be anything but the last time.

Then he remembered that on the floor of the cupboard, to the left, Laide kept her pictures and her letters. Was it wrong to look at them? In the circumstances, that scruple would be the height of imbecility.

He found the cardboard box and sitting on the edge of the bed began to look at the pictures and to read the letters.

There was a half-finished one with no date that she'd written to someone named Stefano Doglia. It seemed to be an attempt to resume an old relationship. "Yes," she wrote, "you took me to dinner and you took me out but every time it was the same. You always talked about your work to your friends, and never a word to me, but what a fuss if I tried to talk to anyone, you know I was in love with you but your continual and ridiculous jealousy was very painful for me.

"Between two people who love each other," she continued with a sudden change of tone, "mutual trust is the only possible basis. But you always treated me as though I was a whore, obviously as far as you were concerned I was only...." Here the letter ended.

He opened another signed by someone named Tani. It was from the period when Laide was in hospital, in answer to a letter Laide had evidently written. "Your letter, my love, has excited me beyond words. If only I'd known before that you liked me so well! Charming Laide, the moment my work permits, and I hope it will be soon, I'll fly to Milan to be with you. Meanwhile I give you all my kisses, all my body, all my love!"

Then he found Marcello's letters. There must have been a dozen of them. One was enough for Antonio.

Marcello wrote from Modena to announce that he had arranged for a room with two beds at the Fonterana hotel. "But I'm telling you right away that we're working continual shifts at the yard now, so it won't be possible for me to spend every night with you...." Then Marcello opened the romantic stop: "I can't tell you, my little star, how eagerly I yearn for your warm caresses, and the black river of your perfumed hair, the beating of your sweet breast, the agony of your endless kisses, your breathless embraces...."

The telephone. "Hello, how long have you been in the house?"

"About half an hour."

"Did you give Picchi his food?"

"Yes. Where are you?"

"At the same old café near the hospital."

"You're not coming?"

"I just can't today. My aunt's had a crisis."

"All right, then listen: wait for me in the bar, I'll be there with you in half an hour."

"I can't, I'm sorry. I've got to go right back."

"A quarter-of-an-hour, that's all."

"I tell you, I can't. I must go."

"Then at least do me a favor, it won't put you out any, give me the number of the telephone where you're calling from."

"It's a public phone!"

"That doesn't matter. It's got a number, hasn't it? Read it to me from the little tag."

"I don't think so, no. What's the point of it?"

"The point of it is you aren't where you say you are. The point as I'm fed up with those lies of yours, the point is I've had enough of being led around by the nose like a complete fool."

"If you're fed up, I don't know what to do about it—"

Laide broke the connection. Her voice had trembled a bit. Pert as always, self-assured, but the earth beneath her feet had begun to crumble. For some days now she'd no longer been able to handle the situation. It was as if something had carried her away; she no longer had time to organize her defenses, nor the desire. She tried hastily to plug the leaks that keep opening everywhere, but she herself had no confidence in her ability. She knew that for her this was defeat, either partial or total, but she didn't know what to do about it. She was no longer the proud and stubborn Laide who walked straight ahead with her head held impudently high. Now she had become a seedy starveling struggling apathetically to stay alive but doubting that she would succeed. What had changed her so? Had she fallen in love? Or was it the world she had tried to escape, her own world, now calling her imperiously back?

Antonio felt anger, fury, hatred, excitement of battle. A desperate and dramatic wind carried him along. He could not remember ever having lived so much in so short a time. Defeated, knocked about, deceived, betrayed, yet alive, stupid, naïve, pitiful, cowardly, yes but still alive. He began to struggle as he headed for the crash. It was the first time he'd ever fought like that.

He left Laide's apartment, went to his studio where he worked hard, and then went out to dinner with friends. For months he hadn't been so gay or sure of himself. At eleven-thirty he left his friends and went back to Laide's apartment. She wasn't there, nor was there any sign she'd been there. No message from her.

He prepared to leave but before doing so he took out Marcello's letter and the other one, put them on the bed and added a note of his own which read: "The choice is yours: don't sleep out, let me come whenever I like, any hour of the day or night, don't go out at night without me. Otherwise we're only friends as before."

That night he slept, perhaps because he'd drunk quite a bit of whiskey, but he slept. He woke in the morning with a mysterious weight on his shoulders; he doesn't care he's furiously angry he's maddened he'll show that bitch that at last he's understood how to treat women, damned disgusting bitch without a drop of Christian charity, he'd like to watch her on the sidewalk in the rain, tired ugly ill, walking up and down hour after hour, followed by the dirty remarks of drunken youth, panting for a chance at a five thousand lire note.

He hurried to Laide's apartment and looked carefully for some little sign. But there was no little sign. She hadn't come, hadn't turned up at all. The two letters left out on the bed had not been touched.

He tore up his own note and wrote another: "Now everything is over between us. Do you by any chance need an explanation? I'll leave the keys with the porter. Good luck. Goodbye."

In the bedroom he saw the two letters he'd left out and, not knowing why, he felt ashamed. He folded them up, opened the wardrobe and put them back in the box.

But once again, seeing all her papers, he felt the need to know. Maybe a secret was hidden there. No, better not look, what he'd already read was enough. But he fingered the things anxiously. A plastic envelope full of photographs. Laide. What was she like? Where had she lived? With whom?

He took out a picture the size of a postcard and saw a little girl about seven or eight years old muffled in a woolen dress with pretensions to elegance. How strange! A little girl. Was it Laide?

A picture taken on a city street, in the background he could make out a bit of sidewalk and the bottom of a house and in the wall at ground level there was an opening to let a little air into the basement but the opening had been cemented over and he could see those little white marks that during the war time indicated an emergency exit for air raid shelters. The picture was some years old then, it was a long time since the last traces of the war had disappeared from the streets of Milan.

The picture had been taken close up and the little girl was looking up toward the camera. She wore a heavy woolen dress that wrapped her up almost entirely but that still made a claim to elegance. In her hands was a teddy bear, or perhaps a doll, it was hard to make out. Her long black hair was tied at the top by a pale silk ribbon and fell down along one side of her round plump face. She was looking up at the lens with a disarming and yet mischievous smile as though to say...to say what? Antonio tried to figure it out, what made up Laide's mysterious pathos?

There was the child, Laide, who as yet knew nothing of life. She looked as if at that very moment someone has arrived with an enormous package for her and refused to open it right away in order to make her yearn for it a bit. But she knew the package was full of presents for her. She didn't know what they were as yet, but she was sure they'd be very fine presents indeed, exactly what she wanted. She knew the waiting was all a game and that's why she smiled in that particular way. How happy she was at that moment, how peaceful, how trusting, at that extraordinary unforgettable moment.

Life itself had brought that enormous package with all its gifts inside and all that had to be done now was cut the colored string and open the wrapping in order to find out what was inside. For such a pretty and innocent little girl, certainly, there should have been wonderful gifts: a carefree youth perhaps, elegance amusement love, fame perhaps, wealth and a house in the green countryside full of sunlight, a handsome good and loving husband, one happy season after another endlessly all the way down to the distant horizon so far away it was not to be seen. Life's gifts.

Life's gifts: in the bedroom on the third floor of the house in Via Schiasseri, the banal furniture, the daily fretful search for something, who knew what? the miserable letters, the jars of cream and the bottles of perfume, the dresses and the shoes in the cupboard, the memories of a hundred unknown men, the disorganized struggle, rushing in taxis from one end of Milan to the other, telephone calls tricks lies rendezvous undressing dressing undressing, brief youth that fades so quickly, the hardly perceptible descent from step to step not aware she was alone though she was terribly alone, for her there was nothing behind all those smiles there was nothing but desire for her body, wanting to make a good thing out of that body of hers, frenzy to get money for her body and the contempt that results, the contempt was hidden now behind extravagant compliments because she was still young and beautiful, but tomorrow when the freshness of the meat began to go off the contempt wouldn't be quite so hidden and one day it wouldn't be hidden at all it would all be out and only one man loved her truly but he was no good to her because she couldn't bear him, for he was an incubus she couldn't put up with any longer, hence her pleasure in betraying him and humiliating him, though even she knew that one day the deception must end but it was more powerful than she was and so she hurtled on among the lights the laughter and the noise and all around her was the city, which with its delicious little whip incited her to go faster, all around was the cold black foggy unfriendly city.

Once long ago the child had looked up with a timid, a mischievous smile: the package is closed—the smile said—but I'm clever, I know what's inside, I know all the lovely things that are inside it. That was why she smiled. Oh if only she could have known. Now the child was gone, she'd been gone a long time and in her place was someone who seemed like a young girl but wasn't a young girl because she knew too much about love, a woman with a haggard face who looked about her like a hunted beast yet kept running stubbornly toward total destruction.

Now Antonio was home again, his furor spent. Night had come, men had finished their work, lights in the houses went out one by one, the world went on as if nothing had happened. At eight that evening Laide had turned up at his studio, she hadn't yet been home, she said, she hadn't yet seen his note. But clearly that was one more lie.

"There's some man, isn't there? some man behind all this?"

She nodded.

He was sitting at his desk, she sat down near him, her legs right in front of him.

"I won't go out any more," she said, "I'll do whatever you want, if you want I'll stay at home all the time."

Stretched out now on his bed, his eyes on those pernicious cracks in the ceiling, he saw her again, her pale frightened face. The altar of the city, that mirage of childhood, that constellation of dim lights and caresses, was shattered and broken.

No, Antonio had told her, it would be useless. He'd look after her for two more months, tomorrow he'd send her a check, but did she know how much she'd made him suffer? She nodded her head. Up into the rosy halo that hangs over that immense conglomeration of houses, float sleepy fumes of oil, overturned banners, and gloomy music like the beat of a hammer that carries her slowly down to the caverns of the south.

Now please go, he had said to her, he had some urgent work to finish. She kept control of herself, she made no scene. Leave him please, otherwise he'd not get it finished in time. As though that idiotic piece of work were more important than she, as though that goodbye was a farewell like any other and tomorrow they'd meet again but they would never meet again, black Milan old and shadowy was about to take her back again and swallow her up, she'd disappear into that labyrinth, for a second her tough little smile would be reflected in the glass door, then in the milling crowd that pushed its way around the passage the back of her neck would vanish amid the distant din of rock-'n'-roll, the distance that separated him from Laide would be boundless, with plains seas and mountains between them, and the curtain of silence and darkness. There was nothing that did not remind him of her: the cracks in the ceiling, the license plate of his car, the armchair, the bottle of lavender water, the wooden animal on the bookcase, the shape of the house across the way seen from the window—everything in the world reminded him of her, without her there'd no longer be any meaning in life nor work nor talk nor food nor clothes, everything was absurd and idiotic without her and thus there opened wide within him an emptiness from here to there, and out of the emptiness flowed a wild river of tears.

Yes, on the whole, it was a ridiculous story, a happening like so many, banal, twisted, funny, mean. How easy it was to realize that it couldn't have ended any way but this, Antonio told himself. So get up, stop crying, goodnight, till tomorrow, don't try to make a tragedy out of it, straighten your tie instead. A needed burst of laughter. Goodnight.

Yet for him it was still the decisive moment of his life, and it was still hell. If he were ill, if he'd got into trouble, if he'd been put in jail, relatives and friends would have come to help him. But not now. Forbidden. Even though his condition was so much worse—thrown to the ground, trampled, battered within and without, left in the dirt, kicked out. Nevertheless there'd be no pity for him.

They would say: Did you try to forget your age? Did you think you could pit your strength against the wickedness of a young girl who was making her own assault on life? Did you insist on playing an unfamiliar game that wasn't for you? Did you suppose you could become a boy again? You'd need some other face than yours. For you the game is over. Doors closing, emptiness, solitude, desolation, silent cries that no one will hear. You're in port, you fool, who thought yourself somewhere else.

Antonio's anguish was a black wave that lifted him up and dropped him sobbing down. Where was she at this very moment? He could hear an occasional car passing in the night streets. Next to the bed stood the telephone over which he had listened to so many stories. Never has it been so black, so motionless, useless, silent, dead.

34

BUT ANTONIO was not one of those people who, when fate has dealt them some severe blows, hold everything inside so that, should you happen to see them, you'd never guess what had happened. After saying goodbye he experienced, naturally, a new access of frenzy, of rage and violence.

Seeing how it was with him, a friend said to him: one day you'll find out that in practice it's not nearly as bad as it seems, I loved this woman I told you about like crazy, day and night I thought about nothing else and the more I followed her around like a dog and kissed her feet the more she treated me like a fool and I went out of my mind (so this friend told him) and I simply couldn't get her out of my mind till one day I said to myself today or never, not that she'd done anything worse than usual—on the contrary that day she'd actually been terribly nice to me but I said to myself do it now friend because otherwise you lose everything you've got, and all of a sudden I said enough and when she phoned I said enough and that's all and she kept at it of course for a few days and even made a scene or two with tears and all but I'd said enough and when I decided to make the break I thought I'd do something foolish or crazy but wonderfully enough at the very moment that I made the decision to break with her—but understand me I really made the decision it wasn't just an idea—at that very moment I felt like a different man and naturally I felt unhappy but the unhappiness was bearable like when you have a tooth pulled that's been hurting you like the devil, I'm not just talking to be talking now I'm telling you from personal experience, so listen to me Dorigo, you can do the same and afterwards you'll begin to laugh when you think how much you've taken from her and all for nothing. That was what his friend told him.

But after the leave-taking Antonio didn't feel like a new man, he didn't begin to laugh. He felt worse because until now at least there had been hope. The daily quarrels, the waiting around, the anxiety, the telephone calls had filled his existence. These were meaningful—in a word, a manifestation of energy and life. Now there was nothing but to go over and over in his mind the same damned things there was no escape because not for a second did his thoughts stray from her: what she was like when she talked, when she walked, when she laughed, every least detail of that extraordinary girl who had destroyed him.

In this blackness of spirit Antonio tried to grab hold of any possible support and so he thought of looking for Piera, a friend of Laide's who came to see her one day when she was in hospital. Antonio had happened to be there at the same time and Piera seemed to him to be both a bright and pretty girl. Laide told him later that Piera had for years had a friend who was old but terribly rich and that she had lost him idiotically enough by letting him find her in bed with someone else. Maybe Piera might be of some help to him. If she agreed, and if he felt like trying it, maybe she'd turn out to be more entertaining and acceptable than Laide, and help him to forget her for a while. Some months before, as a matter of fact, Piera had called him to say she had a fur coat to sell and had given him her phone number.

They made a date to dine out, but the minute Antonio saw her he realized that even to be thinking of a substitute for Laide was ridiculous, and his despair was deeper than before. There was Piera sitting across from him in a fashionable restaurant, looking amused as she watched him.

"Now then," she said, "may I ask why you called me?"

"I don't know," he answered, by now down to earth again, "maybe because you're the type I like."

"Or is it to find something out?"

"What?"

"About Laide. Aren't you satisfied with having been a horse's ass in the eyes of the whole city for over a year?"

"In the eyes of the whole city!"

"Do you still have any doubts on the subject?" She laughed. "Yes, a horse's ass, I could say it by the hour, you horse's ass. Come on, don't look like that. You know you're really very unusual.... A screwball! When I saw you in the hospital and her boy friend was there too, the one with the sheep's face—what's his name?"

"Marcello?"

"That's the one, and you were there looking at her as though she'd knocked you out and she kept calling you uncle, I don't know, I said to myself, is it really possible he doesn't know what's going on, is he such an idiot?"

"I swear to you I—"

"Believed her? I know you believed her. That's why you're the biggest horse's ass that ever lived. You're such a horse's ass you're still not convinced and you came looking for me so I could say no, it's not true, Laide always loved you, she was always faithful to you. Look, you're a nice guy, I know you are, but so naïve, I swear to you, nobody would believe it's possible."

Antonio was silent, overwhelmed by the agony of her words.

"That Laide of yours. I remember the first time I saw her, I went down to the Due with a friend of mine, the man who looks after me, I'm a whore, as you know, and I had my pimp like all the other whores and I supported him. Well, there I saw a girl dancing rock-'n'-roll with long black hair down to her shoulders and the most magnificent legs oh if I had legs like hers, those lovely long thighs and she was wearing a little balloon skirt and nothing underneath and when she twisted she deliberately made the skirt come up to here and you could see everything and every time she did the whole room would howl. I remember that bum Fausta was there too and Fausta introduced us and she came to sit down at our table. Well, if you'd like to know this pimp of mine went to bed with her that night and I'd rather not tell you the disgusting things she did. You're really suffering, aren't you, horse's ass? You'd rather die, wouldn't you, than listen to all this? Should I stop?"

"No. Maybe it's better. Go on."

"Well, so we got to be friends. I liked her, I've got to admit I liked her. In those days she had an old man, so ugly he was frightening. He had a real estate agency but he gave her practically nothing. Every once in a while he'd drop a five or a ten and you wouldn't believe how she had to work for it. Every evening at eight-thirty she had to go to his office and right there on the couch.... I once asked her, I remember, how she could go with a creature like that. Doesn't it make you sick, I said, and she said no he's a real gentleman and he's so good at making love. But of course he wasn't enough. She had debts everywhere, I don't know how she did it. So she had her appointments too.... I remember one evening she said to me, you know something Piera? this afternoon I spent six thousand lire on taxis. Six thousand? I said, how did you do it? Well, as it happens, she said, I had four appointments this afternoon, and if I didn't want to miss any, I had to hop, one at one end of the city one at the other...."

"She did pretty well, then!"

"Of course. One month she told me she made over three hundred thousand lire, but who knows whether it was true? She's got a lot of strange ideas, that one, she's capable of killing herself over nothing. Once she went on a street car all the way to Lambrate and back—to perform a service, shall we say?—for two thousand five hundred lire. Lambrate! I could hardly believe it. She began to laugh. Well, you know, she said, everything helps.... And one night I remember, at a friend of mine's house, I was there too, and a lot of people, boys and girls both, and one man promised her a pinch of coke if she'd pay the penalty."

"What penalty?"

"There are seven men here, says that pig, you've got to amuse all seven of us one after the other. Laide had been drinking that evening. Well, so they all sat down in a circle...Do you want a detailed description?"

"You're a real bitch, you are."

"Don't cry, screwball. A little third-degree is good for you."

"What did she say about me?"

"Now we've got there! About you she said that you were a bore, that you didn't give her a minute to catch her breath, that to keep you happy she had to phone you twenty times a day, that when she had to make love to you she felt she was going to die, that she wouldn't let you set foot in her house at night—"

"It's true."

"So she was free to do whatever the hell she wanted at night. You ought to be proud of yourself. Do you know for a while Fausta was sleeping there with her boy friend?'

"Yes, she told me."

"And did she tell you they were all three sleeping in the same bed with him in the middle? What do you think they were doing, discussing philosophy? . . . What's happened to you? You don't look well. . . . You're as pale as . . . I'm sorry, it's my fault. Come on, let's go, come and have a whiskey at my house and then I'll send you back to beddybye."

Piera lived in a new building, in an apartment with a terrace. The furniture was not bad and there was a huge cupboard full of dresses. But Antonio felt no curiosity, the whole world was whirling inside him.

"Sit down now, your face is like. . . . You felt like dying, didn't you? when I was talking about your love. Yes, I'm a bitch, you know I'm a bitch?"

"You don't look like a bitch."

"A person's got to be bitchy with you. Now I understand a lot of things, if I'd been in Laide's shoes I'd have done worse things to you."

"Why?"

"Because with all your intelligence you're the stupidest man I've ever met. And just as you believed every story Laide told you, now you're believing everything I tell you."

"Isn't it true?"

"How do I know? Some true, some not so true. You needed a good shock and I've given you one." She burst into laughter.

"They're terrible things, understand, for me they're—"

"Of course I understand. Why do you think I told them to you? Now that we've talked about Laide, why don't we talk a bit about you?"

"What about me?"

"Well, for instance, tell me: you hate her now, you despise her, you'd like to see her drop dead, you could strangle her with your own hands, couldn't you?"

"You'll have to admit that she behaved like—"

"Like a whore, is that what you mean? But do you think you're any better than she is?"

"I loved her, I was always straight with her."

"Tell me the truth: would you have married her?"

"What a question! Just think of the difference in our ages, she herself would have said no."

"The difference in our ages! Don't make me laugh. Weren't you in love with her?"

"Unfortunately yes."

"Well, then, would you have married her?"

"Just think of the life she led!"

"That's the point, my dear well-born friend! Middle-class, that's what you are, that's the whole point, disgustingly middle-class, with your head full of middle-class prejudices, proud of your middle-class respectability. What do you think your middle-class respectability meant to Laide? And what do you think you meant to her?"

"I loved her very sincerely."

"Very sincerely? You were sick for her, that's all, you needed her, you did everything you could to get her. But all the time you thought she was bad luck. Is it true or isn't it that you thought she was bad luck?"

"She was, for me, she was bad luck."

"And that's what you call love? Did you ever let her into your life? Did you take her home? Did you introduce her to your family?"

"Don't be absurd."

"Absurd? Yes, I know. I knocked my head against that same damned wall. I had a friend, an engineer, a wonderful boy, he wanted to marry me. He was from the middle class too, but not as middle-class as you. When his mother heard about it, it was the end of the world. If you marry that thing, she said, you'll be dead as far as I'm concerned. A woman of rigid standards, oh how I love rigid standards!"

"Did he leave you?"

"No. We still see each other. But I'm a whore and I'll always be a whore as far as he's concerned. You think of us as a race apart, you members of the bourgeoisie, even when you need us, even when you come crawling at our feet. That's what you call love, is it? Social position, the respect of the world, dignity, family prestige, nice things, but who made us what we are? The hell with your dignity!"

"But there are millions of girls that go to work—"

"I've been waiting for that, I've been waiting for that for half an hour. It never fails: but why don't you go to work? Would you like to know why? Because you middle-class gentlemen, with your filthy money, you've kept us from going to work."

"Are you a Marxist by any chance?"

"Who's a Marxist? I'm a fascist, I am. Where does Marxism come into it? If anything comes into it, it's plain Christian charity. Did you ever wonder where Laide was born, what sort of world she grew up in, what kind of people she lived with, what education she had, who looked after her and really loved her when she was a baby? I've told you some terrible things about her but you know what I tell you now? She's much less of a whore than I am. She doesn't have the craving for it that I have, she thinks of her good name, she doesn't have the courage that I have either and maybe it's because—if you'll allow me to say it—she isn't as intelligent as I am either. If Laide, not me, but if Laide had been born in a family like yours, do you think she'd have become a call-girl? She'd have become a woman of rigid standards. I can see her now, inflexible with girls of easy virtue. Just like my not quite mother-in-law, may she roast in hell."

"Why are you lecturing me, I'd like to know? Do you think I'm a stupid moralist? After all I think I'm pretty broadminded, don't you?"

"When it suits you. But you leave that broad mind of yours outside when you go home."

"All right. But what did she do to try to meet me half way?"

Piera was silent, she looked at him with a sad and kindly smile. "Tell me, screwball. Have you tried putting yourself in her shoes?

Give your brain a workout. You're a girl who gets along as best she can at so much a throw. You meet an older man who says he's in love with you. He's a bachelor, not rich but he makes a good living. This man doesn't offer to marry you, oh no, that's not even to be thought of. Social propriety and all that crap. No, he offers to become your steady lover and he offers you a salary. He wants to buy you, in other words. You make your calculations, you weigh up the advantages, and you accept. He pays you and because he pays you you've got to go out with him, go around with him, go to bed with him. Because he pays you. What's more he's sincerely in love with you, which means he's jealous, suspicious, and boring. But you're not his wife, you're only his secret friend, his kept girl. You're not allowed in his house, you don't go to his friends' houses. He leads a life apart, and you don't even get a sniff at his real life, the life that really counts. Got the picture? Then tell me how that girl, you, can honestly love that man."

"But anyway she's better off than she was."

"Are you sure? Better off from the point of view of the cash yes, but what about her liberty? Sold to the highest bidder, with exclusive rights."

"I never denied her her liberty."

"You've got a nerve! If you'd ever known that she was going to bed regularly with sheep's face—what's his name?"

"Marcello?"

"Yes, if you'd known she was going to bed with Marcello, what would you have said?"

"I think it would have been a bit too much."

"Then what kind of liberty is that? Go easy on the whiskey, chum, even if your heart's bleeding. Not that I'm a miser, anyway it was a present. But that's your fourth if I'm not mistaken and you've got to drive home."

"Just a drop. It's been a fantastic evening."

"Does the truth hurt? Is it true that the truth hurts, screwball?"

"According to you, then, I'm the one that's been wrong the whole time?"

"You couldn't have been wronger."

"What should I have done?"

"Nothing. There was never anything to do. Unfortunately that's the way the world is."

"But you'll have to admit if she'd had a different sort of temperament—"

"You wouldn't have fallen in love with her. That's clear enough."

"No one kept her from being faithful to me—"

"You're the one! You. You bought her at so much a month. She sold you her body and you kept insisting you'd also bought her soul. Can't you understand that there's nothing worse for a girl than that? If she'd been the shinbone of a saint, she'd have had to try to put the horns on you. And if you can't understand that, you'll never understand anything!"

"Whereupon I suppose I ought to forgive her?"

"Forgive her? Don't let that idea even start knocking at your door, screwball. Do you want to destroy yourself completely? Forget her, that's all, as though she never existed. Us too, I think it's better if we don't see each other again. Better for you, get me? You've been an incredible horse's ass but I like you a lot, you're a very distinguished fellow, did anyone ever tell you?" She began to laugh. "I like you very much, if you really want to know. I feel sorry for you. You're like a frightened bird with a broken wing."

"It's true."

"But I think it's better if we don't meet. I haven't seen Laide in months, she's supposed to be mad at me, I don't know why. But I've been her friend, and if you go on meeting me, each time, do you see what I mean? . . . It'll be harder for you to get over it. . . . As far as the rest goes, if you'd like. . . ."

"You're a wonderful girl, Piera, deep down—"

"Oh, I'm a mess! Me too, I'm bad news, that's all. I'm a whore, a whore! . . . O God!"

She threw herself onto the sofa and covered her face with her hands. Her shoulders trembled in silent weeping.

35

A slow web of dreams, drowsiness continuing, silence, vague sound of distant life, abandoned thoughts flying down to the lairs of the past on a hot night in June. Antonio comes slowly out of a nameless valley full of spires that look like trees. He realizes he's in bed, then bit by bit he remembers, he opens his eyes. From the wide opened windows the reflection of the neon lights outside beat onto the ceiling and stretch out into slanting, criss-crossed stripes; the room is dimly visible.

Next to Antonio she sleeps. Altogether naked, she lies supine, her arms crossed on her breast like a princess of the pharaohs, gently her relaxed hands follow the light curve of her breasts and the slow rise and fall of her breath. She sleeps the wholehearted, unreserved sleep of the beasts but the perfection of her pose and the pure serene expression of her face tug at Antonio's heart; he doesn't quite know why; he sees innocence there, and youth, and mortality, sin, time passing and devouring.

How many months have gone by? Antonio looks at her. Is hell contained within that frail body? No, maybe it was something a great deal simpler, maybe it was he who turned the whole thing into a tragedy. But now he struggles no longer against doubts and scruples. Did I do right or wrong to go back to her? Am I contemptible? Abject? The question no longer has any importance.

One evening, after two months and a half of struggle, he gave in. He was in Rome, he remembers the evening well. Silvia was with him, a kind and intelligent girl, and seeing him at such a low ebb Silvia said well after all why not call her? do you want to ruin your health?

what do you want to happen? how can dignity solve your problem? And that was it! He called her from the hotel in Rome, it was around eight at night, not a very good time, she was usually out around that time. But she wasn't out. At first she didn't realize it was Antonio, her voice had not a trace of arrogance in it. "I was going to phone you myself one of these days, to ask you about the rent." "We'll talk about it in Milan," he said, "when I come back I'll call you." And he felt no remorse or shame, he only began to breathe again, and to live.

When he got back to Milan he drove his car out to her house. She came down and sat beside him in the open car and with her right hand played with the safety catch on the dashboard. She looked pale and thin. She was only the shadow of the old Laide, even her nose seemed to have grown longer, but for him she was still love.

She asked him if he could pay her rent for another few months. "Why should I pay your rent?" he replied. "Have I any obligation to you? What will you give me in return?" He spoke thus so as not to admit defeat with the first blow struck, but he knew well enough how it was going to end.

"I haven't anything to give you," Laide answered, "the only thing I can give you is myself, if it doesn't disgust you." "Myself" she said, not "my body," without perhaps even realizing that she had chosen the right word. There were no more discussions, no scenes of jealousy nor tricks nor lies. The story was taken up again slowly and of what had happened neither spoke, never never would Laide have told him the truth, her deceits, her tricks, her intrigues, her liaisons, it was as though her lies were a lost flag she couldn't betray even at the cost of her life, they were the one thing he couldn't ask her about, for her shame, strangely enough, lay there, in those shameless secrets of hers. That night, however, everything seemed to have become at last easy and pure, right and human.

He pulled himself up and sat on the bed, there were only a few cars passing in the street below, it must have been about two or three. In a little while the night would begin to lighten, one could feel a cool breeze beginning. He continued to watch her, wondering what she was dreaming. Every now and then her fingers twitched with a kind of nervous tic, her hands still harmoniously folded like the hands of a medieval statue. Is he happy? For the first time in an age that seemed endless he doesn't have that feeling of anguish in his breast, the red-hot iron stake no longer pierces his gut, it's like the morning when he woke and thought, so mistakenly, that he was cured, and then an hour later while walking through the gardens discovered suddenly that his hell was still inside him. Will he be mistaken again this time? No, out of the utterly relaxed and confident way in which she sleeps he derives a sense of pity and of peace, a kind of invisible caress. Still lying supine on the bed, Laide shudders briefly, murmurs hardly audible moans, strange incomprehensible sounds such as dogs make sleeping. Antonio runs his hand across her sweat-bathed forehead.

Laide opens her eyes.

"What's the matter? What are you doing?" she mutters, with her mouth still pasted shut in sleep.

"Nothing," he replies. "Looking at you."

Her voice, so strangely peaceful now, even thoughtful, the "r" so strong in it, makes a curious sound in the night.

"Antonio, listen, I've got to tell you a secret."

She is silent for a moment. Never, he thinks, has the house seemed so sound asleep, so quiet.

"This month," says Laide, "I haven't had any period."

"Well?"

"That's all. I want to have a little girl."

She smiles. In the dim light the smile is a little white gleam almost phosphorescent. He feels something he has never felt before. Even if he had known what to say, he'd have been too late. Laide's smile fades. Her eyelids close. She drifts back into sleep.

But even in the very dim light Antonio perceives that a trace of her smile still hovers at the corners of her lips and lights her face. "That's all. I want to have a little girl that's all." The echo of her words still sounds through the room, it hasn't sunk yet into the background of silence and it reverberates inside Antonio three four five times. Is this the heartless, frightening girl who was said to be ruining him?

What's happened to her? Who's changed her? Where does she discover in herself the will to have a child, a desire so remote from the racket of night clubs and the making of love for money?

The fact is, no one's changed her, she was always that way, the squalid legends among which she lived—that dark cruel wood—were never hers. Handed down to her in some secret way, from blood to blood, deep at the bottom of her soul lay the desire for simple and eternal pleasures, domestic, reassuring, maybe commonplace too, the pleasures that are the earth's salt.

Of a sudden the secret, sinful and wicked world which stood at Laide's back and out of which she had seemed to come exists no longer. Did it ever exist? Have the sinister fascinating backdrops simply melted away? Have the dangerous phantoms become just nice people? Or have they vanished into a dismayed crowd, among the damp dark ways of the old city? Will she lose then, will Laide lose her romantic halo, her aura of secrecy, now that she is no longer unattainable? Or is still more mystery to be found in a lone lost girl who at her own risk and peril, after having thought about it a long time, decides to put into the world a creature to whom life can offer nothing but scorn, derision, dishonor?

While the misty dawn of Milan rises so slowly, the little tough girl, with her petulant nose in the air, sleeps peacefully. Has she won or lost the personal war she fought day by day, with clenched teeth, in which her weapons were her youth, her wantonness, and her lies? Could she have done differently? Did not Antonio himself, as Piera maintained, force her to defend herself against him and to lie to him? Wasn't she right to be a bitch? Is it only now that Antonio understands who Laide is? and that her meanness came not from herself but was forced into her day after day by the city and the men of the city and even by Antonio himself, and that there was neither guilt nor evil nor shame nor reason for contempt or punishment?

But will the peace last? The truce? Will having a child put an end to that mysterious mania for make-believe and trickery? Or will her strange, undaunted and frightened heart shoot forth its thorns once again against him, its untouchable and twisted thorns? Will she find the strength to renounce her world of unconfessable secrets and throw away that armor of fantastic lies within which she lived? Are new and still more tormenting anxieties being prepared for Antonio?

These are things he no longer even wonders about. As in a lengthy and painful illness, the tired patient at last gives himself up to the sweet drowsiness of morphine and is almost able to convince himself that he's been cured.

The long angry squeal of a brake down in the avenue below, followed by angry voices quarreling. Then suddenly the exchange of insults ends, the car accelerates noisily and then is gone.

Now the city truly sleeps, the sleep that trickles from a hundred thousand rooms and drops down the walls spreads like an invisible shroud over the deserted streets and the tired cars waiting inertly in endless rows beside the sidewalks, a tide foaming gently from one end of Milan to the other, mixing into one breath the breaths of millionaire and beggar, prostitute and nun, athlete and cancer case. Only Antonio is so immensely awake and he savors his peace of mind. As the last shreds of cloud after a storm disappear into the north, so the events of the recent past scurry away, and by now they seem to him like some ridiculous and twisted fable. Into the furthest distance recede the sickly sweet smile of Signora Ermelina (look she's a hot little piece she likes to be bitten and beaten up a bit I'm telling you so you'll know what to do), the squalid afternoon appointments the evil insinuations of friends (you know what her specialty is? I mean in making love? no maybe it's better if you don't know if you knew you wouldn't have the least desire to go to bed with her any more, I'm sure of that, or maybe it would only make you want her all the more you men are such pigs all of you), her awful confessions, the murderous waits in Via Squarcia, the doubts, the phone calls that never come, the sharp spike stuck just here, the sleepless nights, the unhappiness the next morning when on awaking one's thoughts flounder about trying to find something to hold onto, the unhappiness that like a savage horde invades every part of one's being, fantasies faces lights street-scenes rooms stairs halls voices music whispers and the whole world is nothing but Laide, even now as she sleeps beside him the whole world is nothing but Laide, but first there was an ever-whirling vortex a continuing madness a vise that kept on tightening and now this hell seems to have come to an end.

After so long a time, a treaty of peace. Even if he's been defeated, defeated for the second and last time. But even a routed army breathes again once the battle's ended. Silence, the heart thunders no longer, only wisps of smoke here and there.

He looks at her. He wonders whether she'll be able to drive him to frenzy again. He thinks not. If for two or three days he's unable to find her, will he go out of his mind? He thinks not. If he discovers she's been to bed with someone else, will he lose his mind again? He thinks not.

Alas, he's been cured. His hell is over. She sleeps beside him. Then I ought to be happy, he thinks. Am I? No. Fatigue, emptiness, melancholy, one of those overwhelming fits of melancholy that used to take hold of him as a boy at nightfall, save that then the melancholy contained the future, the endless years still to be spent, while now it isn't the thought of the years to come, now the door way down at the end can already be glimpsed, the closed door that opens onto darkness. That's it then, the disquiet the jealousy the despair are ended but so is the storm. It was anger fury frenzy burning speed life, it was youth too, but now, that very night, the very moment that she spoke, that she came out of her sleep for an instant to speak, at that one moment his youth ended, the last patch the last shred of youth so strangely even unwillingly prolonged to the age of fifty. A fire that burns no longer, a cloud that's dissolved into rain, a piece of music that's sounded its last note and will sound no more, fatigue emptiness solitude.

And how about the women to whom Antonio for so many years paid no serious attention save to satisfy his physical needs? What was Laide for him if not the concentration into one person of all those desires that expanded and multiplied without ever being satisfied? He never found the courage to satisfy them. The women he met seemed to him untouchable and useless to think about and so, as a result, they ignored him. They didn't ignore other men. To other men, to his friends, those untouchable creatures smiled, spoke, and said yes. His friends, giving no particular importance to the incident, would tell him about the marvellous girl they'd met at the bar, the *entraineuse*, the model, they'd tell him how they picked her up, took her out to dinner then to bed as though it was all the easiest thing in the world. He too saw those girls, met them, wanted them, but would say to himself each time how ridiculous, never would that one work out. So he passed them by, never daring to try them, held off by that mournful dignity of his, and then it was too late.

Such an easy thing. A game. Even splendidly beautiful girls. But you've got to know how. He never knew. Let him say a word to them, they seem bored and annoyed; let him look at them, they turn their heads away at once. It's always been that way. Especially the ones he liked the best. Some of the others sometimes seemed friendly and maybe even willing. But never the women he liked the best. Never the bold snubnosed girls from the suburbs, the slow deceitful girls with the sly look in their eyes. He used to see them with other men, on other men's arms, eating with other men, driving with other men, but if he looked at them they'd turn their heads away annoyed, it's always been like that. Who were the men they were with? Billionaires, movie stars, apollos? No. They were just any kind of people, nobodies, with big bellies, unable to discuss anything but football, vulgarians, ugly too but apparently with the right kind of look, they knew two or three stupid remarks that the women liked—just thinking about it made him feel so angry so furious so full of regret but without bitterness by now, by now even if he knew now it was too late.

Looking at men his age—he realizes it only now—he always used to wonder: Whom do they make love to? Judging by their allusive conversation, their self-confidence, their implicit contempt for easy girls, they must have had millions of opportunities. He was struck especially by the way most men, as soon as they met a desirable woman, considered her as prey, not a being like themselves with a world of interests and desires and preoccupations as important as theirs, but only as a body to be enjoyed and they regarded it as almost her duty to yield to them and were amazed if by some quite intolerable caprice she refused them. It was this conviction which provided them with their strength and their success. To Antonio who all his life had encountered nothing but indifference and who the few times he'd found the courage to try had only battered his head against an unyielding wall, what was most astonishing of all was the way women accepted this inferiority of status, their willingness to be considered objects of pleasure and to be enjoyed for an hour or two, as though they were happy, and indeed proud, to be courted, knowing well that man's desire is single and once it's been attained they'll be chucked away like so many useless rags, knowing full well that man, following his ancient and outrageous tradition, will despise them once his desire is satisfied and think of them as whores. Antonio could never understand—here his resentment became confused with envy—why on earth women were willing to admit, thus tacitly, that they belonged to an inferior race and to allow themselves to be treated like slaves. But at least he now understood why, when particular circumstances reversed the normal order of things, and the man fell in love and the woman therefore had the power, why it was inevitable and reasonable for her to make the man suffer, even if only for a little while, the kind of humiliation to which other men had for so many long years exposed her. But wasn't it odd, and wasn't it just a bit funny too, that these ideas should have started buzzing about his head only now at the tender age of fifty? Most of his contemporaries, he knew, were well beyond all that, they thought about it no more, and if they went on making love, it was no longer a problem to them. While he, on the other hand, had never taken it seriously enough; he was like someone who walks by a spectacular shop window without really noticing it and only after he's gone a long way past does he realize what marvellous things lay inside and so he turns and goes back only to discover that they've already turned out the lights and are now closing the shutters. He had never taken it seriously enough and now he was paying bitterly for his remissness, with regret, with envy, with the torture of having too little time ahead, with loneliness.

In the truce he now enjoys, his anxiety has lessened, while she lies sleeping on the bed, her hands crossed over her breasts, and he sits beside her and runs his fingers lightly over her thigh, the long thigh of a girl who has frenziedly danced rock'n'roll, the arrogant leg that has been wrapped around so many male legs, but there's no longer any evil there—if there ever was any evil there, which he still doesn't know—and there comes back into his mind an idea that for many months had been driven out by his illness.

He thinks of himself as a small smooth stone tied to a string and made to swing faster and ever faster, and swinging him was the wind was the autumn tempest was despair, love. And swinging madly he no longer knew what shape he was, he became a kind of fluidly moving circle.

He was a jousting horse and at one point the tournament began to spin crazily about him, faster and ever faster, and goading it on was Laide, was autumn, was despair, love. The horse whirling so fast lost the shape of a horse, he became a quivering white garland, a quivering white curtain with gold fringe, he was no longer himself, he was a being no one knew and you couldn't get in touch with him because he wouldn't listen to anyone he listened only to himself hissing through the wind, there was nothing for him but Laide, that dreadful speed, and in the whirlpool he couldn't even see the world around him, all other life had ceased to exist, it existed no longer, it had never existed, Antonio's mind had been entirely sucked out of him by her, by that dizziness, and it was painful it was a terrible thing, never had he turned so fast, never had he been so alive.

But now the tourney's stopped, and stopped is the stone tied to the cord, the horse has crystallized into the shape of a horse, and the stone tied to the cord hangs motionless and at last one can see it's a stone. Antonio is no longer hurtled along by the tempest, Antonio has stopped and has gone back to being Antonio and once again he begins to see the world as it used to be.

He looks around in the night. God what is that high dark tower that hangs over him? The old tower that had always been hidden deep in his soul since he was a boy. A little while ago, when he was in the whirlwind, he completely forgot that terrible tower, the speed with which he whirled had made him forget that great inexorable black tower. How could he have forgotten something so important, the most important thing of all? Now it was there again, it rose as terrible and mysterious as always, it even seemed somewhat higher and closer. Love had made him forget entirely the existence of death. For almost two years he hadn't thought about it once, it had seemed like a legend to him—to him, who had always had the obsession of death in his blood. Such was the power of love. Now suddenly it had reappeared before him, its shadow was over him the house the district the city the world and it was growing slowly closer.

But meanwhile, sleeping deeply, unaware of the harm she's done and will do, she floats under the rooftops the skylights the terraces the pinnacles of Milan, she's a naked thing, a soft white suspended grain of flesh, or maybe of soul, dreaming a beloved impossible dream. Through the layers of mist, the rosy reflection of the street lamps that are still turned on have lit her kindly, making her glisten with pity and mystery. It is her great hour, without her knowing it the great hour of Laide's life has struck, and maybe tomorrow everything will be as it was, and the shame and the bitchery will begin again, but now for this one second she is greater than everything, she is the most beautiful, precious, and important thing in the world.

But the city slept, the streets were empty, no one, not even Antonio, raised his eyes to look at her.

OTHER NEW YORK REVIEW CLASSICS

For a complete list of titles, visit www.nyrb.com.